FALCON QUINN AND THE CRIMSON VAPOR

JENNIFER FINNEY BOYLAN

FALCON QUINN
AND THE
CRIMSON VAPOR

 KATHERINE TEGEN BOOKS
An Imprint of HarperCollins*Publishers*

Katherine Tegen Books
is an imprint of HarperCollins Publishers.

Falcon Quinn and the Crimson Vapor
Copyright © 2011 by Jennifer Finney Boylan

Library of Congress Cataloging-in-Publication Data
Boylan, Jennifer Finney, date.
    Falcon Quinn and the crimson vapor / Jennifer Finney Boylan.
— 1st ed.
        p.   cm.
    Sequel to: Falcon Quinn and the black mirror
    Summary: Born in the reality stream but with both the heart of a
monster and the heart of a guardian, thirteen-year-old Falcon Quinn is
not sure what path to follow until he fastens an amulet with a red jewel
around his neck.
    ISBN 978-0-06-172835-8 (trade bdg.)
    [1.   Monsters—Fiction.   2.   Animals,   Mythical—Fiction.
3. Angels—Fiction. 4. Junior high schools—Fiction. 5. Schools—
Fiction. 6. Friendship—Fiction. 7. Identity—Fiction. 8. Fantasy.]
I. Title.
PZ7.B696415Fac   2011   2010024717
    [Fic]—dc22   CIP
                                                                     AC

Typography by Amy Ryan
11 12 13 14 15   LP/RRDB   10 9 8 7 6 5 4 3 2 1
❖
First Edition

FOR ZACH AND SEAN, AGAIN.

Sons good.

Well, the Sasquatch girls are hip,
I love their fur all splotched with crud;
And the vampire girls, with the way they bite,
They knock me out when they suck my blood.
Egyptian pharaoh's daughters really make you
    lose your head,
And the Frankenstein girls, with the bolts
    in their neck,
They bring their boys back from the dead.

I wish they all could be zombie mutants
I wish they all could be zombie mutants
I wish they all could be zombie mutant girls.

                    —Traditional

Contents

1

MONSTER ISLAND

1
The Glory of Everything

The sun shone on Monster Island. Falcon Quinn, standing behind the counter of a lemonade stand, looked down the midway of the all-mutant amusement park. A world of unlikely creatures strolled through the fairgrounds. There they were: reflected in the Hall of Broken Mirrors, bouncing in the Antigravity Bumper Cars, staring in astonishment at the macabre picket fence that surrounded the Unhaunted House.

It was a very good place to be, thought Falcon, this lemonade stand at the heart of Monster Island, with its groaning Frankensteins, the hot summer sun, the passage of Sasquatches, the loyalty of Chubakabras, the nearness of vampires, the smell of zombies, and the glory of everything.

The summer was nearly at an end. In a matter of days Falcon and his friends would return to the Academy for Monsters on Shadow Island. For now, the sun was bright and the air was filled with the smells of hot pretzels and mummified flesh and sweet Italian sausages. He thought of the favorite phrase of his best friend, Max the Sasquatch: *Our lives are unbelievably, amazingly great!*

"Hey, gimmee an egg cream," said a deep, growling voice, and Falcon, the young angel, turned to see a were-rhino, a guy named Snort, standing there. Steam rumbled from Snort's nostrils, and there was mud on his horn. He wore a New York Yankees cap.

"What?" said Falcon. In addition to his wings, Falcon had two eyes of shockingly different colors—one blue, one black. The black one, at this moment, began to burn.

"I said an egg cream already," said Snort. "Hey! *I'm waitin' here!*"

Falcon tried to be gentle. When it came to wererhinos, it was best to be diplomatic. "Listen," he said. "I don't have any—uh, egg creams. But this lemonade is really good. You want some lemonade?"

"Lemonade," muttered Snort, turning his back. He walked about twenty paces from the stand. Snort pawed the ground and lowered his enormous horn, preparing to charge. "I didn't *want* to have to stampede ya," he said. "Wasn't *my* idea."

"Hey—," said Falcon. "Hey, Snort. Seriously—"

The steam from Snort's enormous nostrils was coming out in gushing clouds now, as if issuing from the spout of the world's largest teakettle.

"Dude!" said a happy voice. Falcon looked over to his

left and saw his friend Max, who was wearing a Hawaiian shirt and baggy shorts. The Sasquatch was holding a three-foot-long frankfurter, slathered with onions and chili and relish and cheddar cheese and hot mustard. "Check out this super chili cheese dog! It's got *bacon!*"

"One!" shouted Snort from across the midway.

"Max," said Falcon. "You don't want to be here right now."

Max stuffed the whole chili cheese dog into his mouth. "Of course I want to be here right now," he said, chewing. "This is like, the best possible place to be! You and me, Monster Island! A beautiful summer day! Our lives are unbelievably, amazingly"—Max spread his arms—"*great!*"

"Two!" shouted Snort. Over Max's shoulder, Falcon could see the wererhino preparing to thunder toward them.

"Max," said Falcon. "I'm serious! You do *not* want to be here right now!"

"You keep sayin' that," said Max. "But you're wrong. I'm thinking of moving here. Building, like, a little house! With a porch and junk!"

"Max, you don't understand," said Falcon. "I've got a problem with—"

"Dude," said Max. "Your problem is in your *mind.* You want to be happy, you got to get with the program. Got to shake out all that tension! Here, take a deep cleansing breath, man. Go on—inhale! Exhale! Inhale! Exhale. You see how that releases the toxins?"

"Max," said Falcon, pointing now over his friend's shoulder. "Run!"

"Run?" said Max. "What do you mean, run?"

"Three!" shouted Snort, and began to charge.

"I mean *run!*" said Falcon. Max, just barely beginning to understand that something was going on behind him, slowly turned as the thundering rhino bore down upon him, horn first.

"Duuuuude," Max yelled, and jumped up in the air. A moment later he came down, although unfortunately for the Sasquatch, he landed directly on the back of the charging wererhino.

Falcon spread the enormous white wings that until now had lain flat against his back. With a sudden pulse, they lifted him out of the lemonade stand just as Snort crashed into it. There was the sound of splintering wood as the stand smashed into thousands of pieces, and lemons went flying in every direction.

"Hang on, Max," said Falcon, and swept toward him.

"Dude!" shouted Max. *"I'm totally on top of a charging rhino!"*

Sonahmen Ankh-hoptet, the teenage mummy, was sitting in the audience at the Hall of Boxing Robot Presidents, wondering whether her friend Lincoln Pugh, the were-bear, was ever going to work up the courage to hold her mummified, gauze-wrapped hand. Looking down at her fingers, Ankh-hoptet rather wished she'd remembered to wrap herself in fresh bandages this morning; the gauze that encircled her was still stained with a few splotches of tomato sauce from a pizza party the night before. *It's because of me*, the mummy thought. *He doesn't want to hold my hand because he doesn't like my wrappings.*

At the moment Lincoln was in his human form, a small, pale boy with red hair. Usually he also wore a pair of especially ugly, rectangular, orange spectacles; but he'd misplaced these recently, making him, on the one hand, somewhat less ridiculous looking but, on the other hand, terribly nearsighted. Lincoln and Ankh-hoptet sat in the dark and watched the show. In the boxing ring, lit by spot-lights, a robot Abe Lincoln was beating up a robot Richard Nixon. Lincoln was fast on his feet, and in no time at all the Great Emancipator had Nixon pinned up against the ropes. He connected with a left to Nixon's jaw, and Nixon went down. The crowd roared. Lincoln raised his hands in the air. "I am the greatest!" he said.

At this moment a rhino horn plowed through the ring, like the dorsal fin of a shark, ripping through the canvas and sending Abe Lincoln flying into space. Just behind the moving horn was a Sasquatch, yelling at the top of his lungs.

"What's going on?" said Lincoln Pugh. "I can't see without my glasses!"

"It's Max," said Ankh-hoptet. "He's—"

"Somebody help me!" shouted Max. "I'm stuck on a rhino!"

The rhino turned around and stabbed the Richard Nixon with his horn at the very moment the Nixon was finally back on its feet. There was a flash of sparks. "I am not a—*werrp,*" the robot said, and its arm fell off. *"Werrrp."* The sweat on the robot's upper lip burst into flames.

"Uh-oh," said Lincoln Pugh.

"You should transform into your bear self," said Ankh-hoptet. "And put a stop to this charging rhino."

"Maybe," said Lincoln nervously as Snort stampeded through the hall.

"Lincoln," muttered Ankh-hoptet. "This moment calls for a hero."

"Yes, well," he replied. "Sometimes the most heroic thing you can do is nothing."

"This is your philosophy?" said Ankh-hoptet. "The philosophy of nothing?"

"It's worked out okay for me so far."

Now Falcon Quinn flew into the auditorium, his wings beating. He tried to swoop down and get hold of Max, but Snort's movements were unpredictable.

"What's that?" said Lincoln Pugh, squinting. "Is that Falcon Quinn?"

"It is Falcon Quinn indeed," said Ankh-hoptet with a sigh. "The angel! The hero!"

"There, you see," said Lincoln Pugh. "I told you it would all work out."

Falcon dove toward Max once more, but Snort lowered his horn and thundered toward the far wall of the room. Young monsters scattered and screamed as the rhino crashed through the wall and back out into the crowds of Hematoma Boulevard, Monster Island's main street. There was a band of middle school marching goblins passing in front of the Hall of Boxing Robot Presidents at that moment. Snort, with Max still stuck upon his back, charged directly into the trombones. "It's the end of the world!" shouted Elaine Screamish, a banshee who'd been watching the parade.

"That's not the end of the world," said a minotaur named Picador, who was also the president of the student body. "That's Falcon Quinn!"

"What's he doing?" said Maeve Crofton, a fire elemental who was also Picador's girlfriend. She looked at Falcon flying around in circles above Max's head.

"Hey!" said Picador. "He's attacking Snort!"

At this moment there was an ear-piercing, brain-rattling trumpeting, and everyone—Snort, Falcon, Max, the goblins—stopped in their tracks and recoiled from the blasting sound. The director of the park, an elephant man named Mr. Trunkanelli, was standing in the midst of the melee, blasting on his long, gray trunk. The trumpeting sound was so loud it knocked people over and left them stunned and half dazed upon the pavement of Hematoma Boulevard.

"What's the big idea?" shouted the elephant man.

"That kid attacked the other one," said Picador. "Falcon Quinn, the angel. He was flying around, trying to hurt the rhino."

"Oh, he was, was he?" said Mr. Trunkanelli, narrowing his eyes. "I've heard about you, Mr. Quinn. I've heard *all* about you."

"Everybody's heard about Falcon Quinn," said Picador.

Snort looked at Mr. Trunkanelli and started to cry. "I just wanted a little egg cream," he said, sniffing. "That's all I ever wanted. I guess that's a crime!"

Mr. Trunkanelli wiped his big, gray head with one hand. He looked at Max. "What's all this about?"

"I don't know, man," said Max. "I was just, like, eatin' this big ol' hot dog when all of a sudden, I was, like, ridin' this rhino-cyclone!"

"And *you*, Mr. Snort," shouted Mr. Trunkanelli. "I warned you about the stampeding! What is the law, Mr. Snort? Tell me the law!"

A big tear rolled down Snort's face. He lowered his horn almost to the ground. "No stampedin'," he said.

"And yet here we are," shouted Mr. Trunkanelli. He blasted his trunk again, and everyone covered their ears. "Goblin trombones—flattened! A lemonade stand—reduced to splinters!"

The robot Abraham Lincoln stumbled out of the hole in the side of the Hall of Boxing Robot Presidents. "Four score—*werrrp*—," he said, smoke billowing from his ears. "And seven—*zzzz*—" With this, the president's head fell off, leaving nothing upon his neck but a vibrating spring. For a moment, headless Abe Lincoln stumbled around the porch. Then he tripped on his own decapitated head and fell over.

"My Abe Lincoln!" shouted Mr. Trunkanelli, and he trumpeted again. *"You busted my Abe Lincoln!"*

Falcon looked over at the weeping wererhino and felt sorry for him. "It wasn't Snort's fault," he said.

"What's that?" said Mr. Trunkanelli.

"It wasn't?" said Snort.

"No," said Falcon. "I—I guess I forced him into it. I—tricked him."

"But *why*?" said Mr. Trunkanelli, reaching into his pocket for some peanuts. "Why would you do this? Why?"

"I don't know," said Falcon. "I thought it would be funny, I guess."

Mr. Trunkanelli looked at Snort. "Is this true? Did this angel deliberately mislead you?"

Snort shrugged and mumbled something.

"What was that?'

"Yes," said Snort. "He did! He tricked me into it! I didn't wanna stampede! Honest I didn't!"

Mr. Trunkanelli sighed and wiped his face with his hand again. "Bludd Club," he said. "Tonight. The both of you, busing tables." He trumpeted. "Understand?"

Snort looked a little pale. "But—that's where the vampires—"

"I said Bludd Club!" yelled Mr. Trunkanelli. "Tonight!" He trumpeted again, so loudly that Max covered his ears. He turned to the goblins. "What are you all looking at? Start the parade again!" The elephant man walked into the Hall of Boxing Robot Presidents to inspect the damage. The goblins looked at one another, then at their drum major, an orc with an ornate mace. She pounded the ground with her mace four times, and the goblins began to march once more, some of them playing instruments that Snort's stampeding hooves had bent into unrecognizable shapes. The trombones now made odd, squeaking sounds, like kazoos, and the crowd that had gathered around the three young monsters dispersed. "You know, I like that sound *better* than trombone," said Max. "It's relaxing!"

"Thanks for nothing, Falcon Quinn," said Snort. "Now I gotta bus tables tonight. In the *Bludd Club*!" Steam blew out of his nostrils.

"You're welcome," said Falcon.

"One of these days," said Snort, "you're going to realize your little routine doesn't fool nobody. Everybody knows what you're trying to do. What you are."

"What am I, Snort?" said Falcon, his dark eye growing hot.

Snort looked at the angel, his wings spreading angrily, one of his eyes beginning to glow with fire. "You tell *me*, angel face. What *are* you?"

With this, Snort turned from Falcon and Max and walked away.

"Man, what a sorehead," said Max.

"What did he mean, everybody knows what I'm trying to do?" asked Falcon.

"What did he mean? Nothing, man! He's a doofus!"

"Yeah, but Max, what was he saying—that people think I'm . . . against them or something?"

"Nah," said Max. "Nobody says that. Only the doofuses." Max looked nervous. "They don't know what they're talking about."

Falcon's angel wings folded down flat against his back. "So people do say things," he said. "Sometimes."

"Yeah, well, people say all sorts of stuff," said Max.

"What are you going to do, man, spend all your time listening to everything somebody says?"

"What do they say?" said Falcon. "Max? What?"

Max blew some air through his cheeks. "Are you hungry?" he said. "I'm totally starved."

"Max," said Falcon. "Tell me."

Max sighed again. "Well, when we left the Academy? Last spring? That whole adventure seemed kind of wonky to some people, after it was over. I'm not saying I thought it was wonky. I'm just saying."

"Wonky how?" said Falcon.

"Well, 'cause Megan Crofton . . . never came back. That's got some people kind of grouchy, especially her sisters. You know? And then Jonny Frankenstein kind of . . . disappeared. And Peeler and Woody got, like, toasted. So, you know. Some people—the stupid ones—say they never got the whole story. That it was all part of some crazy plot or something."

"What kind of plot?" said Falcon. "What are you talking about?"

"Well , it's like—everybody knows your mother's, like, the *enemy*. The leader of the monster killers and stuff. You can see how it'd make people antsy."

"But, Max," Falcon said, "they know I escaped from her. That I got away from the Island of Guardians and came back to rescue everybody. They know that, right?"

"Sure," said Max unconvincingly. "Sure, they know that."

"I'm going to find Megan," said Falcon. "I swear it. And Jonny too! I'll find them!"

"Dude," said Max. "I know all that. C'mon. Dim your headlights."

"Okay," said Falcon. "What's the problem then?"

"Problem?" said Max. "Who said there was a problem?"

At that moment, a fifty-foot robot approached. "Destroy—Falcon Quinn!" it said. "Destroy! Destroy!" The robot was covered with flashing lights and had a square head that looked sort of like an old-fashioned washing machine, and two shiny, reticulated arms that resembled the exhaust hose from a clothes dryer. Falcon and Max stood motionless for a moment as the gigantic robot staggered down Hematoma Boulevard toward them, waving its arms around.

"Dude," said Max regretfully.

"Destroy Falcon Quinn!" shouted the robot. "Destroy! Destroy!"

Falcon looked up and down Hematoma Boulevard. Some of the other monsters were looking at the approaching robot with anticipation. It was one of the park's attractions, that giant robots occasionally appeared and destroyed things with their cyborg lightning or crushed various objects with their hydraulic arms.

"Stand back!" said Falcon as his majestic wings unfolded above and behind him once more. They quivered in the air threateningly. Now the robot made a strange electronic sound, like *HAUGH-HAUGH-HAUGH*. It took a moment for Falcon and Max to realize that the robot was laughing at them.

"Who are you?" said Falcon. "Where do you come from?"

"Do—you—not—know?" said the electronic voice.

Max and Falcon looked at each other, slightly embarrassed. "Dude," said Max. "Do you know the robot?"

"I don't think so," said Falcon.

Now the robot's head popped up, revealing a small trapdoor in the automaton's neck. A tiny, familiar face appeared out of the door and said, "I am—¡la *Chupakabra!* The famous goatsucker of Peru!"

"Pearl!" shouted Falcon as the pixie-sized Chupakabra flew out of the control booth in the robot's head and swept toward them on her tiny wings.

"Dude," said Max, smiling broadly.

"It is myself!" said Pearl with her usual bravado. "Operating the controls of this gargantuan machine! Providing entertainment and a touch of danger for all whom I encounter!"

"They got you working the robot," said Max. "Excellent!"

"'Excellent' does not describe the interior of the robot's control chamber," she said, buzzing on her tiny wings and hovering above Max's head, "which is devoid of fresh air and light! However, 'excellent' *does* describe many other fine things, not only Señor Falcon Quinn, angel at large, but Señor Maxwell Parsons himself, the Sasquatch to whom I am pledged henceforward!"

"Aw," said Max.

"And greetings to yourself, Señor Falcon," said Pearl. "I trust I am not interrupting a conversation of grave importance!"

"Max was just telling me about some of the bad things people are saying about me," said Falcon.

"Those who besmirch your name," said Pearl gravely, "shall find themselves facing the deadly poisons that I bear!"

"Rrrr," said a voice. "Destroy!"

Falcon turned to see several of his other friends standing in the bright sunshine of Abominationland. There was Destynee, the enchanted giant slug, currently in her humanoid form, as well as Weems, the ghoul, wearing his tattered black rags. Sparkbolt, a young Frankenstein, stood just behind them, growling.

"Hi, Falcon!" said Destynee, blushing slightly. "How are you?"

"I'm good," said Falcon.

"But how are you *really*?" said Destynee.

"Greetings to you all, my companions!" said Pearl. "I bid you good day!"

"Rrrr," said Sparkbolt again.

Weems cleared his throat. "We cannot linger," he said.

"Yeah?" said Max. "What's up?"

"We're going to the Unhaunted House," said Destynee. "Do you want to come, Falcon?"

"I am not sure there will be room for—," said Weems.

"Dude, I have so wanted to check out the Unhaunted House!" said Max. "This is great! Let's check it out!"

"I too have nourished a curiosity about this place of grotesque normality!" announced Pearl.

"Well, what are we waiting for?" said Destynee. "Let's do it!"

Weems sighed. "Always it is like this," he muttered.

"Like what?" said Max.

Weems shook his head. *"This."*

"Are you having a good day, Falcon?" said Destynee. "I hope you are!"

Falcon looked at the faces of his friends—the brave Chupakabra, the enormous Sasquatch, the enchanted slug and the ghoul and the Frankenstein. He felt his two hearts pounding.

"Yeah," said Falcon. "It's a great day."

"Friend good," noted Sparkbolt.

They walked to the Unhaunted House and joined the long line of monsters waiting to get in. A group of vampire girls in stretchy tank tops and short shorts looked curiously at Falcon and his friends. One of them whispered something to the others, and then they all laughed.

"I don't know about you guys," said Destynee, "but I can't wait until we get back to the Academy. There's something weird about this place. An amusement park brings out the worst in monsters, if you ask me."

"Amusement bad," said Sparkbolt.

In the long line before them were dozens of other monsters—goblins and banshees and leprechauns and ice worms. Most of these creatures spent their days in disguise, out in the Reality Stream, living among humans, their true selves cleverly camouflaged. For many monsters, their annual vacation to Monster Island was the only time all year they got to be themselves.

The doors to the Unhaunted House opened, and the line of monsters moved inside. The line snaked into a small dark chamber with oil paintings of skeletons and vampires on the wall. "Welcome!" said a cheerful voice. "To the Unhaunted House! A place where behind every corner lurks something—*normal!*"

Everyone screamed.

"Take this chamber, for instance. It might seem like a nice, clammy room, a good place for sucking blood or

performing horrible experiments. But beneath this monstrous exterior lies something *lighter*, something *fluffy*,
something *wholesome*! Ha! Ha! Ha! And do note—there
is no way out! Your first challenge? To find the exit! Ha!
Ha! Ha!"

There was a sudden flicker of the lights, and the room
seemed to be growing taller, although whether this was
because the ceiling was rising or the floor was dropping
was not immediately apparent. The pictures on the walls
were changing, and where the vampires and skeletons had
been before were now insurance salesmen and nice ladies
in book clubs. All of the monsters screamed.

All at once the room filled with happy music, and
the walls rotated back to show a panorama of dancing,
happy children from many nations all singing in perfect
harmony. "Monsters rowed the boat ashore!" they sang.
"Kumbaya!"

"*Rrrraarrwwww!!!*" shouted Sparkbolt in horror, and
charged through the wall, screaming and waving his arms
wildly. Now there was a Sparkbolt-shaped hole in one wall.

Pearl looked at her companions. "It seems as if our
large, green friend has located the exit!"

The others stepped through the hole and into a kind
of loading zone, where people in straw hats and seersucker
suits helped people onto cars shaped like minivans and
station wagons.

Sparkbolt, Falcon, Pearl, Max, Destynee, and Weems found themselves in a car together—Falcon and Destynee up front, Max and Pearl in the middle, and Weems and Sparkbolt in back. Soon they were being wheeled through a vast universe of pastel colors. There was a new song playing in their ears now, which sounded like a mixture of "Polly Wolly Doodle" and "Oops! . . . I Did It Again." The car entered the first chamber, in which a dad was sitting in a big easy chair as his two children, each wearing baseball uniforms, sat in front of the TV. The dad picked up a remote control and pointed it at the TV. A mom came into the room with a big platter.

"Who wants nachos 'n' baco-bits?" she said.

The monsters all screamed.

Then they wheeled into another room in which some kind of party was taking place. There were guys eating crispy orange balls of cheese out of a giant plastic bag.

"I like Harry Potter!" said a boy who was building a model rocket out of a kit.

Weems covered his face with his hands. "Tell me when it's over," he said.

Sparkbolt groaned. "Sparkbolt not allowed to read Harry Potter. Sparkbolt told it *bad influence.*"

The car crashed through a pair of black doors, and now they were in what looked like some kind of lunchroom. On the wall was a sign: PTA MEETING. Two middle-aged

women with frameless glasses were reading from a piece
of paper as a dozen other women listened. "Okay," said
the woman on the right. "For our spring fund-raiser, we're
selling gift baskets! And magazine subscriptions! And pop-
corn! And lightbulbs! Who wants to be in charge of the
gift wrap committee? We need volunteers! Patty? Margie?
Jane?"

"Sparkbolt want OUT!" shouted Sparkbolt, but he
was held in place by his safety belt. "OUT!"

On and on it went—a room full of white-haired
people playing bingo; another room with two men in
hunting outfits shooting a duck; a living room with a wall-
mounted TV screen that displayed some cable news show
where fat, angry guys yelled at each other. In a classroom,
a teacher pointed to a blackboard on which was written
The Importance of Flossing. By the time they got to the last
room, Falcon and Sparkbolt and the two zombies were
exhausted. Now "Kumbaya" was starting up again.

"We hope you've enjoyed your trip to the world of
human beings," said the laughing, macabre voice. "But
before you go, do be careful of hitchhiking humans! They
might just FOLLOW YOU HOME!" The cars passed in
front of a mirror, and briefly Falcon and his friends saw
themselves reflected. But then they saw the shadow of a
human who appeared to be sitting between Falcon and
Weems—a round woman holding bottles of cough syrup

that she poured into a small teaspoon. "This cough syrup is for if you have mucus!" said the hologram. "This other cough syrup is if you have a cough *and* mucus! This third cough syrup is if you have a cough, and mucus, and a sore throat! This fourth cough syrup is if you have a cough, mucus, a sore throat, and postnasal drip! This fifth cough syrup is if you have a cough, mucus, a sore throat—"

The monsters screamed in horror. Then the car bumped through a set of doors again, and a moment later they were back in the dim lights of the house's outer chambers. A man in a straw hat and a seersucker suit helped the children out of their car. A moment later, they exited into the light of Monster Island once more.

"I never want to do that again!" said Destynee. "Ever!"

"Unhaunted house BAD," said Sparkbolt.

"You can say that again," said Weems.

"Unhaunted house BAD!" said Sparkbolt. "Humans destroy!"

"You really think they're so much stranger than we are?" asked Falcon. "Seriously?"

"Dude," said Max. "All those ladies playing bingo? And the guys shooting ducks with their big, blammo guns? That is seriously messed up."

"Yeah," said Destynee. "And what was with that lady with all the cough syrup?" She shuddered. "Creepy!"

Falcon and his friends stopped in the crowds of

Hematoma Boulevard in front of the Five Cent Kandy
Korner, a store where a huge machine stood in the window
whipping saltwater taffy through the air. Falcon felt his
twin hearts pounding in his chest. He was reminded that,
of all his friends, he was the only one with two hearts.
He had a monster heart, of course, but he had a guardian
heart as well. Most of the time, these two hearts lived in
equilibrium with each other, their pulses in harmony. At
other times, like now, he felt strangely out of sync.

"Hey, Falcon," said Max. "You okay? You look kind of
wonky."

The marching goblin band passed by again, and the
air filled with the sounds of drums and godzookas and
squeakaloes.

"I'm fine, Max," said Falcon.

From a blue, endless sky, the sun shone down on the
monsters of the world. There were ogres with digital
cameras, banshees with cheeseburgers, dryads with violet
sno-cones.

But the parade contained no angels.

2

THE FILCHERS

An hour later, Falcon stood on the beach throwing stones into the Sea of Dragons. He watched as they fell into the water with a soft *plunk*. Falcon could hear the sounds of the monster amusement park less than a mile away down the beach, the calliope in the Misery-Go-Round, the screams of vampires rushing down the flume ride in Plasma Falls. He bent down and picked up a small conch shell and held it to his ear. He heard the whisper of the sea.

Falcon unfolded his angel wings and stretched them high over his head. He felt the wind blowing against them, and he thought, briefly, about taking flight. But instead he remained on the ground, feeling the ocean wind gust against his wings.

He remembered the words that Snort had spoken. *Everybody knows what you're trying to do. What you are.* And his reply: *What am I, Snort?*

He would have liked to ask his parents for the answer to this question. But his mother, the queen of the monster killers, lived far from here, on Guardian Island. And his father, the Crow, was exiled to the Tower of Souls in Grisleigh Castle. Most of the time, his parents seemed more concerned with trying to kill each other than with their son's fate. What did Vega, or the Crow, know about being an angel? What did anyone?

Falcon walked down the beach, listening to the crash of the waves upon the shore. From a long way off, he saw something running toward him, a small creature darting and cavorting along the waves. There was something in his mouth.

"Hey," Falcon shouted. "Hello?"

The creature appeared to be a black Labrador retriever, except that instead of four legs he had eight rubbery tentacles. His face came alive with happiness as he drew close to Falcon, and he bounded toward him on his squiggly appendages. He opened his mouth and dropped a book at Falcon's feet. The octopus retriever barked once and began to wag his tail.

Falcon bent down and picked up the book. On the cover was Sparkbolt's handwriting: "Poetry Book of Rhyming Poems."

"Hey," said Falcon. "That's my friend's book. Where did you get this?"

The creature barked again, chomped down on Sparkbolt's poetry journal, then turned and bounded down the beach with it.

"No," said Falcon. "Bad dog. I mean—dog thing. Come back. No! Bad!" Falcon ran after the creature. The octopus retriever bounded across the sand and into the thick, wooded area beyond it. There was a trail here that cut through the woods. Falcon hurried down the path, past ferns and tall mushrooms and thick pine trees. The forest floor was brown with fallen needles and enormous pinecones.

"Oh," said a voice. "Falcon Quinn. You found the dog."

Falcon turned to see a faun sitting on a stump, smoking a pipe. He was an older man with deep, thoughtful eyes. Two goat horns sprouted from his head. His legs, which were covered with fur, were crossed in front of him. He had two mud-covered hooves for feet.

The octopus retriever sat at the faun's side, the book of poems in his mouth. He wagged his tail when he saw Falcon.

"That's my friend's book!" said Falcon. "It's—" His voice sounded unpleasantly loud in that quiet place. Wind blew softly through the trees. The faun sucked on his pipe, then blew a thick smoke ring up in the air. "Did you hear that, Lumpp?" said the faun. "It's his friend's book."

Lumpp, the octopus retriever, looked mournful.

"Drop it!" said the faun. Lumpp whimpered. "I said drop it." Lumpp lowered his head and deposited the book on the forest floor.

"There you go," said the faun. "All's well!"

"What?" said Falcon. He looked at the faun, his merry eyes taking Falcon in as if enjoying a very pleasant joke. "Who are you?" Falcon said.

"I'm Mr. Sweeny," said the stranger. "And that's Lumpp." He sucked on his pipe and then exhaled. The smoke came out purple. Mr. Sweeny smiled as he looked at the smoke. His hairy face crinkled with lines. He turned toward the forest. "You can all come out," he shouted. "It's all right."

There was no reply. Mr. Sweeny smiled thoughtfully. "They don't want to come out," he said. "They're a little skittish."

"Who?"

"My companions."

"What did he do to the dog?" said a voice, and Falcon turned to see a beautiful girl standing there. She had long, black hair, black eyes, full red lips, and two pointed ears. She appeared to be about Falcon's age, but her eyes seemed as old as the Earth.

"He *found* the dog," noted Mr. Sweeny.

"Is that what he says?" said the girl.

"'Tis," said Mr. Sweeny. "Falcon, this is Clea."

The girl looked annoyed and bent down to pat Lumpp on the head. "Poor baby. What did he do to you?"

"Behold!" said a loud voice. "The Squonk!"

The most hideous creature Falcon had ever seen

stepped out from behind a tree. His skin was green and covered with hundreds of warts. Some of his warts had warts. In one hand the Squonk carried a birdcage.

"Falcon Quinn," the man shouted, extending his horrible, wart-covered green hand. "Meet the Squonk!"

"I wouldn't shake his hand," said Clea. "It's contagious."

Falcon shook the Squonk's hand nervously. The Squonk looked at Clea, his feelings hurt. "It is *not* contagious!"

"I didn't mean you," said Clea.

"So you're the famous Falcon Quinn," yelled the Squonk, who apparently yelled everything. "Son of the Crow! Son of the guardian queen! The angel!"

"Yeah," said Falcon. "And you—"

"I'm Squonk," said Squonk. "I'm *the* Squonk." He looked at Falcon as if he ought to have heard of the Squonk before. "You know. The terror of the Pennsylvania forest?"

"He's never heard of you," said Clea contemptuously. "No one's heard of you."

"Well, there's a reason for that," said the wart-covered creature. "You got something like this goin' on, you don't want word to get around!"

"Who are you?" said Falcon. "Where did you come from?"

"We are known as the Filchers," said Mr. Sweeny. "We live apart."

"We're *outcasts!*" shouted the Squonk.

"How many of you are there?" said Falcon.

"Me?" said the Squonk. "I told you. I'm one of a kind!"

"No, I mean—here. Your group."

"We are seven," said Mr. Sweeny, "plus Lumpp, who is not really one of us but who enjoys Mrs. Grubb's cooking."

Lumpp nuzzled close to Falcon's leg. Falcon stroked Lumpp's soft face, and the octopus retriever wagged all of his tentacles happily.

"I think he's found a new friend," said Mr. Sweeny.

Falcon looked at Mr. Sweeny, and Clea, and Lumpp, and the Squonk. "I only see four of you."

"Aye," said Mr. Sweeny.

"That," said a gravelly voice, "is because some of us prefer not to be seen." Falcon turned and saw a crooked man in tattered, black clothing—a coat and vest, a pair of trousers held up with suspenders. He wore frayed, finger-less gloves on his hands. "'Tis a pleasure, Falcon Quinn," said the man. "An honor, indeed."

"This would be Mr. Grubb," said Mr. Sweeny. Mr. Grubb looked at a conch shell in his hands. It took Falcon a moment to realize that this was the same shell he'd picked up on the beach.

"You picked my pocket," said Falcon, unsure whether to be angry or amused.

"Aye," said Mr. Grubb.

At this moment the bird in the Squonk's cage began to

squawk. "Awe! Awe!" it said. "Awe! Awe!"

"Squonk," said Clea. "Please. The bird."

The wart-covered man held his finger over the top of the bird's cage. "Quiet," said the Squonk. "If you know what's good for you." One of the man's fingers seemed to dissolve, and it dripped like hot solder into the cage. The drop landed on the mockingbird's perch with a hot *hiss*.

"I didn't say fry it," said Clea. "I said silence it."

The Squonk held up his hand. A new finger oozed into the place where the old one had been. After a moment, warts sprouted on this one as well.

The bird sang a sad note and fell silent.

A woman wearing a gray apron and holding an enormous wooden spoon appeared before them. "Luncheon's ready," she said. "Although it's not much. And it'll be less, with the extra mouth." She glowered at Falcon. "I'm not used to feedin' angels, and if he thinks he's getting's special treatment 'e'll 'ave me to contend with. Oo, 'e's an angel, I s'pose we're all s'pose to bow down to 'em, well 'e's wrong if 'e thinks that, 'e'll eat slops like the rest of us, slops and burnt varmint roasted on a spit, and that ain't to 'is liking, 'e can feed off 'is own filth. Come on now, the varmint's getting cold. And me shoes aren't comfortable."

"Ah," said Mr. Grubb. "It's the missus." He walked toward the woman, who was nearly as round as she was tall. Her angry face was framed by a head full of boiling gray curls. "Come, me honeydew," he said. "I'd like you to meet our guest, Mr. Falcon Quinn! Say hello to our visitor, dearest!"

Mrs. Grubb just stamped her foot. "Another mouth," she said. "'E better not be stayin' for dinner, that's all I can say."

"That's okay," said Falcon. "I'm not hungry."

Mrs. Grubb's face grew redder and angrier, and there was a short moment of silence.

"Falcon," said Mr. Sweeny reproachfully. "You've been invited to break bread with us. I'm sure you'll do us the honor."

Mrs. Grubb looked like she was going to explode. "Yes, of course," said Falcon.

"Well, it's all set then," said Mr. Grubb. "Come along. Just like one big 'appy family."

"'Appy," muttered Mrs. Grubb. "Turnin' 'is nose up at me fine victuals and 'e says we're 'appy."

"Oh, I'm sure it'll be a fine feast, my little mountain flower," said Mr. Grubb. "My little crumpet!"

"Don't you 'crumpet' me," said Mrs. Grubb. "Come along then. Nothin' worse than cold varmint."

"Aye," said Mr. Sweeny. "We'll come." The faun guided Falcon through the woods to another clearing, where a campfire was softly crackling. There was a large, flat stone covered with food: cheeses and sausage, raspberries and blueberries, and loaves of fresh bread. There were bottles of clear liquid and bottles of blue liquid and a pitcher filled with milk. A chocolate cake stood at one end of the table, and next to this, two pies, still freshly steaming. A large roast beef lay next to a whole chicken. There were mushrooms and asparagus and fiddlehead ferns, huge slabs of butter and jams and cauldrons of Irish stew and green pea soup and beef Stroganoff. There were Mexican tamales and *entomatadas* and a plate of sushi. There was a platter of Szechuan orange beef and another of Rhode Island–style breaded calamari with jalapeños. There was roast duckling and homemade ravioli and a plate of steaming corn on the cob.

"It's not much," said Mrs. Grubb. "But it'll have to do."

"Go on," said Mr. Sweeny. "Help yourself."

There was a stack of clay plates at one end of the table, and Falcon took one. Mrs. Grubb began to heap the plate with the food, giving him a huge portion of everything. After she was done with Falcon, she did the same for Mr. Sweeny and the Squonk. She even set up a plate for Lumpp, which she then placed on the ground. Lumpp began to eat heartily from his dish.

They all sat down on two fallen logs that lay adjacent to the stone table. There was lots of talking and joking as the Filchers ate their food, and Mr. Sweeny and Mr. Grubb in particular drank a great deal from the bottle of blue liquid. The food on Falcon's plate was the most delicious he had ever tasted—the beef was rare and salty, the vegetables fresh and crunchy, the pie and the cake sweet and buttery. Perhaps the best thing on his plate, however, was the homemade brown bread, which smelled like molasses. The crust crunched against his teeth; the inside of the bread was as soft and sweet as cream.

"She's good with the vittles, isn't she?" said Mr. Grubb.

Falcon was just about to agree when he noticed someone sitting by herself at the edge of the forest. She was a pale, young girl with pointed ears and long, yellow hair. She had something in her lap that occupied her whole attention. "Who's that?" said Falcon.

Mr. Sweeny followed Falcon's gaze. "That's Fascia," he said. "The brownie. Very determined."

"Doesn't she—eat?" said Falcon.

"Not while she's working," said Mr. Sweeny. "She's kind of single-minded that way."

"What's she doing?" said Falcon.

"She's fixing shoes," said Mr. Grubb. "It's her calling, you know."

"Hey," said Falcon, recognizing the shoes now. "Those are Destynee's sandals. She burned a hole in them with her slime." The others took this in. "She's an enchanted slug," he explained.

"We know all about Destynee Bloodflough," said Clea.

"You do?" said Falcon.

"We know about all your little friends," said Clea contemptuously. "The whole pathetic story." Falcon noticed that on the elf's plate was only a mound of red cherries. She ate them one by one. "The Sasquatch. The Chupakabra. That Jonny Frankenstein. And the wind elemental who vanished—what was her name?"

"Megan," said Falcon. "Megan Crofton."

"Ah yes," said Clea with a derisive laugh. "The invisible woman!"

The Squonk got out a paddleball and tried to whack it with the paddle, but he missed. The ball bounced up and down on its elastic string.

"Hey," said Falcon. "That's Weems's paddleball. He was looking for that."

"He wasn't usin' it," said the Squonk.

"So, wait," said Falcon. "You just steal things? Is that it?"

"Aye," said Mr. Sweeny. "It's just as you say."

"Now, you're a bright lad, Falcon," said Mr. Grubb. "I wonder if you can guess the biggest thing we've ever stolen. Go on. You try and guess."

"He won't guess," said Clea. "How could he?"

"An elephant," said Falcon.

"Bigger," said Mr. Grubb.

"A whale," said Falcon.

"I told you he couldn't guess."

"Sing us a song now," said Mrs. Grubb.

"A what?"

"Here," said Clea. "Maybe there's a song in here." She picked up the "Poetry Book of Rhyming Poems."

"That's Sparkbolt's book," said Falcon. "Lumpp was chewing on it!"

"Aye," said Mrs. Grubb. "I thought we could boil down the cover, but it's too tough. I'm going to have to make a marinade for it, and I just don't have the time! And my back hurts."

"But these are his poems," said Falcon. "This is important to him."

"Then he should have taken better care of it," said Mr. Grubb, laughing. "Instead of just leaving it out where a body might nick it!"

"But these poems are like Sparkbolt's heart and soul," said Falcon. "It matters to him. Just like that paddleball matters to Weems."

"And that Lincoln Pugh's glasses are important to him," said Mr. Grubb, pulling a pair of large, ugly, orange spectacles out of his jacket.

"And the Sasquatch's bananas!" said Mrs. Grubb, pulling out a slightly bruised banana from her apron. All the Filchers laughed.

Falcon just looked at them, irritated and a little embarrassed.

"Falcon," said Clea. "They're just *things.*"

"But they're important things," said Falcon. "They're important to the people who own them."

"Falcon," said Mr. Sweeny, sucking on his pipe. "Things don't matter. What matters is *life.*"

"Aye, life," said Mr. Grubb. "The pleasures of the table! Songs and stories! The blue of the morning sky!"

Falcon looked at the Filchers in astonishment. He had to admit there was something appealing to their lives, at least if he could judge it on the basis of Mrs. Grubb's cooking.

"Hey!" shouted the Squonk. "Maybe it's time for me to play—the saxophone!" He jumped to his feet happily.

"You'll do no such thing," said Mrs. Grubb. "You know the effect your saxophone has on the innocent!"

"But I thought that he was going to join us!" said the Squonk. "If he's one of us, he won't have the problem!"

"He hasn't joined us yet, has he?" said Mr. Sweeny.

"Well—," said the Squonk. "Not—technically—"

"And what happens when others hear your saxophone?" said Mrs. Grubb. "Do you have no memory at all?"

The Squonk sat back down, dejected. "I remember."

"What happens?" said Falcon.

"Their brains explode," said Clea.

"It's because I never get to practice!" said the Squonk.

"'Explode' is putting it too strongly," said Mr. Sweeny. "But it's not a pleasant thing for the brain, at

least not for the uninitiated. It does leave one's thoughts
a bit bruised."

"I'm an acquired taste!" shouted the Squonk. "I'm very
special!"

"Come on then, Fascia," said Mr. Sweeny. "Leave your
cobbling for a while and let's hear a bit of the fiddle."

Fascia sighed and put down her sandal and her hammer. She brought out a violin and tucked it under her chin.
Clea played something that looked like a large mandolin.
The others clapped along with the tune, and the Squonk
got up on the table and danced. Mr. Sweeny picked up
and played a set of Uilleann pipes, which were like a small
set of bagpipes except that instead of blowing into them,
Mr. Sweeny filled the bag with a bellows strapped under
his right elbow. Their tone was haunting and sweet.

Mrs. Grubb sang the tune:

The man in the moon told me, "Please keep it down.
All the church bells are waking up the dead.
A fool looks better than a headless clown.
Send yourself to bed."

Once on the gray and foam-covered shore,
Fezriddle walked all alone,
Saying, "We shall not see our little houses more.
No more shall we see home."

He laughed and he cried and flew through the air
Till he crashed on the sand on his knees,
And he said three times, "It's just not fair!
Everything comes in threes."

He sobbed in his hands and his beard grew long
And the faeries upon him sprang,
Saying, "Before you go, won't you sing us a tune?"
So he threw back his head and he sang:

"The man in the moon says, 'Please keep it down.
All the church bells are waking up the dead.
A fool looks better than a headless clown.
Send yourself to bed.'"

"I love the way you sing that one, my love," said Mr. Grubb, resting the thumbs of his hands behind his suspenders. "My little potato blossom."

"Why, Mr. Grubb," said his wife. "The things you say."

"Where did you all—come from?" said Falcon.

"Oh, there's always been Filchers," said Mrs. Grubb. "Livin' on the outskirts of things. This particular group's been together, what, seven or eight years now?"

"The brownie was the last to join," said the Squonk, looking at Fascia. "She thought it'd interfere with her work!"

"I didn't like the idea of always moving around," said

Fascia. "It's a grave responsibility. Fixing the shoes of the world."

"Oh god," said Mrs. Grubb. "Here we go with the shoes."

"Who would fix the shoes were it not for me?" said the brownie. "Who?"

"Now, now," said Mr. Grubb. "Everyone respects your trade. Don't we, my rose petal?"

"Do you see this hammer?" said Fascia, holding up her small cobbler's tool. "This is a most important hammer, Falcon Quinn. The key to everything!"

"Important?" said Falcon. "Important how?"

Fascia smiled. "It fixes more than shoes," she said.

"Who knows you're here?" said Falcon. "Does the Academy know?"

"No one knows about the Filchers," said Clea.

"Except Falcon Quinn," said Mr. Sweeny.

"Aye," said Mr. Grubb. "No one but Falcon Quinn."

"Do you live in this forest?" said Falcon. "Is this your home?"

"We go where we please," said Clea. "In search of cherries. In search of streams of clear water. We care nothing for your world of monsters, and guardians, and other such nonsense."

"There are worse things than guardians!" yelled the Squonk.

Lumpp growled softly. At the edge of the clearing a soft, twinkling light shone in the air, drifted toward them, and then went out. The Filchers stood still. The Squonk sniffed the air. Clea closed her eyes as if deep in thought.

"Something's coming," she said.

"Frankenstein," said the Squonk. "From the smell of it."

"We have to be off, Falcon," said Mr. Sweeny sadly.

"What was that light?" said Falcon.

"Willa," said the Squonk. "The wisp. Flickers when there's danger. Or when she's happy!"

Clea looked at Mr. Sweeny. "Tell him," she said. "While there's time."

The faun blew some smoke up in the air and rubbed his chin thoughtfully.

"Tell me what?" asked Falcon.

"Falcon Quinn," said Mr. Grubb. "You're a remarkable chap, really."

"Escaping from the Pinnacle of Virtues," said Clea, her dark eyes glowing.

"Outwitting your mother," said the Squonk.

"Outwitting the father as well," said Mr. Sweeny. "Entering the black mirror, and choosing your own path. You're quite a fellow, Falcon. Quite a fellow indeed."

"How do you know all that?" said Falcon.

"We were passing through," said Clea.

"You mean—you were following me around?"

"We follow no one," said Mr. Sweeny. "But our paths have crossed yours now and again. And with good reason."

"What reason's that?" said Falcon.

"Because, my boy," said Mr. Grubb. "You're one of us."

"What do you mean?" said Falcon. "You mean—you're angels too?"

Clea began to laugh. "Angels," she said as if this was the funniest thing anyone had ever said. "He thinks we're angels."

"Not angels!" shouted the Squonk. "Outliers! Outcasts! Rejects!"

"What?" said Falcon. "I'm not a—" He looked at the Filchers. "I'm part of the Academy," he said. "Me and my friends."

"You never guessed the riddle," said Clea.

"What riddle?"

Mr. Sweeny blew a smoke ring. "Mr. Grubb asked you what the largest thing is you could imagine we've taken. You never guessed."

"I said a whale," said Falcon. "I said an elephant."

"Wrong," said Clea. "And wrong."

"There may come a time," said Fascia, taking Falcon's hand and staring at him with her pale blue eyes. "When you realize you don't fit in anywhere. When you decide that your fate lies outside the world of monsters, or guardians, or any other creatures. That there is no place for you.

And when that time comes, remember us. You will always find yourself welcome among those who live apart."

"The thing we stole, Falcon," said Mr. Sweeny. "The big thing." He smiled kindly. "Don't you see? We stole *ourselves*."

"You stole yourselves?" said Falcon. "I don't understand. What does that mean?"

"Out of the world, Falcon," said Mr. Sweeny. "We stole ourselves out of the world, and have kept ourselves safe and happy, here. On the fringe."

The bird in the cage twittered and flapped its wings. "Awe," it said.

"What kind of bird is that?" said Falcon.

"Oh, that's no bird," said Mr. Grubb. "It's some sort of creature put under an enchantment. It was spying on us."

"Awe," said the bird, looking at Falcon.

"It hates being in this cage," said the Squonk sadly. "I should let it go! Seriously! I should just let it go!"

"Who would spy on you?" said Falcon.

Mr. Sweeny smoked his pipe thoughtfully. "The Watcher, I think," he said. "He's trying to find us."

Falcon seemed to remember something about the Watcher from his Monster Ed class back at the Academy. The Watcher was a kind of shepherd of the monstrous world, supposedly, although no one at the Academy, so far as he knew, had ever actually seen him. He lived on something called the Island of Nightmares, where he tended the dreams of living things. "Why would the—"

But at this moment Willa glowed again, more brightly this time.

A twig snapped in the woods, and Falcon looked down the path that led from the clearing. Something groaned. Then there was the sound of footsteps, and a moment later Sparkbolt appeared.

"Falcon Quinn—," said Sparkbolt, surprised.

Falcon turned to the Filchers, to let them know that Sparkbolt presented no danger to them.

But except for Lumpp, the Filchers had vanished completely. There was no sign of them. The table full of food, and the fire, even Destynee's sandals—all were gone. The octopus retriever whimpered softly, then looked at Falcon and wagged his tentacles. In his mouth, once again, was Sparkbolt's poetry book.

Sparkbolt stepped toward the place where Falcon was standing. "Falcon Quinn—," said Sparkbolt. "With squiggle-dog!"

"Yeah," said Falcon. "This is—uh—Lumpp." Sparkbolt tried to remove the book of poems from the creature's mouth, but Lumpp thought it would be fun to play tug-of-war with it. His tail wagged happily as the Frankenstein pulled on the book.

"Rrrr," shouted Sparkbolt. "Poems—*bitten!*"

"Drop," said Falcon commandingly, and Lumpp let go. The book fell onto the ground. Sparkbolt picked up the journal, which was now covered with saliva and had four deep bite marks in it.

"Bad dog," Sparkbolt muttered darkly. "Dog bad."

3

THE CRIMSON MADSTONE

Max was sitting on a beach chair watching the vampire girls play volleyball in their bikinis. The sun was setting over the sea behind them, bathing the girls in golden light. Around the bonfire to his right, a zombie named Mortia was playing her guitar.

Well, the Sasquatch girls are hip,
I love their fur all splotched with crud;
And the vampire girls, with the way they bite,
They knock me out when they suck my blood.
Egyptian pharaoh's daughters really make you
*   lose your head,*
And the Frankenstein girls, with the bolts
*   in their neck,*
They bring their boys back from the dead.

I wish they all could be zombie mutants
I wish they all could be zombie mutants
I wish they all could be zombie mutant girls.

Transylvania's got the castles
And the girls all get so pale
When the sun goes down and all the banshees come out,
They knock me out when I hear 'em wail!
The leprechaun chicks in Ireland,
When they drink they get so smart,
And the Chupakabras on the coast of Peru
They put a stake right through my heart!

I wish they all could be zombie mutants
I wish they all could be zombie mutants
I wish they all could be zombie mutant girls.

Weems, the ghoul, came over and sat down next to Max and Pearl.

"Love Mortia's tunes, man," said Max. "You love this song? I do."

"Is someone singing?" said Weems. "I hadn't noticed." He looked discouraged.

"Señor Weems," said Pearl. "Your spirits seem diminished!"

"I have misplaced the paddleball," said Weems. "I am angered by its absence."

"Hey, what's the deal with you and the paddleball, anyhow?" said Max. "It's kooky."

"I find it soothing when my nerves are frayed," said

Weems. "When I find myself trying to make peace with the constant tide of deceit, and cruelty, and betrayal."

"You should have one of those foot-long hot dogs, dude," said Max. "Beats paddleball."

A gorgeous young vampire named Vonda came over and sat near Mortia. She was yanking a hunchback girl along on a chain. Twisty, the hunchback, had hair the consistency of tangled spaghetti.

"Hey, Vonda," said Max. "What up!"

"Tell him not to talk to me," said Vonda.

"She says not to talk to her," said Twisty.

"And yet we send you our greetings notwithstanding," said Pearl.

Weems dug down into a bucket of eyeballs, put one on a stick, and started roasting it.

"Hey, Vonda," said Max. "You want Weems to make you a s'nasty?"

Weems picked up a pair of graham crackers. "They are so squishy and sweet," said Weems.

"Twisty," said Vonda, "tell them not to talk to me!"

"She says—"

"I know what she says," hissed Weems.

"Hey," said Falcon, walking up to his friends. At his side was Sparkbolt, carrying his book of poems. Just behind them was Lumpp, who now had a large sea sponge in his mouth.

"It is Falcon Quinn," said Pearl. "And Señor Sparkbolt, the well-regarded Frankenstein author of sonnets and verse! We welcome you to our celebration!"

"Rrrr," said Sparkbolt.

"Hey, Pearl," said Falcon.

"And they got some kind a squishy dog with 'em too!" said Max excitedly. "Whoa! He's excellent! Where'd the dog come from, Falcon?"

"His name is Lumpp," said Falcon. "I—uh—found him in the forest."

Lumpp dropped his sea sponge at Max's feet. Max picked it up and threw it. Lumpp tore off across the sand to retrieve it. The octopus retriever came back in a flash, dropped the sea sponge at Vonda's foot this time. He looked hopefully at the young vampire.

Vonda kicked the retriever and laughed. He looked unharmed, although his eyes looked as if his feelings had been hurt.

"Hey!" said Max. "That's not cool! All he wants is a little love and affection!"

"I hate animals," said Vonda. She turned to Twisty. "Tell them."

Twisty hitched forward and looked at them with her goggle eye. "She says she hates animals."

"All Sparkbolt want!" said Sparkbolt. "Is love! And affection!"

"Dear god, here we go," said Vonda.

"Can I have it?" said Twisty, looking at the sea sponge at her mistress's feet. "Please, just one time? Can I be the one who has it?"

"Here," said Vonda, and threw the sponge in Twisty's face. "Ha! Ha! You're stupid!"

"Thank you for throwing the sponge at me!" said Twisty. "I'm so grateful!"

"Why are you grateful to her, Twisty?" said Mortia. "She's so awful to you!"

"She's so *pretty*," said Twisty. "And that's the most important thing in the world! Being pretty!"

"Hey, man!" said Max to Falcon. "Weems is makin' s'nasties! You want one?"

"Maybe later," said Falcon. "I have to work at the Bludd Club in just a few minutes."

"How come you have to work at the Bludd Club?" said Max. "Snort was the one who stampeded *you*, man."

"Señor Max," said Pearl. "Our friend Falcon has done this deed out of the nobility of his own heart! To save even his own enemy from expulsion!"

"I know, I know," said Max. "It's just kinda—wonky, that's all."

"'Wonky,'" said Pearl. "I do not understand this 'wonky'!"

"I didn't think about it that much," said Falcon. "It

was just something I could do for him. So I did it."

"Hey, I got another question, about vampires," said Max to Vonda. "How come you guys can just walk around in the middle of the day? Isn't the sunlight supposed to turn you into—dust?"

Vonda turned to Twisty. "Tell him not to talk to me!"

Twisty hunched forward. "She says—"

"But it is an intriguing question!" said Pearl. "I too have wondered about this!"

Twisty's bulbous eye twitched. "It's because they wear sunscreen," she said. "It protects them."

"You're kidding," said Falcon.

"It's, like, SPF ten thousand!" said Twisty. "That's how Vonda stays so pale! And pretty!"

"Señor Falcon," said Pearl. "Where have you been in the hours since the altercation? I have been concerned, in the time intervening, by your mysterious absence!"

Falcon thought about his afternoon with the Filchers and considered telling his friends about it. But then he thought better of it. "I just went for a walk," said Falcon. "There's nothing mysterious about it."

"Falcon Quinn," said Sparkbolt. "Find poetry book of poems. Lost! In forest!"

"Curses," said Weems. His eyeball on a stick burst into flames. He pulled the eyeball out of the fire and blew on it.

Something wet and squishy bounced off of Falcon's

face. He looked down to see a moist sea sponge at his feet.

"Hey, Lumpp," said Falcon. He leaned down to pat the octopus retriever on the head. "You're a good boy!" Lumpp looked at Falcon with an expression that looked very much like love.

"What's so good about him?" said Vonda. "He's boring! I hate being bored!" She looked at Twisty. "Don't I?"

"She does," said Twisty.

"Here you go, Lumpp," said Falcon, throwing the sponge. In an instant, the octopus retriever cantered enthusiastically after it. Max and Pearl and Falcon watched as the creature swam out into the waves, grabbed the sponge with one tentacle, and then returned to the shore. He shook off the water that clung to his fur, then trotted back to the monsters, dropped the sponge, and pointed once again.

"Dude," said Max. "Now you have an animal friend!"

Lumpp started to dig down in the sand with his foretentacles. He seemed to be sniffing around with his big, furry head, plunging it into the hole that he was digging. After a moment, Lumpp's head disappeared entirely into the earth. Dirt flew over the creature's shoulders as the hole got bigger.

"He's going way down," noted Max. "Look at him! I mean, he's goin' waaaaayyy down!"

A moment later the retriever pulled something out of the sand with his tentacles.

"What is it that this creature has unearthed?" asked Pearl.

"I don't know," said Falcon, going over to Lumpp. "Hey, fella. What you got there?"

Lumpp held a sand-covered pendant on a long chain up in the air. It dangled from his tentacle. Falcon took it from him.

"It is an amulet," said Pearl, "of most mysterious design!"

"An amulet?" said Max. Falcon was rubbing the sand off of it. It was a golden disk with a ruby-red jewel in its center.

"There's writing on it," said Falcon. He rubbed the flat disk some more.

"What is this writing?" asked Pearl.

Falcon squinted. "I can't read it. It's a bunch of strange runes."

"Let me see," said Max, taking it from him. "I'm good at Sudoku and junk!"

The bigfoot squinted at the strange lettering, but, like Falcon, he could not make sense of the symbols. "Kooky," Max said, then put the amulet around his neck.

"Señor Max," said Pearl. "I would not be placing an amulet of unknown properties upon my person without first researching its nature."

"C'mon," said Max. "It looks all hippy-dippy, doesn't

it? Anyway, what could hap—"

Max's sentence was left unfinished, however, for at this moment he vanished into a glowing crimson vapor and the amulet fell into the sand. The red mist hung in space for a moment, a shadow-version of the giant Sasquatch, before drifting toward Sparkbolt.

"Dude," said Sparkbolt, looking at himself in astonishment. It was Sparkbolt's body, but Max's voice was coming out of it.

"Check it out! I'm a Frankenstein!" said Sparkbolt's body with Max's voice.

"¿Señor?" said Pearl.

"Sasquatch!" shouted Sparkbolt in his own voice. He raised his green hands to his head. "IN BRAIN."

"Hey, man, how do I get out of here?" shouted Max with Sparkbolt's mouth. "It's nasty!"

"SASQUATCH DESTROY!" yelled Sparkbolt. "RRRRR! RRRRR!"

"Señor Falcon," said Pearl. "We must free our friend from his Frankenstein prison!"

"SASQUATCH DESTROY!" shouted Sparkbolt. "DESTROY! DESTROY!"

"Dude," said Max from inside Sparkbolt.

"Wait," said Falcon, slipping the amulet around Sparkbolt's neck. There was, once more, a cloud of crimson mist as the Frankenstein dissolved. A moment later,

Max fell onto the sand, out of the bottom of the cloud, and the amulet dropped onto the beach next to him.

"*¿Señor?*" said Pearl.

Max dusted himself off. "Okay," he said. "I'm not doing that again."

"It is a relief to have you in your original form once more," said Pearl.

"I tell you what," said Max. "Being stuck inside of Sparkbolt kind of opened my eyes, man."

"In what way," said Pearl, "have your eyes been opened?"

"About what Frankensteins are up against. I mean, while I was inside his skull I could feel all—you know, dark and lurchy. What's that old saying, about how you can never really understand somebody until you've walked a mile inside their brain? Turns out—that is so totally true!"

"Where *is* Sparkbolt, anyway?" said Falcon. "That mist must have gone somewhere."

They looked around the beach. There was no sign of him. Over at the fire pit, Mortia was still singing her folk songs. Lumpp wagged his tail, hoping someone would throw the sponge. Vonda lay on a beach towel as Twisty rubbed sunscreen onto her back. Ankh-hoptet, wearing a strange bikini made entirely out of mummy bandages, sat in a folding chair next to Lincoln Pugh.

"Dude," said Max. "The smoke. Maybe it blew out to sea."

"Oh no," said Falcon, picking up the "Poetry Book of Rhyming Poems," which had fallen into the sand. "We've lost him!"

"Dude," said Max. "This is bad."

Vonda got up from her seat and walked toward them. Twisty followed behind her. Vonda looked at Max and Pearl and Falcon with her usual disdain.

"Hey, Twisty," said Falcon.

Twisty looked thoughtful for a moment. Then Sparkbolt's voice came out of her mouth. "Rrrrr! Twisty bad!"

"Oh no," said Max.

"What did you do to her, Falcon Quinn?" said Vonda.

"Me?" said Falcon.

"Yes, of course you. Everyone knows what you're trying to do, Falcon Quinn."

"Rrrr!" said Sparkbolt's voice. "Twisty destroy! DESTROY!"

"It's not Falcon, man," said Max. "It's this creepy amulet. It turns people into this nasty red mist, and then the mist drifts into people's brains."

"I was not speaking to you!" said Vonda, wrinkling her nose.

"Help me, Falcon," said Twisty in her own voice.

"Please! Don't let the Frankenstein take over my brain!"

"You should be ashamed of yourself," said Vonda.

"Me?" said Falcon. "I didn't put Sparkbolt in her brain."

"Destroy!" shouted Twisty with Sparkbolt's voice. She picked up a rock. "Must destroy!"

"Get the Frankenstein out of her brain!" said Vonda. "I demand it! This instant!"

"Hey, man," said Max. "You can't just order people around!"

"Ow!" said Twisty as she crushed a rock against her skull. "That hurt!"

"Must destroy!" shouted Sparkbolt's voice, and Twisty bent down to pick up another rock to smash against her head.

"This cycle of violence cannot continue!" said Pearl.

"Falcon," said the hunchback, her eyes wide and sad. "He's going to make me smash my head with a rock again."

"Destroy! Destroy!" shouted Sparkbolt's voice.

"Help her," said Vonda. "I demand it! Undo this damage you have done!"

Falcon sighed, then put the amulet around Twisty's neck. The hunchback vanished, and a moment later, Sparkbolt, wholly restored, fell onto the sand. The red vapor drifted through the air once more.

"Ah! Ah! Ah!" said Sparkbolt. "Sparkbolt *Sparkbolt!*"

"Dude," said Max.

Vonda looked angrily at all of them. "I am totally upset!" she said. "I need a massage! Twisty, tell them I want a massage!"

But Twisty wasn't there anymore.

"Twisty?" said Vonda. "Where are you?"

Then Vonda's beautiful face took on a distinctly odd expression, one eye larger than the other, and for a moment she seemed to hunch forward. The girl looked at her own body with shock and amazement, as if seeing it for the first time. "I'm—*Vonda*," she said, but she said this with Twisty's voice. "I'm—*pretty*—!"

"Twisty?" said Falcon. "Are you in there?"

"I am," she said with amazement.

"Put on the amulet," said Vonda's voice. "Hurry." Falcon picked up the necklace and held it out toward her.

But Twisty's expression spread once more over the lovely girl's face. "No," she said. "I don't think I will."

"What are you talking about?" said Vonda's voice.

"I think I'm going to stay here," said Twisty's voice. "I—like it here! I like being—*pretty*."

"I demand that you leave this body this instant!" said Vonda. "I demand that you—*grrrkkk*!" Vonda's face turned purple for a moment, then Twisty's expression returned. This time, Vonda's expression did not come back.

"Vonda's going away for a while," said Twisty's voice,

and a sly smile spread over her features.

"Twisty?" said Falcon. "What happened to Vonda?"

Twisty's voice laughed softly. "I chained her to a log!" she said triumphantly. "I chained her to a log—in her own brain!!!"

"I do not understand," said Pearl. "You are saying that you have seized control?"

"I have," said Twisty's voice.

"Dude," said Max, shaking his head. "This is better than video games. I'm serious."

"Ah! Ah! Ah!" said Sparkbolt. "Twisty FRIEND!"

"It's not Twisty," said Twisty. "It's Vonda."

"Listen," said Falcon. "Not that this isn't entertaining and all. But I have to get over to the Bludd Club to bus tables."

"I'm pretty!" Twisty shouted, starting to do a little dance.

"Okay, man," said Max. "We'll be here! Eatin' s'nasties!" He glanced over at Twisty. "Watchin' the show."

"S'nasties bad," said Sparkbolt.

"And I'll walk around being—pretty!" said Twisty jubilantly. "Everyone will be amazed—at how pretty I am!"

Sparkbolt groaned to himself. Falcon nodded to his friends and began to walk back toward the amusement park. Lumpp scampered after him.

"Hey, wait up," said Max. He put his arm around the retriever's squishy neck. "You gotta stay with us, fella. No octopus retrievers in the Bludd Club."

"Thanks, Max," said Falcon.

"Also," said Max, "don't forget your amulet thing." He put the necklace in Falcon's hand.

"Okay," said Falcon. He started to walk away again, but Max called to him one more time.

"And dude," said Max, "one last thing? Be careful tonight, okay? Those vampires—they're—well, you know. They're kinda wonky."

"I'll be careful," said Falcon. He squeezed his friend's large, hairy shoulder. "You're a good friend, Max. I mean it."

"That's right," said Max. "I'm awesome!"

Lumpp wagged his tail.

"You're a good friend too, Lumpp," said Falcon. The octopus retriever had gotten hold of Sparkbolt's poems again, and once more he stood there with his tail wagging and the leather journal in his rubbery mouth.

"I gotta go," said Falcon.

"Later," said Max, and headed back toward the ocean, Lumpp at his side.

Falcon looked at the amulet in his hand. He remembered the sound of Max's voice coming out of Sparkbolt's mouth. He looked over at the bonfire, where even now

Twisty was walking around saying "I'm pretty!"

This thing is dangerous, Falcon thought. *I should get rid of it.*

Falcon held the amulet in his hand for a moment longer, looking at its mysterious runes. Then he threw it as far as he could. It soared above the beach, over a volleyball net, and landed in some sand dunes.

Then Falcon turned his back and headed toward Abominationland, and the Bludd Club.

Mortia, firelight flickering off of her half-decayed face, was still singing her zombie song.

I wish they all could be zombie mutants
I wish they all could be zombie mutants
I wish they all could be zombie mutant girls.

Lumpp, meanwhile, had not taken his eyes off Falcon, even as Max led him away. As the amulet sailed through the air, the octopus retriever dropped Sparkbolt's "Poetry Book of Rhyming Poems" and let it fall into the sand.

A moment later, Lumpp was running across the beach, his eyes focused intently on the place in the dunes where the amulet had come to rest.

4

THE BLUDD CLUB

Falcon walked from the beach back to the amusement park. At this hour, just after sunset, many of the monster families were leaving the park for the evening. They left the sections of the park with the rides—Yesterdayland and Abominationland—and made their way toward the exits, where hearse cars or Viking funeral boats would take the visitors back to their hotel rooms at the Waldorf-Hysteria. The night creatures, however, were just beginning to come out, and an equal number of weredogs and vampires were pouring into the park at this same hour. A long line for the evening buffet at Dracula's Castle had formed, and from the Plasma Falls water park, Falcon saw a coffin-shaped flume boat emerge from the gushing summit of Thrombosis Mountain and plummet down the five-hundred-foot waterfall of roaring, thundering blood.

The Bludd Club was a dark-looking pub between Plasma Falls and the Waldorf-Hysteria. The hotel, which was run by Mr. Trunkanelli's wife, Pachysia, flickered with the lights of candles. Bats circled around and around its towers. From the Bludd Club came the sound of harp-sichord music. Falcon sighed.

"Whatsa matta?" said a familiar voice. "Ya don't like harpsichord?"

Falcon looked over. "Hi, Snort," he said.

"I been in here once before," said Snort. "By the end of the night that harpsichord music was like nails on a blackboard."

"When were you in here before?"

Snort shrugged. "Last time I stampeded somebody," he said.

They opened the thick, oaken door to the Bludd Club, and Falcon and Snort walked inside.

The loud, raucous room was abundant with vampires of many varieties. There were old-school vamps in tux-edos and slicked-back hair; there were younger ones with crew cuts and pool cues over at a billiard table. There were girls with navel rings and tattoos; there were middle-aged blond women who looked like the hosts of cable news shows. At scores of tables sat the undead creatures, talking animatedly with one another, laughing, cavorting. They were an exceedingly attractive group of people, their teeth shiny, their hair perfect.

"Boy!" shouted a hearty young man. "Boy! I need a clean spoon."

Falcon was still staring at the interior of the Bludd

Club. There was an outer chamber called the Crypt, in which the vampires drank blood from pint glasses. Beyond this was the Coffin Room, a fancy restaurant in which a man with deeply wrinkled skin and bloody slits for eyes sat behind a harpsichord playing Bach.

"Boy!" shouted the hearty young man again.

"He's talking to you, Falcon," said Snort. "You take care of the Crypt; I'll cover the Coffin Room." He nodded. "Go on, see what he wants. They get mad if you keep them waiting."

"Yes?" said Falcon to the young man. "Can I help you?"

"I said I need a clean spoon. Do run along and get me one. Spit spot!"

"Spit spot?" said Falcon.

"There's a good man," said the vampire. He gave Falcon a fifty-dollar bill. "And please do take good care of the ladies." The young man nodded to the women at his table.

"Where's Vonda?" said one of the girls. "I don't see Vonda!"

"She's back at the Monster Beach party," said Falcon.

There was a moment of shocked silence. "Did you just speak to me?" said the girl in a tone of outrage. "Reevey! Make him stop!"

"Say, you're Falcon Quinn, aren't you?" said the young man. "I'm Reeves Pennypacker Sherrod-Waldow

Binswanger III." He nodded to the women. "This is Dominique and Muffy." The girls looked away. "You're new here, aren't you? Haven't learned your place?"

"I guess not," said Falcon.

"Well, you will," said Reeves. "You will."

"Right," said Falcon, and turned toward the back of the room, where the kitchen was. As he stepped forward, Muffy swung her leg out and tripped him, and Falcon fell onto the floor. Everyone laughed.

"Look, everybody!" said Reeves. "A fallen angel!"

This witty comment made all the vampires laugh even harder. Falcon's black eye began to burn with fire. He got back on his feet and as he did, his wings began to spread above and behind him. He looked more than a little menacing, standing there by the vampires' table, looking at them all with hatred. Reeves looked back at Falcon with widening, hypnotic eyes. Conversation in the Crypt fell silent as the vampires turned to watch the standoff.

Reeves and Falcon stared at each other for a few seconds more, then Falcon lowered his wings again and turned his back on them. As he walked across the room holding the spoon, he felt the vampires' gaze upon him. Conversation began again—a series of whispers at first, followed by laughter.

From behind a small, elegant wooden table, a man with a red carnation in his lapel watched Falcon as he headed toward the kitchen. He fingered a rich ruby ring on his right hand and then looked once more at Falcon with a cruel and cunning smile.

Back on Monster Beach, the campfire had burned down to coals. Mortia sat on a large rock, playing her guitar and singing softly. Max, Sparkbolt, and Pearl were now gathered around her. Lumpp sat at their feet. Waves crashed on the dark shore. Out on the ocean, a soft yellow light flickered on the horizon.

Mortia sang.

> *All I wanna do*
> *Is suck some blood.*
> *I got a feeling*
> *I'm not the only one.*
> *All I wanna do*
> *Is suck some blood*
> *And watch the sun come up over Hematoma*
> *   Boulevard. . . .*

Lumpp turned his head toward the ocean. His eyes settled on the small, yellow light in the distance. It was moving.

The octopus retriever growled softly.

"Dude," said Max, looking at Lumpp. "What's with

the growling? Now's not the growling time. Now's the sit-around-and-be-excellent time!"

"Our many-tentacled friend has a feeling of discontent!" observed Pearl.

Lumpp's tail stood out straight behind him. He raised one of his front tentacles to point. He growled again.

Mortia put her guitar down and looked in the direction Lumpp was pointing.

"Hey," she said, looking at the moving light. "What *is* that?"

"Light," Sparkbolt said. "Belong dead."

Lumpp growled more loudly now. His tail quivered.

"Dude," said Max. "Something's coming."

"Falcon Quinn," said a waitress named Cuttles. "I heard you and Snort were coming to help out tonight." She was a kind of enchanted squid, with ten long rubbery arms. Cuttles wore a pink waitress uniform.

"Yes, ma'am," said Falcon.

"Oh, don't you 'ma'am' me, hon," said Cuttles. "Put on an apron and start working the room. You'll figure out the drill soon enough." She picked up two plates of food with a pair of tentacles and shoved a pile of plates onto the conveyor belt for the dish room with several others. Cuttles was a whirlwind of moving arms and legs. "It's a fine place to work. I don't know why Mr. Trunkanelli thinks it should be a punishment. Me, I'd come in here on my day off, if I wasn't too tired. It's good to be busy!" As she said this, another pair of tentacles picked up a plate with a juicy steak on it, plus nine pints of blood, each of which was stuck to another of her sucker disks.

"What do I do?" said Falcon.

Cuttles was still moving. "You see your friend the rhino, over there in the Coffin Room? Do what he does. Clear the plates. Get the bloodsuckers what they want. If you don't know what to do, tell me, and I'll take care of it as soon as I can. But don't expect any miracles! I only got ten arms!"

"Okay," said Falcon. He held up Reeves's dirty spoon. "What do I do with this?"

"Conveyor belt," said Cuttles, grabbing the spoon with one tentacle and putting it on a moving belt that led toward the dish room. "Copperhead will wash it in the back room. Oh, and don't talk to Copperhead, okay?"

"Why not?"

"She's a Gorgon, hon. Snakes for hair, the works. She wants you to come into the back room so she can turn you to stone. So don't listen to her! Just keep moving!" Cuttles reached toward the counter and picked up a piece of pie on a plate. "That's what I do!"

"Okay," said Falcon.

"And don't talk to the vampires either!" she shouted.

"They don't like it! Just stay busy! Busy! Busy! Busy!"

Falcon watched as Cuttles swept through the Crypt like a cephalopod tornado. As she moved, she carefully placed the steaks and pints of blood on the vampires' tables while simultaneously gathering up used plates and cutlery.

"Boy," said a vampire, and Falcon turned to see a distinguished, older man looking at him. He had a red carnation in his lapel. Falcon went toward his table and began to gather the dirty dishes.

"So you're the famous Falcon Qvinn," said the man. There were points of silver light in the man's eyes.

"How do you know my name?" asked Falcon.

"Now, now," said the man. "Everyone knows your name. You're all anyvun can talk about. Especially after the ewents of this morning. Attacking the"—the man looked at Snort with distaste—"*ungulate.*" He shuddered. "Tearing up the park. And of course, the matter of your parentage. The mother. The father. Really, it's a vonder anyone can speak of anything else."

"I wish they didn't," said Falcon, feeling strangely ashamed. "I wish I was like everyone else."

"But of course you do not vish this," the man whispered. "This is not the vish for Falcon Qvinn."

"I don't know," said Falcon.

"I think you do," said the man. "I—am Count

Manson. Vun of the instructors at the *Academy.* Ve have been vatching your progress, Falcon Qvinn, my colleagues and I. Vatching vith a sense of fasincation—and *vonder!*"

"Yeah?" said Falcon. "Well. I'm interesting, I guess."

"Oh, much more than interesting. A remarkable case—the boy born to a demon and—our adversaries. A creature from the land betwixt and between! There are those, I am sure you are avare, who vonder vhich side you are on."

"I'm on nobody's side," said Falcon. "Or everybody's, maybe. I don't know."

"Ah," said the count. "I vonder if you think it vill be possible to live a life vithout choosing a side."

"Yeah, well," said Falcon. "I vonder that too sometimes. I mean—wonder."

The count laughed as if this was a deeply humorous thing to have said.

"I suppose," he said darkly. "Ve vill see. Von't ve?"

"Yeah," said Falcon. "I guess ve vill." He collected the dirty glass from the count's table and took it back to the dish room. As he walked away, he felt Count Manson's gaze still upon him. It was as if the man's glance was burning a hole into the back of his head.

"Help me," moaned a low voice, and Falcon turned toward its source—the small hole in the wall with the conveyor belt that led to the dish room. Falcon unloaded the dirty dishes and plates from the Crypt onto the conveyor, and as he did, the voice called out again.

"Is anybody there?" it said.

"I'm here," said Falcon.

"Help me."

"Who are you?"

"I'm Copperhead. I'm in the dish room. Can you let me out?"

"I'm sorry," said Falcon. "I was told not to."

"Who are you?" she said. He heard the clattering of plates and the rushing of water in a sink.

"I'm Falcon Quinn," he said.

"Falcon Quinn," said the voice breathlessly. "I know you! You're the angel!"

"Yeah."

"Won't you come in and talk? Just for a second!"

"Cuttles told me not to talk to you," said Falcon. "You've got, like, snakes for hair. If anybody sees you they turn to stone."

There was a long pause. Falcon heard the sound of more splashing water, the clink of glasses in a sink. "You don't have to look at me," said Copperhead. "I have this bag I can put over my head."

"I'm working," said Falcon, and he turned with his empty platter back toward the Bludd Club. He walked through the Coffin Room, busing tables, as the young vampires laughed at their private jokes and the harpsichordist continued playing in the corner. Suddenly Falcon felt an unexpected jabbing in his rear end, and he shouted, nearly dropping his platter of dirty glasses on the floor. He turned around and saw Snort standing there, hot steam curling out of his nostrils.

"Poked ya," said Snort.

"What?" said Falcon, confused.

"Poked ya," said Snort again, and chuckled.

"Did you want something, Snort?" said Falcon.

"Thought you were pretty funny today," said Snort to Falcon. "Making me look stupid. In front of everybody."

"What?" said Falcon.

"Getting me in trouble with Trunkanelli. Making everyone *laugh* at me." More steam blew from his nose. "But who's laughing now, Falcon Quinn? Tell me that!"

"I wasn't trying to get you in trouble, Snort," said Falcon. "I was trying to help you."

"Why would you help me?" said Snort, his voice cracking for a moment. "Nobody wants to help me!"

"I don't know," said Falcon. "It just seemed like the—"

But Falcon paused midsentence. A strange hissing noise, like the voices of hundreds of approaching snakes, was slowly rising in the room. A blue fog crept across the floor.

"What's this fog?" said Reeves at a nearby table. "It's not very sporting!"

"I think I'll just have a little nap," said Muffy, laying her head down on the table. "So tired!"

"It's really getting *sleepy* in here," said Dominique, looking around. A lot of the vampires were yawning now, closing their eyes, resting their heads on their hands.

"Cuttles—," said Reeves. "Be a good girl and have them stop this fog. It's making everyone so"—he yawned—"so *piqued*."

"Vait!" said the count suddenly. *"Don't you see? They're here! They're here!"*

"Who?" said Falcon. "What are you talking about?"

It was at this moment that Falcon saw a figure he recognized emerging through the mist. Cygnus, the guardian general, walked into the Bludd Club and looked around with an air of amusement. At his side was a man with a large white mustache and a monocle. He wore a pith helmet atop his head and with one hand he carried a large elephant gun.

"I say!" shouted the man with the pith helmet. "Here's some game worth hunting!" He aimed his elephant gun at the slumbering crowd.

"Colonel," said Cygnus. "Please. We mustn't be hasty." The general searched the room until his eyes fell upon Falcon. "Ah, Prince Falcon," he said. "There you are. Your mother sent us."

"What do you want?" said Falcon. "You aren't allowed here!"

"But Falcon, don't you see?" said Cygnus. "We've come to rescue you!"

"Rescue me?" said Falcon, astonished. "I don't need rescuing!"

Cygnus shook his head. "Oh please," he said. "It's not going to be like that, is it?"

"What's that?" said the colonel. "Says he doesn't need rescuing? Curious! Highly irregular!"

"A sleeping grenade," said Count Manson in a voice of contempt. "I am disappointed in you, Cygnus. I should have expected you vould at least be villing to fight—one gentleman to another."

Cygnus gave a sneering laugh. "You're no gentleman, Count," he said.

"Right," said the colonel. He raised his elephant gun to his face, closed one eye, and pulled the trigger. There was a blast of white smoke and a loud explosion, and Count Manson was propelled across the room. The vampire smashed through a far wall.

"I say," said the colonel. "A direct hit! Bully!"

"There will be no more violence," said Cygnus. "If you'll just come peacefully, Falcon!"

From the hole in the wall came the sound of Count

Manson groaning. "I vill get—*rewenge!*"

"I say," said the colonel. "That fellow's not dead!"

"He's a vampire," said a familiar voice. "You can't kill him with bullets."

A girl about Falcon's age stepped forward through the fog. She was carrying a large bullwhip. Falcon's jaw dropped open as he looked at her.

"Megan?" he said.

5

THE RESCUE

The girl glanced around the room uncertainly. "Whoa," she said. "Monsters!"

"Don't worry," said Cygnus. "The vampires are all asleep. As for the rest of them"—he cast a glance at Falcon—"I think they're *harmless*."

"Megan," said Falcon, moving toward her. "It's me."

The girl pulled out the whip and cracked it in the air. "You stand back, you," she said. "Don't come near me!"

"What have you done to her?" said Falcon to Cygnus. The girls's hair was blond, not black, and her arms and shoulders were well muscled. These differences aside, Falcon could swear she was his friend from Cold River. "What have you done to Megan?"

"Megan?" said Cygnus. "This is *Gyra*. One of our most prized cadets. And one of your subjects, Prince Falcon."

"No it's not," said Falcon. "That's—"

"All right, you," said a stern voice. "Outta my club!" They turned to see Cuttles rushing toward the invaders, wiggling on her many tentacles. "This is a nice place! We don't need no roughhousing here!"

But the colonel aimed his elephant gun at Cuttles, and a moment later there was another blast and a puff of white smoke, and the waitress flew across the room and out the same hole that Count Manson had opened.

"Another direct hit!" said the colonel. "Bully! I say, I can't wait to describe this conquest in my memoirs!"

"Falcon, please," said Cygnus. "Is this really what you want? A slaughter?"

"I say, I want that one for my trophy room!" said the colonel. "Awfully nice trophy, a giant squid. Last one I bagged I believe was back in eighty-six! No, eighty-seven. Same year I contracted malaria from one of the banshees of Tasmania!"

"Colonel, please," said Cygnus. "This is not the time for one of your stories."

"A rum go, malaria!" said the colonel. "Feared for my life! If it wasn't for an elixir I procured from one of the natives, I'd have—"

"Look out!" shouted a voice. "I'm *stampedin'*!"

Snort thundered across the room, his horn lowered in order to skewer Cygnus. But Gyra cracked her whip on Snort's backside, and the rhino, enraged, spun around to impale her. Gyra, however, took a step to one side, and Snort stampeded past her and straight into a wall, imbedding his horn firmly in the wood.

"I got him," said Gyra, surprised at herself. "Did you see? I got him!"

"Bully for you," said the colonel. "Still, I *did* suppose they'd have more fight in them than this, this lot. Rather disappointing, I should think. Not much sport in them at all!"

Cygnus narrowed his eyes, peering through the mist that was still drifting through the Coffin Room. "Don't underestimate them, Colonel," he said. "They're *cunning!*"

The vampires did not seem cunning at this moment, though. One by one they were waking from their slumber, and then, in that same instant, transforming into bats. The air filled with fluttering, leathern wings, and the bats flew out the Bludd Club's broken windows and into the night.

Falcon felt his left eye burning with heat. An orange fireball shot out of his dark eye and hurtled toward the colonel. But the man just swung the butt of his rifle like a baseball bat, and he knocked the fireball across the room, where it exploded against the back of the bar, shattering bottles into thousands of tiny pieces and setting the splintered fragments of the bar aflame. The fire caught quickly and began to crackle up the wall.

"Bully," said the colonel happily. "Now we've got a conflagration!"

"Megan," said Falcon. "What did they do to you?"

The girl looked at Cygnus, uncertain. "Why does he keep calling me that?" she said.

"Come, Falcon," said Cygnus. "Let us go."

"Go? Go where?" Falcon said.

"Back to your own kind," said Cygnus. The fire behind the bar was starting to spread now. "Back to your friends."

"He's right, you know," said Gyra. "You *should* come with us."

"Why would I go with you?" said Falcon.

"For a better life?" said Gyra. She held out her hand.

Falcon felt his hearts pulsing as he looked at the girl's extended hand. He remembered standing with Megan in front of the clock face, up in the Tower of Souls, last spring. He remembered the way the wind had lifted her hair, how the ticking of the clockworks had pounded in his ears.

At this moment, however, a sea sponge bounced off of Gyra's face. Gyra and Falcon both looked at the wet, round sponge as it rolled around on the floor.

"*Who*—," said Cygnus angrily. "Who threw that?" Something swept through the air, circled him, and jabbed him with a sharp object. "Ow!"

"It is I!" shouted a voice. "*¡La Chupakabra!* The famous goatsucker of Peru!" Pearl jabbed Cygnus with her stinger, then circled around Gyra and Falcon and the colonel. "And I have come to defend Falcon Quinn! To whom I have pledged my life!"

"Dude," said Max, roaring through the door. "*We're* his friends!"

"Max!" shouted Falcon. "Pearl!"

Cygnus looked at Pearl with contempt. "You're going to need poison more powerful than that," he said, "if you're going to battle me, Chupakabra."

"I have all the poisons that shall be required," shouted Pearl, buzzing toward the guardian general once again. "I am *¡la Chupakabra!* The famous goatsucker of P—"

But Cygnus just swatted Pearl out of the air with the back of his hand.

"Hey," shouted Max. "YOU HURT MY FRIEND!" He ran toward Pearl, who lay on the floor, her wings buzzing softly.

"General," said Gyra, looking worried. "You said that Falcon would join us without a fight."

"I'm not going with you!" Falcon shouted.

Gyra looked disappointed. Her lips parted.

"I say, old chap," said the colonel to Cygnus. "We seem to be losing our advantage!"

Weems and Destynee now ran into the Bludd Club. Weems opened his mouth and let forth a blasting sound known as the Crystal Scream, shattering all of the Bludd Club's remaining windows. Behind them, Sparkbolt lurched forward, groaning angrily. The Frankenstein was followed by Mortia and Ankh-hoptet and Lincoln Pugh in his giant bear form. The light from the crackling, spreading fire reflected off the monsters' faces.

"General," said Gyra, her voice rising in panic. "We're surrounded!"

But Cygnus did not seem concerned. "Let us withdraw, then," he said. "Until next time, Falcon Quinn. You will see. They will turn on you. One by one."

"General," said Gyra as the monsters bore down upon her. "Do something!"

"Colonel, if you would, please," said Cygnus.

"Bully," said the colonel, and turned and shot the wall behind them with his elephant gun. There was a deafening explosion and a flash of light, and then the air filled with drifting smoke and the smell of sulfur.

"Guardians destroy!" shouted Sparkbolt.

"After her," said Falcon, "I mean—*them*." Everyone ran outside, pursuing the invaders.

"We must not let them escape!" said Pearl, now recovered from the blow Cygnus had struck. "We must pursue them to their death!"

But the guardians had fled without a trace. "Dude," said Max to Falcon, "are you okay?"

"I'm all right," said Falcon, coughing a little from the smoke.

"We must seek the count," said Ankh-hoptet. "And

the serving squid!"

"They had Megan," said Falcon. "Did you see? They did something to her—erased her brain or something—made her into one of *them*."

"You are referring to whom?" said Pearl. "The girl with the whip of the bull?"

"That wasn't Megan, man," said Max.

"I tell you, it was her," said Falcon. "I know it!" At this moment the roof of the Bludd Club exploded with fire.

"Snort," said Destynee.

"I fear our friend Señor Snort may find himself hopelessly trapped," said Pearl. "His horn, when last observed, was still imbedded in the wall of this tavern!"

"The rhino," said Ankh-hoptet. "By the tomb of Amen-toth!"

"Dude—," said Max. Falcon was looking into the distance, in the direction Gyra had fled.

Then he sighed, and turned, and flew back into the burning building.

"Falcon, wait," shouted Destynee. "Be careful!" She turned to Weems. "Weems, stop him," she said. "Oh, if anything happens to Falcon, I'll just—"

Weems sighed. "Always Falcon Quinn," he said.

The inside of the Bludd Club pulsed with flames. "Help," said a voice, and Falcon turned to see Snort, struggling against the far wall. The flames were growing closer.

"I'm burnin' up here!"

"Hang on," said Falcon, moving quickly toward him.

"Stay back, you!" said Snort.

"Snort, it's okay," said Falcon.

"I said get back! You're the one who *brought them here!*"

"Maybe they came here because of me," said Falcon. "But I'm not with them. I'm with you. And I'm going to help you, Snort."

Falcon tried to get the rhino's horn out the wall, but Snort was firmly stuck. He looked around the room for something he could use as a crowbar, but there was nothing at hand that would work. The flames were almost upon them now, and Falcon began to cough in the thick smoke.

"If you're gonna kill me, just do it and get it over with," said Snort. "What do I care?"

"I'm not trying to kill you," said Falcon.

"I don't believe you!" shouted Snort.

A rafter began to sag and creak above Snort's head. Fingers of flame consumed it. The heat scorched Falcon's face.

"Snort," shouted Falcon. "Close your eyes."

"What? Why should I?!"

"Fine," said Falcon, and then he concentrated on the wall just above Snort's imbedded horn. He felt his black eye growing hotter and hotter, and he tried to focus on the exact spot he was aiming for. Then a fireball shot out of Falcon's eye and burst through the wall, making a hole just big enough for Snort to free his horn.

"What are you doing?" said Snort.

"Let's go!" shouted Falcon. "Come on."

But at this moment the burning rafter above their heads snapped in two, and Falcon and Snort were both knocked to the floor, pinned beneath the heavy beam.

"Augh!" shouted Snort. "What a day I'm havin'!" He struggled against the rafter, but he was trapped again.

Snort looked over at Falcon, who was pinned under the charred rafter next to him. His eyes were closed. "Hey, angel. You all right?"

Falcon said nothing. His wings fluttered, then were still.

"Seriously," said Snort. "Angel. Say something. Falcon?"

Max and his friends stood outside the burning building.

"Where's Falcon?" said Destynee, her voice rising in panic. "Where is he?"

"Friend?" said Sparkbolt, looking at the Bludd Club sadly. "Smoke?"

"It seems that our friend has been consumed," said Weems with an unsettling grin. "His flesh burned all crispy."

"Shut up," said Destynee. "Why do you have to talk that way? Why?"

Weems looked crestfallen. "It is a way that I have."

"Well, I hate it! I hate it!"

"My friends!" said Pearl. "We should not abandon hope for Falcon Quinn! Surely he shall yet emerge, triumphant!"

But now another part of the roof fell in, and the flames roared toward the sky.

"Dude," said Max.

"What is going on?" said a voice, and they turned to see Mr. Trunkanelli rushing toward them. "What *is* this?" At his side was his wife, Mrs. Trunkanelli, and their little elephant boy, Peanut.

"The guardians attacked the Bludd Club," said Mortia.

"Guardians!" said Mr. Trunkanelli. "Here? Impossible! We have a treaty! This island is off-limits to them!"

Peanut squeaked his tiny trunk. "I'm scared, Mommy!" he said. "I'm—" Then he looked confused. "What were we talking about?"

"Guardians," said Mrs. Trunkanelli. "On Monster Island!"

"Pachysia," said Mr. Trunkanelli to his wife. "Get Peanut back to the hotel. This is no place for an elephant boy."

"Why is everyone upset?" said Peanut.

Count Manson drew near now, followed by Cuttles. The vampire's clothes were smoking. "Because the enemy has attacked us," he said angrily. "Because ve have been betrayed—by Falcon *Qvinn*!"

"Hey, Falcon didn't betray anybody!" said Max.

"He brought them here!" shouted the count. "Told them how to attack us!"

"My club," said Cuttles sadly. "Ruined!"

"I'm scared, Mommy!" said Peanut. "I'm—" He scratched the top of his head with his trunk. "Uh—were we just saying something?"

Mrs. Trunkenelli shook her head and walked away with her child. Mr. Trunkanelli watched his wife and son as they made their way back to the Waldorf-Hysteria.

"Is anyone hurt?" said Mr. Trunkanelli.

"Hurt, yeah, somebody's hurt!" said Max. "Falcon's in there! With Snort!"

"Falcon," said Destynee. "Falcon!" Her voice broke, and a tear began to trickle down her cheek. As the salt tear met her slug skin, her face began to melt.

Weems sighed. "Always Falcon Quinn."

"Wait," said Pearl. "A figure emerges from the con-flagration!" They watched as someone stepped out of the flames. It was a small, bent creature in gray rags. It was wearing a bag over its head.

"So—lonely," it said. "So terribly, terribly alone!"

"Copperhead," said Mr. Trunkanelli. "You're alive."

Copperhead coughed. The snakes beneath her bag

hissed. "If you can call it that."

"Did you see anyone else in there?" said Destynee. "Were there any other survivors?"

"I saw no one," said Copperhead.

They all fell silent. The flames from the Bludd Club rose into the sky. The count chuckled to himself, then turned to the others. He readjusted the flower in his lapel and cleared his throat. "Good *evening*," he said, and then slowly walked away.

"Friend?" said Sparkbolt. "Friend?"

Pearl's buzzing slowed down until she landed on Max's shoulder and her wings fluttered to a halt. There was a long silence as the friends stood in a semicircle watching the Bludd Club burn.

Suddenly there was a thundering *smash*, and Snort burst out of the burning building. Falcon was on his back.

"Stand back!" shouted Snort. "Comin' through!"

"*¡Señor!*" shouted Pearl. "Have you survived once more and returned to us alive?"

Falcon, his clothes smoking, looked at his friends and smiled wearily. "I'm all right," he said.

Snort galloped around the monsters triumphantly, steam puffing from his nostrils.

"Dude!" said Max to Falcon. "*You're totally on top of a charging rhino!*"

Falcon raised his wings as his friends gathered around

him in a circle and shouted happily. But even as he bathed in the glow of their affection, he found himself looking toward the Sea of Dragons.

Why would I go with you? Falcon had asked the girl who looked so much like Megan.

For a better life? she'd said.

II

SHADOW ISLAND

6

THE LIBRARIAN

Four figures stood at the end of a long dock on Shadow Island, watching the *Cutthroat* enter the harbor bearing its monster passengers. The ship's red mizzen sails and spinnakers rippled with wind. Mrs. Redflint, the dean of students at the Academy for Monsters, glanced at her watch.

"They're late," she said.

Dr. Cortex, head of the Academy's Wellness Center, turned to her and nodded. "Indeed," he said. His giant exposed brain pulsed and the black veins that encircled it wriggled and throbbed.

For many long years transportation between the amusement park and the Academy had been subcontracted to a group of monsters known as the Mutant Corsairs. These creatures lived on an island of their own, called Pirate Island, and devoted themselves to the pirate lifestyle, with its all-consuming obsession with the burying of treasure. The Mutant Corsairs even operated their own school upon their island, the Pirate Conservatory, which taught its pupils the finer points of swordplay, rum swizzling, and cartography. They were a breed apart, the pirates, and over time they had come to think of themselves as a society wholly separate from that of their monster cousins. Still, there was no one as dependable for traveling across the high seas as the pirates, and their privateer, the *Cutthroat*, with its many decks for passengers, was the traditional means of transport between Shadow and Monster islands.

Pirate swabs, holding coils of thick rope, now stood by the rails as the *Cutthroat* prepared to dock in the harbor of Shadow Island. Other corsairs hung from the rigging, looking toward the towers of Castle Gruesombe through spyglasses.

"*Yargh!*" shouted a young buccaneer from the crow's nest, speaking in the nearly incomprehensible pirate jargon. "*Tar tar jack skoggin!*"

Mrs. Redflint sighed. "I hope we can get the students safely to their dorms without the usual disturbances. It would be nice if the pirates would spare us the traditional burning and looting this year, given what the students have been through."

"Why do we put up with them?" asked Dr. Cortex, his engorged brain pulsating. "They give me such a headache."

Dr. Cortex was the associate of Dr. Medulla, the former head of the Academy for Monsters' Wellness Center, who had been turned to stone the previous spring.

"I like pirates!" said Mr. Hake, the vice principal, who was also, on some occasions, the Terrible Kracken. At present he was in humanoid form, wearing a cardigan and a pair of tennis shoes. He licked a melting Creamsicle. "They're funny!"

"They're not so funny when they set fire to things," said Mrs. Redflint, the dragon lady. She puffed two large smoke rings from her nostrils. "They're not so funny when they lie in the center of the academic quad singing songs about—well, you know. *Wenches.*"

"But it's tradition!" said Mr. Hake. "Tradition is good! It connects us to our grampaws!"

"Traditions should be examined from time to time," said a man with tangled, yellow hair and a scraggly beard. "To see whether they still serve their proper functions."

There was silence for a moment. The four of them watched the *Cutthroat* draw near.

"Mr. Lyons. Are you saying you doubt the usefulness of our pirate friends?" said Dr. Cortex to the bearded man.

"Not their usefulness," Mr. Lyons replied in a deep, rumbling voice. "But their loyalties."

"Their loyalties?" said Mrs. Redflint. "They have been ferrying our students from the Academy to Monster Island for long years now. "

"Yes," said Mr. Lyons. "But still. Now and again, I wonder if the pirates are wholly on our side."

"They are on no side at all, I should think," said Mrs. Redflint. "At this point they serve anyone who will provide them with—what is the term? *Booty*. Which, indeed, we do."

"My point exactly," said Mr. Lyons. "I wonder, given the changing circumstances of the world, if there are others who have considered providing them with terms better than our own." He growled softly. "For if there is a price we pay for protecting our students, for bearing them away from harm, then surely there is a price that might be paid—by others—to lead them directly into harm's way."

"Yes, well," said Dr. Cortex. "I imagine many things will be examined in days to come." He looked at Mrs. Redflint. "Has the headmaster been kept informed of the events on Monster Island? This unprovoked attack?"

"He has," said Mrs. Redflint.

Mr. Hake's Creamsicle slid off of its stick and slapped onto the dock. "My ice cream fell down," he said sadly. "Go boom-boom!"

Dr. Cortex's brain veins throbbed again. "What do you do when you're sad, Mr. Hake?"

The vice principal thought about it. "I suffocate things with my tentacles."

"That's good," said Dr. Cortex. "You don't want to keep things bottled up inside."

The *Cutthroat* was nearly at the dock now. Two pirate

swabs in striped shirts and tricorn hats stood by the railings, holding coils of rope.

"I wonder if that's true," said Mrs. Redflint.

"Therma?" said Dr. Cortex.

"I said I wonder if that's true. That it is best not to bottle things inside."

"Of course it's true," said Dr. Cortex. "Is that not the credo of our school? That we should accept ourselves and live our truth in the open?"

"I know, Doctor," said Mrs. Redflint, a trace of smoke once more drifting from her nose. "You need not remind me of our principles. I merely wonder if we understand what we are asking of our young people when we ask them to live an authentic life."

"An authentic life is its own reward," said Dr. Cortex. "Is it not?"

"Perhaps," said Mr. Lyons. "But the challenge of living this authentic life, it seems to me, can be its own burden as well."

On the *Cutthroat's* promenade deck, the young vampires drank plasma smoothies and ate little pieces of raw meat served on stoned wheat crackers. A jazz band played "I've Got You Under My Skin." As they drew near the harbor, the students could see the gray wall that surrounded the Academy and, rising just beyond this, the towers of the academic buildings, castles Grisleigh and Gruesombe.

"Look, look," said Muffy to a small group of her friends. "I can see Saphenous Hall!" She turned to Dominique. "We are going to have the best year ever, in our own double room! You and me, VFF!"

"I hope so," said Dominique in a tremulous voice.

"Dominique," said Reeves Pennypacker Waldow-Sherrod Binswanger III, who was wearing a blue sport jacket with small gold buttons that had anchors embossed on them. "Surely you're not still distraught over the unpleasantness at the Bludd Club!" He looked surprised.

"No," said Dominique softly. "Course not. But I'd feel a little better if my friend Merideath was here. We were best friends when we were little. We used to suck the blood out of her gerbils."

"I heard about her," said Reeves. "Expelled last spring, wasn't she? After failing the test of the first semester?"

"That test was rigged against her!" said Dominique. "The way they always rig things against us! I hate it when we don't get our way! It's so unfair!"

"Don't you worry about Merideath," said Muffy.

"What do you mean, don't worry about her? She got permanently expelled!" said Dominique.

"Nothing's permanent," said Muffy. "Except us."

Several levels down, the rest of the monster students were crammed into something called the grease deck.

Weems and Destynee and Ankh-hoptet were wedged into a single seat. Just behind them, Pearl, Max, Mortia, Falcon, and Lincoln Pugh stood in a small space between the seats and the bulkhead. The grease deck emitted a unique stench—a combination of old garbage and frying fat. There was a pirate in a uniform speaking into a microphone. "Please take a minute to—*argh, tar tar!*—check the area around yer seat," she said. "Fer your *tar tar tar tar!*—personal belongin's. *Argh! Argh!* Captain Hardtack will give ye the two-bell signal— *tar tar!*—indicatin' it's safe to walk about the cabin."

"I, for one, shall be cheered to disembark from these close quarters!" said Pearl. "I feel as if I have been flattened like a cake of the pan!"

"I'm hungry," said Max. "They didn't even give us anything to eat except biscuits. Who eats biscuits, man? Nobody!"

"I like biscuits," said Lincoln Pugh. He was still half blind without his glasses. "They're tasty."

"Biscuits bad," said Sparkbolt.

"You know what I wonder?" said Mortia. "Do the monsters from the Reality Stream put up with this? When they take their vacation on Monster Island? Do they have to ride these crummy pirate ships too?"

"No way," said Max. "They take the magic bus, man. Remember how we got to the Academy in the first place? They got these excellent magic buses that are all wonky-do."

"I do not understand this wonky-do!" said Pearl.

"Well," said Max. "You oughta."

The ship lurched suddenly as the *Cutthroat* bumped against the dock. The monsters belowdecks heard the sounds of pirates leaping onto the dock from outside and the sounds of hatches opening and gangplanks moving.

"All ashore that's *gargh* ashore," said the pirate steward. The monsters on the grease deck all stood up and grabbed their luggage, then moved toward the metal stairs that led up to the exit. The staircase was jammed. All the disembarking monsters were shoved toward the gangplank. There was a cacophony of growling and laughing as the students jostled against each other.

"We're totally smooshed!" said Destynee.

"Yes," said Weems happily. "We are."

"Wish I had some more of those biscuits," said Max.

"You said you did not enjoy these biscuits of the sea!" said Pearl.

"I said I didn't like them. That doesn't mean I don't want some!"

"Señor Falcon," said Pearl. "You will have to explain the language of the Sasquatch to me. At times I find it difficult to translate into Chupakabra." Pearl looked around her, at the crammed-together crowd of monsters. "*¿Señor?*" she said uncertainly. "Señor Max?" she said. "Where is Falcon Quinn?"

"I don't know, man," said Max. "Wasn't he with you?"

Pearl looked anxiously at the encircling throng. There were creatures with antennae, things with claws, entities with stingers and fur and razor-sharp teeth. There were no angels.

"Falcon?" she said.

"We're back!" said Muffy, coming down the gangplank. "Be glad, everyone! Muffy's here!!"

"Miss Ventricle," said Mrs. Redflint. "How was your summer?"

"Divine!" shouted Dominique.

"'Divine' is a word that means happy," said Mr. Hake with a smile. "And happy means happy! Yes! Yes! That is what it means! Happy!"

"Attention, please," said Dr. Cortex. "If all vampire students would follow me, please, we'll get your things and head over to Saphenous and Arterial."

"Good afternoon, Muffy," said Mrs. Redflint. "It's a pleasure to see you!"

"Oh, Mrs. Redflint," said Muffy, bursting into tears.

"Now, now, dear," said Mrs. Redflint. "You're back among vampires and zombies and mummies. Nothing can hurt you here."

"It was so terrible!" said Muffy. "They attacked us, out of nowhere! They sprayed us with this sleepy fog!"

"There, there," said Mrs. Redflint. Dr. Cortex nodded gravely.

"It was the Quinn boy," said Reeves Pennypacker Waldow-Sherrod Binswanger III. "He brought them."

"Dr. Cortex," said Mrs. Redflint. "I do think we ought to offer counseling services to the students. It must have been a terrible shock."

"I don't want counseling," said Muffy, wiping her eyes. "I want revenge!"

"Revenge," said Mr. Lyons, shaking his head. "Do you think revenge will solve your troubles?"

Muffy wrinkled her nose. "Who's he? I've never seen him before!"

"This is Mr. Lyons," said Mrs. Redflint. "The librarian. He just joined us over the summer."

"You will find a number of interesting books on the consequences of revenge in the stacks," said Mr. Lyons. "I can prepare a reading list for you."

"I don't want a reading list," said Muffy bitterly. "I want them to punish Falcon Quinn!"

"Revenge is a happy way to make people pay!" said Mr. Hake. He turned his arms into tentacles and waved them around exuberantly. "Revenge is a kind of happy. My, my! If you think about it, there really are so many *varieties* of happy!"

"Let us first find out the truth," said Mr. Lyons, "before

we start doling out revenge. There can be no justice without truth."

"Yada yada yada," said Dominique. "We all know the truth."

"Miss Ventricle," said Mrs. Redflint. "You will not say yada yada to a member of the faculty."

"He's not faculty," said Dominique contemptuously, nodding toward the bearded man. "He's just a librarian!"

"Rrrr!" shouted an angry voice at the top of the gangplank. "Destroy! Destroy!"

"Ah, Mr. Sparkbolt," said Mrs. Redflint. "How nice to see you again!"

"*Cutthroat* bad!" said Sparkbolt. "BAD!"

"Ugh," said Destynee, walking behind him. "He's right. I've never been so squished in my life. The whole ride I've been jammed right up next to Weems in that horrible tiny chair!"

"I didn't think it was so bad," said Weems, looking at Destynee with his sad, hollow eyes. "Was it really so bad, being so close?"

"The worst!" said Destynee.

"Mr. Weems and Mr. Sparkbolt," said Mrs. Redflint. "You're in Dustbin Hall. And Miss Bloodflough, you're in Heimlich, of course."

"Rrrr!" shouted Sparkbolt.

"Mr. Sparkbolt," said Mr. Lyons, checking his name

off on a clipboard. "I'm Mr. Lyons, the librarian. I'm told you're a talented poet. Miss Wordswaste-Phinney speaks highly of your work."

"Aw," said Sparkbolt. "It nothing."

Mr. Lyons gave Sparkbolt a small handwritten note. "I've drawn up a list of books you might find helpful. Sharon Olds. Elizabeth Bishop. Sylvia Plath. Young writers sewn out of dead body parts such as yourself find these authors highly inspirational."

Sparkbolt murmured, "Inspiration good."

Destynee looked up at the crooked mass of Castle Grisleigh. "We aren't in Grisleigh this year? I liked Castle Grisleigh," said Destynee. "The towers, and the catacombs. It was homey."

"Heimlich Hall is homey too!" said Mr. Hake. "Every house is a home where someone's happy!"

Mr. Lyons licked his lips as he noted the disembarking students. After Destynee came Ankh-hoptet and Lincoln Pugh, and Mortia and Crumble, and Snort and the Crofton sisters and Picador. The teachers stood at the bottom of the ramp, welcoming each of the monsters back as the ship emptied itself of the entire student body. It took almost fifteen minutes to unload them all and to get everyone's luggage squared away. Max and Pearl were some of the last off the boat.

"And so!" shouted Pearl triumphantly. "Once more

I return to the Island of Shadow! To continue my quest toward illumination! I am *¡la Chupakabra!* The famous goatsucker of Peru! I disembark!"

"Miss Picchu," said Mrs. Redflint. "How nice to see you. This is Mr. Lyons, our new librarian at Screamer."

"Señorita," said Mr. Lyons. *"¡Bienvenido a casa!"*

Pearl curtsied in midair. "I am most pleased to hear the Spanish within my ears!"

"Dude," said Max petulantly. "I don't understand Spanish! At all!"

"'*Doodah*' is from the German," noted Mr. Lyons. "It means 'fool.'"

Max looked crushed. "Dude," he said.

"Here," said Mr. Lyons, handing Max a book, *In Pursuit of Excellence*. "I have reserved this for you."

"Excellent!" said Max.

"Indeed," said Mr. Lyons.

"Señora Redflint," said Pearl. "Where is our friend Señor Falcon Quinn? We seem to have become separated from him, and I was most hopeful of finding him on the dock, waiting for us."

"Falcon Quinn?" said Mrs. Redflint. She looked over at Mr. Lyons.

"He has not disembarked," said Mr. Lyons.

"Hmm," said Mrs. Redflint. "Curious."

Dr. Cortex led the vampires toward their digs in

Saphenous and Arterial, and Mr. Hake guided the other students toward Dustbin and Heimlich. Max and Pearl remained on the dock, looking back at the *Cutthroat*.

"Wait"—said a voice at the top of the steps—"for—me—"

For a moment, Pearl and Max—not to mention Mrs. Hake and Mr. Lyons—looked up at the gangplank hopefully.

Turpin the wereturtle appeared in the hatch and then slowly began working his way down the gangplank.

"Ah," said Mrs. Redflint with what almost sounded like regret. "Mr. Turpin. I almost forgot."

"Hello," said Turpin. He took another slow step down the gangplank.

"Argh yar jack skoggin," said one of the pirates, and the other pirates began untying the ropes.

"Strange," said Mrs. Redflint. She turned to Turpin, who was still only halfway down the gangplank. "Did you see Falcon Quinn, Mr. Turpin? The angel?"

"No," said Turpin.

"Very strange," said Mrs. Redflint.

Mr. Lyons rumbled softly. "They have him," he said.

"What?' said Mrs. Redflint.

"The boy," said Mr. Lyons. "They have him." He gave his clipboard to Mrs. Redflint. "Excuse me."

"I warned our friend to be on his guard!" said Pearl.

"I implored him to maintain the highest level of caution!"

"Mr. Lyons," said Mrs. Redflint. "We have no evidence—"

"*Argh tar har yo!*" said the first mate, now nearly finished untying the ropes.

Mr. Lyons walked up the gangplank. "*Argh tar yo skoggin!*" shouted the first mate, and instantly a half dozen other pirates appeared on the deck. They drew out their swords.

"Avast!" said Captain Hardtack, appearing in the hatch. "You've not been given permission to come aboard me vessel!"

"I cannot tell you how terribly, terribly sorry I am," said Mr. Lyons in his deep, sad voice. "But it would appear as if one of our students has not disembarked! I just thought I'd have a look around. To be certain, you see."

"Impossible!" shouted the captain. "Ye shall not pass without me own word!"

"I'm sure you'll give me your word then," said Mr. Lyons softly. "Won't you? You've always been known for your fearless heart."

"Nay!" shouted the captain. "I'll not be contradicted! I'll stand no words of mutiny! This ship has been emptied of its cargo! And those that deny me shall stand ready to forfeit their lives."

"Ah, I see," said Mr. Lyons. "I am so, so sorry." He did

sound sorry for whatever it was that was about to happen. Mr. Lyons reached forward with one of his hairy hands and pushed the captain back slightly, as if he was pushing open a door.

"I said avast!" shouted the captain, brandishing his sword.

"I know," said Mr. Lyons, pushing the captain back again. "I heard you." The two of them disappeared into the dark hatchway of the ship and vanished from view. Mrs. Redflint, Max, and Pearl stood at the bottom of the gangplank, watching anxiously. The other pirates looked into the doorway, frozen in place, waiting to see what would happen next. For a few moments there was silence.

"*Yo?*" said the first mate.

Then there was an earsplitting roar, followed by a scream. There came a second roar, louder than the first, and then there was a soft *clump*. A long moment passed. Then the body of the captain was thrown out of the hatch and landed in a heap at the foot of the gangplank.

"Whoa," said Max, looking at the captain's chewed-up form.

Mrs. Redflint looked at the pirates and shrugged. "He did say he was sorry," she said.

"*Argh yo tar tar!*" said the first mate, astonished.

Mrs. Redflint nodded. "Exactly," she said.

A moment later, Falcon Quinn emerged from the

Cutthroat, looking more than a little scuffed up. He walked down the gangplank toward his friends.

"Dude! What happened to you?!"

"I don't know," said Falcon. "I was getting ready to leave with everyone else, when suddenly someone snuck up behind me and hit me. They stuffed me in this room without any windows and said they were going to take me—"

Falcon blew some air through his cheeks.

"Where did they say they would take you?" asked Mrs. Redflint.

Falcon looked embarrassed. "Home," said Falcon. "They said they were going to take me home."

"But surely you are home now," said Pearl. "Once more among your friends, on Monster Island!"

"Yeah," said Falcon, looking up at the spires of Castle Grisleigh. "I guess."

The air thundered with a deep roar, and then a magnificent, enormous lion bounded through the hatch of the *Cutthroat* and paused on the gangplank. It stood, illuminated with light, its tail undulating softly.

"Dude," said Max. "Now we have a *lion* friend."

7
DUSTBÍN

They walked across the campus toward Dustbin. To get to the Upper School, they had to pass through Grisleigh Quad, and as they walked past the castle, Falcon looked up at the Tower of Souls. There, leaning against a pillar, was a dark silhouette. Falcon paused to wave. The figure remained motionless, except for an almost indiscernible quivering of its enormous black wings.

"Hey," said Max, following Falcon's gaze and seeing the dark shadow in the tower. "Who's your daddy?"

"¡Señor!" said Pearl. "The question of Falcon's parentage is surely no mystery at this time. His father is the headmaster of this institution, the Crow, whom we can discern even now, observing our progress from his mysterious perch in the Tower of Souls. And his mother—"

"Pearl, man," said Max. "Turn it down a thousand, okay? I know who Falcon's daddy is. Everyone knows who Falcon's daddy is."

"But you yourself have just inquired as to the identity of his father!"

"Yeah," said Max. "But when I say 'Who's your daddy,' it's not like I'm actually asking who's his actual daddy, okay?"

"Then what can be the meaning of this phrase?" shouted Pearl. "You are suggesting it has a meaning other than the meaning which it appears to have!"

"Yeah, okay, now you got it," said Max.

"What is it I have?" said Pearl, more furious than ever.

"You got me," said Max.

Pearl sighed. "It seems at times as if the more we converse, the less I understand!"

"Now you got it," said Max happily.

"What have I got?" said Pearl. "What?"

"I just told ya!"

"Mr. Lyons," said Mrs. Redflint as they approached the large stone wall that separated the Grisleigh campus from the Upper School. "I am grateful that you retrieved our straggler. But I'm sure you understand that there are likely to be—ahem—*consequences*—for your actions?"

Mr. Lyons, who had reverted back to human form, shrugged. "Actions always have consequences," he said.

"True enough," said Mrs. Redflint. "But I wonder if it was wholly necessary for you to chew the captain into such tiny shreds. Our relationship with the pirates is always fraught. I cannot help but think that they will interpret the devouring of Captain Hardtack as an act of hostility."

"Yes, I suppose," said Mr. Lyons. "But then, imprisoning one of our students against his will—this was an act of hostility as well."

"It would have been nice to know upon whose orders Captain Hardtack was proceeding, wouldn't it?" said Mrs. Redflint. "Whether the guardians have infiltrated their ranks, or whether he was acting of his own accord, or whether there was—uh—some other party who wished this student enslaved. But now we won't be able to find out the answers to those questions, will we? Since you sliced him with your razor claws and imbedded your giant teeth in his heart?"

"I am sorry if I've disappointed you, Mrs. Redflint," said Mr. Lyons.

They passed through the gates of the Upper School campus. Each of the massive doors in the wall was affixed by a golden hinge to a large, stone column. At the top of the right-hand column was a gargoyle shaped like a young man, his mouth frozen open in terror. This was Scratchy Weezums, a human student who had apparently been admitted by accident to the Academy years and years ago and who had been turned to stone so that he could not return to the Reality Stream and tell the world of humans what he had seen.

As they passed through the gates, Falcon took one last look back at the Tower of Souls. But his father was no longer there.

The Upper School campus of the Academy for Monsters looked a little like a college campus, with its old stone buildings and its wide green lawns. Castle Gruesombe, the primary academic building, was larger and even more dilapidated than Castle Grisleigh. It had four large towers of varying heights. The largest was missing, however, as if it had been shot off, or crumbled of its own accord, at some time in the distant past. There was a deep, swampy-looking moat surrounding the castle. A large drawbridge, currently in the down position, traversed the moat, and a spiked portcullis ornamented the main gates. On either side of the castle were other academic buildings, including, to the left, the Hall of Unspeakable Tongues, the Hall of Horrible Experiments, and the Hall of Revolting Observations; directly across from these, on the other side of the academic quadrangle, was the Hall of Dismal Sciences and the Center for Social Disengagement and Disintegration. Beyond these was a smaller, rickety-looking building, the Hall of Pus. It was in this building that Falcon and some of his friends had found the secret entrance to the Academy dungeon last spring. It was also in this same place that Falcon had, after many, many years, first met his father, the Crow.

"Ah, here we are," said Mrs. Redflint. "Dustbin Hall." She gave Falcon and Max two sets of keys and nodded to them. "I trust you'll find your lodgings. Miss Picchu, if you'll follow me, I'll get you settled in Heimlich."

"I do not wish to be separated from my friends, to whom I have sworn my everlasting loyalty!" said Pearl.

"Yes, well, girls are in Heimlich. Boys are in Dustbin. You can be loyal all you like from Heimlich."

Pearl nodded. "So shall it be. But my friends, if at any moment you need my aid, simply call out the name of *¡la Chupakabra!* The famous goatsucker of Peru! And it is I who shall appear in an instant, ready to lay down my life on your behalf!"

"Okay, man," said Max. "See you at dinner, okay?"

"Let it be done," said Pearl.

Mrs. Redflint sighed. "Mr. Lyons, you'll be at assembly tomorrow?"

"Indeed," he said.

"Very well," she said, and walked toward Heimlich with Pearl buzzing over her right shoulder.

Mr. Lyons looked at Falcon and Max. "She is a good friend, isn't she?" he said, purring deeply.

"Dude," said Max. "She's awesome."

"Gentlemen," said Mr. Lyons. "I suspect this semester may be something of a challenge, particularly for you, Falcon. There are many forces in the world, and it is your misfortune, perhaps, that you are torn between so many of them. Remember—it is not always for us to choose our fate. But we can embrace our fate with faith, and courage, and wisdom."

"Dude," said Max. "That is so awesome."

"Awesome, yes," said Mr. Lyons. "Oh, and Falcon. This is for you." He handed Falcon a copy of *Stuart Little*. "Perhaps you'll find this of interest."

"I read that when I was a kid," said Falcon, slightly perplexed.

"Of course," said Mr. Lyons. "But perhaps you might revisit it again. The situation—a child so unlike his parents! I thought it might speak to you."

"He's a mouse," said Falcon.

"Yes, and what happens to him in the end? He has to leave them, doesn't he? And seek his fortune, alone, in his invisible car?"

"I always thought that book was kind of wonky," noted Max.

"Wonky! What a delightful word," said Mr. Lyons, and then shook Max's hand. "From the Old German 'verklonklich,' meaning 'remarkable.' Well done. Carry on, gentlemen." He turned and walked away from them with an air of great dignity. For a moment they watched as he walked in the direction of a massive structure that looked like a fortress. In front of the building was a sign: SCREAMER LIBRARY.

"Hey, man," said Max. "We totally have a *lion* friend!"

"We have lots of friends," said Falcon. "Come on, let's find our rooms."

The first floor of Dustbin was a long, dark hallway with a half dozen doors on either side. Some of these doors were open, displaying the rooms of the various monsters, each of which was decorated—or undecorated—according to the nature of the monster within. Owen Fitzhugh, the abominable snowman, for instance, had set his room up very neatly, with his books all evenly arranged and a single poster of the Manchester United football club on one wall. Snort, on the other hand, was sitting in the middle of his room as they passed, surrounded by piles of wrinkled clothes and papers and garbage all over the floor.

"What are you looking at?" said Snort.

"Nothing," said Max. "Just passing through."

Next to Snort's was a door marked SERJ & OZZIE. It was closed at the moment, but from behind it came the sound of blasting heavy metal music.

"Here's your room," said Falcon, looking at the door across the hall.

The door opened, and Weems was standing there. "Why, Mr. Parsons," he said. "I thought you might be dead."

"Dead? No way, man. We're roomies!" said Max. His face lit up with happiness, and he picked Weems up in the air and hugged him. "Dude! This is so excellent!" He turned to Falcon. "Hey! I'm roomies with Weemso!

I love this guy! I love him!"

"Put me down," screeched Weems.

"Aw, you can't kid me, man," said Max. "We're like peas in a pod, you and me! We are going to party up! Seriously! Then we're going to party *down*!"

"I think you're insane," said Weems.

"I think you're right, man!" shouted Max.

"Okay," said Falcon. "I'm going to get settled. I'm just down the hall, I think."

"Okay!" said Max joyfully. "Me and Weems are going to start workin' on all our special roommate stuff!"

"Why is it always me," hissed Weems. "Why?"

"Why you what?" said Max, starting to unpack his duffel.

"Why is it that I must live this life? And not some other?"

Max turned his duffel upside down, and clothes, beach balls, and banana peels scattered everywhere. "I don't know, Weems," said Max. "You're just lucky, I guess!"

Max picked up his triangle, which was his instrument in band, and he rang it with a small metal mallet. "Ding!" said Max.

Falcon left the two of them behind and walked down the long hallway toward the last room on the right. *I hope my roommate isn't someone who hates me,* he thought. When he reached his door, Falcon found that someone had ripped off the name tag that had been affixed to it. He sighed and put his key in the lock. The door squeaked heavily on its hinges as it swung open.

There at a table, writing with a quill pen, was Sparkbolt. He looked over at Falcon and then slowly put his pen down. Sparkbolt stood up, and then his face transformed into a look of happiness and of light.

"Falcon Quinn!" shouted Sparkbolt. "Ah! Ah! Ah!"

"Sparkbolt," said Falcon.

"Falcon Quinn GOOD!" said Sparkbolt, and lifted Falcon up in the air. "FALCON QUINN—*FRIEND!*"

The next day after breakfast, the students made their way toward Castle Gruesombc for the first day of fall classes. A deep bell rang from the Tower of Souls, and the boys from Dustbin walked across the Upper School campus in groups of twos and threes, carrying their books. Falcon and Sparkbolt caught up with Weems and Max, and found Max smiling from ear to ear and Weems appearing more than a little worn down and shell-shocked.

"Sparkbolt!" shouted Max, who was holding the copy of *In Pursuit of Excellence* Mr. Lyons had given him. "You're looking excellent! For a guy that's all green, I mean."

"Green bad," said Sparkbolt sadly.

"Hey, man, you can't be thinking that way. Green's the color you got, right? So you might as well make it as excellent as you can!" He smiled and turned toward Weems. "Am I right, Weemso? Tell him I'm right!"

"Is it true a person can lose his hearing if something explodes next to him?" asked Weems.

"Why, you got something you want to blow up?" said Max.

"Perhaps," said Weems.

Other monsters poured out onto the quad now. There was Snort and Lincoln Pugh and Turpin the wereturtle. There were other upperclassmen whom Falcon did not know—goblins and leprechauns and a Sphinx. There was even a kind of molten, burning slime named Quagmire, who bubbled down the front stairs of Dustbin like lava.

"Ah, Sparkbolt," said a voice with a distinctly British accent. This was a Frankenstein named Crackthunder, the editor of the school's literary magazine. "Good to see you, old man. All settled into your flat?"

"Flat good," said Sparkbolt. "This Falcon."

"Falcon Quinn," said Crackthunder, shaking Falcon's hand. "Charmed."

"Hey, Crackthunder," said Falcon. The three of them joined the long line of students now pouring onto the quad from Heimlich and Arterial and Saphenous and walking toward Gruesombe.

"I've been meaning to ask you, old boy. Do you write? I do hope we can count on you to contribute to *The Gullet* this semester. It's going to be a special issue on limericks."

"Once was monster named Stu!" said Sparkbolt suddenly. *"Who got himself job! At the zoo!"* Sparkbolt growled to himself for a moment, then continued. *"Him gorged the hyena. On lard and farina! Then him say, 'Now the last laugh on you!'"*

"Good heavens, Sparkbolt!" said Crackthunder. "Right out of the blue, you're composing verse! I have never seen such an intuitive understanding of the mechanics of literature."

"Showing good," noted Sparkbolt. "Telling bad."

The three monsters were nearly knocked over as two young creatures rushed past them on black skateboards. They were small, nimble beings with pale skin, jet-black hair, and pointed ears. They wore ripped-up black leather pants and torn white T-shirts.

"Rrrr," said Sparkbolt. "Destroy!"

"It's all right, Sparkbolt, old man," said Crackthunder. "It's just Serj and Ozzie. Dark elves, you know."

"Dark elves bad!" shouted Sparkbolt.

"No, no, dark elves good," said Crackthunder. "You just have to—well, let them pursue their own path. Their ways can be hard for us to fathom. But they are good souls, the dark elves. They live for music and the dance."

The vampires from Saphenous and Arterial were now joining the throng, and the well-dressed young creatures entered the long line on their left and right. Now they were all crossing the drawbridge that led over the moat that separated Castle Gruesombe from the rest of the campus. Below them the turgid waters of the moat bubbled and churned, and the air was ripe with the stench of sulfur.

The old castle was a magnificent place. There were rich tapestries of faded crimsons and blues on the wall, depicting monsters in various scenes of triumph over their adversaries. There were suits of armor and swords and pikes and shields mounted on the wall.

The monsters moved through the hallway to an immense stone staircase that rotated in a clockwise fashion up and around the inner walls of the sanctuary. As they ascended the stairs, Falcon saw a group of blackbirds flying in circles around a central chandelier that hung down on a long, pendulous chain from the impossibly high, vaulted ceiling.

"Dude," said Max, who'd caught up to Falcon and Sparkbolt. "Check out the crows! It's like some total bird party, man!"

"Oh, those aren't crows," said a voice, and they turned to see a small, gawky boy with a long neck and large, ovoid eyes. "Those are Gruesombe ravens, *Corvus gruesombus.* Count them—there are—*raawwk!*—there are thirteen."

"Hey, man," said Max. "You've kind of got a bird thing going on your own self, don't you?"

"*Rawwk,*" said the boy. "Not really."

"I'm Falcon. This is Max. And Sparkbolt."

"I'm Squawker," said the boy, his head bobbing in and out as if he was pecking at something. "I'm a vampire. *Raawk!*"

"Dude," said Max. "You're no vampire. Come on! You're like a birdman or something. I mean, don't mess with our minds, okay?"

"Vampire," said Squawker. "Not birdman! *Raawk!*"

The students in Falcon's cohort found their way through the castle to the first class of the day, Language and Fabrications with Willow Wordswaste-Phinney. Willow, a dryad, looked a little different than she had last spring; now she appeared much more treelike, with a few leaves crackling in her hair and her limbs much longer and more branchlike.

"Greetings, students," she said as they all took their seats. "The first text for the semester is *Hamlet*, as written in the original Frankenstein dialect."

"Rrrrr," said Sparkbolt.

"Shakespeare," explained Willow, "was of course one of our most successful monsters, and he succeeded in the Reality Stream how? By translating his work from the tongue in which it was composed into something incomprehensible that humans could pretend to admire. But listen to Hamlet's soliloquy, and compare this with the

translation. You'll discern in the original monster-tongue
so much more subtlety and shadow! Mr. Sparkbolt, could
you read for us?"

Sparkbolt cleared his throat and blushed slightly. It
was already clear that this semester, as last, he was going
to be Willow's prize student.

"Be. Not be.
That question.
Suffer bad. Oppose troubles? Bad!
All bad! Bad! Bad! Rrrr!
Die! Heart-ache end. Die and sleep.
Dream? Rrrr! That rub. Calamity! Stab!
Dread after-things. Make coward.
Life, death have smell, liverwurst.
Weird country, destroy.
Prince belong dead!"

"Very nice, Timothy," said Willow. "Now Falcon,
would you read the translation. please? And class, note
how ridiculous this sounds when Falcon reads it. Would
you start with the line, "The insolence—"

"The insolence of office, and the spurns,"
read Falcon,
"That patient merit of the unworthy takes,

When he himself might his quietus make
With a bare bodkin? who would fardels bear,
to grunt and sweat under a weary life,
But that the dread of something after death,
The undiscover'd country—"

Everyone laughed at this, and although Falcon understood that the laughter was not aimed at him specifically,
it felt personal to him, somehow.

"All right then, please, let's try to contain ourselves,"
said Willow. "Now why would Shakespeare use such
ridiculous words? 'Fardels'? 'Quietus'? 'Bodkin'? Honestly!
Why would he not express his words with more lyricism
and grace, as in the original that Sparkbolt read?"

"Because," said Reeves Pennypacker Sherrod-Waldow
Binswanger III. "Humans like to think they're smart. It
helps them feel better about being so—pathetic."

"But why would humans feel better about a poem they
can't understand?" said Willow.

"Maybe if they pretend they understand it, it makes
them feel like they have something over people who actually *don't* understand it," said Mortia. "It's important for
humans to feel like they have something over somebody."

"Why?" asked Willow.

"Because they're inferior," said Reeves Pennypacker
Sherrod-Waldow Binswanger III.

"So if they feel like they have an advantage over someone else—," said Willow.

"They forget that they're mortal," said Ankh-hoptet. "That they have no powers. That they are but *dust!*"

"Dear, dear, Mr. Quinn," said Willow, looking at Falcon. "You have the greatest frown upon your face. Do you disagree with the lesson that Shakespeare provides us?"

"I don't know," said Falcon. "I just think—the English version of it isn't so bad."

"I'm not sure I understand you," said Willow. "You mean, you don't like the monster original? You're saying you see poetry in the English, but you fail to see poetry in the language of Frankensteins?"

"Rrrrr!" said Sparkbolt. "Poetry good. Language bad."

"Listen to him," said Muffy. "He prefers the language of humans to the language of his own kind!"

"But they're *not* his kind, are they?" said Reeves Pennypacker Sherrod-Waldow Binswanger III. "Monsters, I mean. Come to think of it, I don't know what his kind is! Is there angel poetry?"

Everyone laughed at this. "You mean *guardian* poetry," said Muffy.

"Now now," said Willow. "I'm sure Falcon's just trying to—"

"*I'm* sure he's trying to destroy us!" said Dominique. "That's what Count Manson said. Why do they even let him stay at our school, anyway? I want him to leave! Why doesn't someone *make* him leave?"

"*Bwaak,*" said Squawker. "Father headmaster! Only reason! *Bwaak!*"

"Stop it," said Falcon, his wings rising on his back and his dark eye heating up. An angry red fireball unexpectedly launched out of his eye. It flew across the room, smacking into a bust of Shakespeare with a loud explosion and cracking the bust evenly in half. The two pieces of the Frankenstein of Avon fell to the floor and shattered into even smaller pieces.

"Rrrr!" said Sparkbolt angrily. "Shakespeare explode!" Everyone looked surprised, including Falcon's friends. Ankh-hoptet and Max and Pearl and Destynee all sat in their chairs wearing expressions of dismay.

"Cluck cluck cluck *cluck!*" said Squawker disapprovingly.

"Falcon!" said Willow. "That will be five unhappiness stars for you! Really, I'm shocked at you!"

"Don't be shocked," said Muffy. "It's what he does. We'll all wind up like Shakespeare if he has his way."

"I didn't mean to—," said Falcon, but at this moment the bell rang and all the students got up, grabbing their backpacks and thundering out into the hallway. Falcon was one of the last out of the room, and as he headed out, Willow shook her head sadly. "Falcon," she said. "What are we going to do with you?"

"Do?" he said. "What do you mean, do?"

"You're on very thin ice, Falcon. After the attack on the Bludd Club, there are lots of monsters just looking for a reason to—well. Just please—be more careful."

"I didn't have anything to do with that attack!" said Falcon. "They just came for me—Cygnus and the others. Tried to kidnap me!"

"I know," said Willow. "I understand that." A few of her leaves turned yellow and slowly fell to the floor. "But that's not how some of your—adversaries—see it. There are many here—including members of the faculty—who think you led them there."

"Count Manson," said Falcon.

"The count and others," said Willow. "Please. If you would try not to shoot any more fireballs at anyone, I personally would be very grateful."

Falcon sighed. "I just can't win," he said.

"Of course you can win," said Willow. She clapped him on the shoulder with one of her branchlike hands. "In fact, I don't see that you have any other choice."

After morning classes, Falcon headed down to the cafeteria for lunch and stood in the long line for food, a line in which neither the monster ahead of him—Bonesy, the skeleton girl—nor the zombie Crumble, who stood just behind, spoke a word to him.

The cafeteria lady stood motionlessly behind the counter with her spatula and her apron and her lizard face. Her long tongue darted out of her mouth and captured a fly and then returned it to her mouth. She chewed silently.

"Good morning, Cafeteria Lady," said Falcon.

"I don't like you," she said.

Falcon took a plate from underneath the heat lamp—they were having clamburgers—and thought, *Join the club.* In the cafeteria he saw Sparkbolt at a table of other Frankensteins—Crackthunder and Stinkfinger and some of the other guys from the literary magazine. There was no room for Falcon.

He looked around the cafeteria for a place to sit but couldn't find a free table. Everyone seemed to be sitting with their friends—Max and Pearl with a group of leprechauns, Destynee and Weems with Lincoln Pugh and Mortia and Ankh-hoptet, even Turpin the wereturtle with a group of banshees and harpies and jelly-blobs. In the end, Falcon sat by himself at a long table, disconsolately picking at his clamburger with a fork and wondering how it was he'd come all the way to the Academy for Monsters only to wind up in a situation that felt, in so many ways, exactly like one he'd faced back at Cold River Middle School in Maine. There, he'd had to negotiate his way between the various factions and cliques of emos and goths, jocks and freaks and nerds, skateboard punks and juvenile delinquents. It seemed as if he'd traveled a long way in order to wind up back at the same place he'd started.

"Can I sit here?" said a voice, and Falcon looked up to see Copperhead standing there, her burlap bag covering her head.

"Sure," he said. "If you don't mind sitting at the outcast table."

"You think you're an outcast?" said Copperhead, sitting down. The snakes beneath her burlap bag hissed softly. "Please."

"Yeah, well," said Falcon. "At least everyone doesn't think you want to destroy them."

"But I *do* want to destroy them," said Copperhead. "For their cruelty, and their savagery. Don't you?"

"I don't want to destroy anybody," said Falcon. "I just want to—" He shrugged. "I don't know."

"You just want to fit in, you were going to say?" said Copperhead. She lifted the bottom of her burlap bag slightly so she could get her fork to her mouth. Falcon saw what looked like pale, soft skin.

"Yeah, maybe. But I guess it's a little late for that." He sighed. "I had an accident in Willow's class today. Shot off a fireball with my eye."

"So I heard," said Copperhead. "Let me ask you something. Why do you want to fit in with people who hate you?"

"Because," said Falcon, "they only hate me because they don't know the truth."

"Oh, I see," said Copperhead. "If only everybody knew the truth about you, they'd all stop being so judgmental and hateful. You think the truth will open their eyes."

"You don't?"

"I think they're judgmental and hateful," said Copperhead, "because that's the way they are. I don't want to open their eyes. I want to blind them."

"Why don't you just take the bag off your head, then," said Falcon. "Turn everyone to stone?"

"I want them to realize how wrong they are first," said Copperhead. "To beg me for forgiveness. Then I'll take the bag off. There's no satisfaction otherwise."

"Why wouldn't you just forgive them?" said Falcon. "That's how I'd get revenge on people. By forgiving them."

Copperhead shook her head. "Boy, you *are* an angel, aren't you? All you want is to love, and forgive. That's so . . . *perverse.*"

Copperhead picked up a cup of Jell-O and stuck a straw into it. She sucked the wiggling purple Jell-O into her mouth.

"How do you see with that bag over your head?" Falcon asked.

"I don't know, Falcon. How do you see with a bag over *yours?*"

"Seriously."

Copperhead got up to take her tray back to the dish room. "How do you suppose?" she said. "I am guided by my hate."

Falcon was surprised to see Quagmire, the puddle of bubbling glop, during band the next day. Apparently the pool of glup had a lovely singing voice, which Falcon and the other monsters learned as they were practicing an orchestral version of "Vhat a Vonderful Vorld." They played a short intro, and then a mouth opened up in the midst of Quagmire's slime and began to sing with a clear tenor.

"I see skies aflame,"
sang the puddle of glop.

"Madwomen insane!
Mutants with giant, pulsating brains!
And I think to myself—vhat a vonderful vorld!"

"Very nice," said Mr. Largo, stopping the music for a moment. "I wonder, Mr. Quagmire, if you might be more *adagio.*"

The puddle of glop boiled, and several bubbles emerged from it and floated in the air.

"How come *I* don't get to sing the solo?" asked Muffy. "I want to sing!"

"But Mr. Quagmire has such an affecting tenor," said Mr. Largo.

"I can be affecting too!" said Muffy.

"I understand that."

"I want to sing!" she whined. "I can have you fired!"

"Please," said Mr. Largo. He walked over to have a private conference with Muffy. As they conferred, Weems—who was playing the didgeridoo—turned to Falcon. "I wonder what they will serve at dinner tonight," said the ghoul. He smiled with his horrible triangular teeth. "I am hoping it might be—*finger food.*"

Weems's eyes shone brightly.

"Funny," said Falcon.

"All right then, let's try again," said Mr. Largo. "From the top. And one, two, three . . ." The band began to play, but when they reached the moment Quagmire was supposed to sing, there was only silence. Everyone looked around for the bubbling puddle, but there was no sign of Quagmire. "Stop, stop," said Mr. Largo, exasperated. "Where is Mr. Quagmire?"

"He was just here," said Weems.

"*I* can sing!" said Muffy.

Mr. Largo's ears quivered back and forth. "Students," he said. "Let us just play the piece and hope that Mr. Quagmire returns from wherever he has gone. All right then? From the top. Five, six, seven, eight . . ."

The band began to play again. But this time Falcon had a hard time with his godzooka. He blew into the mouthpiece, but the sound coming from the bell was muffled. "Stop, stop," said Mr. Largo again.

He walked over to Falcon and said, "Mr. Quinn. What

seems to be the problem?"

"I don't know," said Falcon.

"Did you empty your spit valve?" said Mr. Largo.

Falcon was still getting used to the godzooka, which seemed to have less and less in common with the tuba the longer he played it. Now he found a small valve on the side of the huge coil of intertwined brass tubes, and he opened this and blew into the mouthpiece again.

A giant spray of bubbling glop soared across the room and hit Mr. Largo in the face. The glop dripped onto the floor and re-formed itself. It was Quagmire.

"Good heavens," said Mr. Largo, wiping the slime from his clothing. "How did Mr. Quagmire get inside your godzooka?"

"I don't know!" said Falcon.

"Are you all right, Mr. Quagmire?" The puddle of gunk boiled furiously.

Mr. Largo looked cross. "Mr. Quinn," he said. "Did you put Mr. Quagmire inside your godzooka on purpose?"

"Did I—? No!"

"Tell me the truth!"

"I didn't!"

"Well, Mr. Quagmire didn't get into your instrument by himself."

"I swear, I don't know anything about it! Weems and I were just talking—I wasn't paying any attention! Then, when I tried to play—"

"You did it on purpose, admit it!" said Picador, the minotaur. He played the bass guillotine.

"What?"

"Mr. Quinn," said Mr. Largo. "I'm very disappointed."

"But—"

"Enough. Mr. Quinn, perhaps you might absent yourself from rehearsals until you've gained a little more maturity."

"But I'm—"

"Excused," said Mr. Largo firmly.

Falcon left the rehearsal, his dark eye hot in his face, and walked by himself from the rehearsal hall in Castle Grisleigh all the way down to the beach. He looked out at the Sea of Dragons, feeling angry with Mr. Largo and with everyone for assuming that whatever had happened with Quagmire was somehow his fault.

He remembered the words of Copperhead at lunch the day before. *I am guided by my hate.* He did not agree with Copperhead and could not imagine seeing the world through the fabric of a burlap bag, as the Gorgon did.

But he could understand how someone could wind up guided by their hate. *It would be easy to give in to it,* he thought. He looked over his shoulder, up at the dark Tower of Souls. *Especially if you had no one to guide you.*

8

ROAD NOT TAKEN DESTROY!

A few nights later, after dinner, Falcon returned to Dustbin Hall to find Sparkbolt in his bed, writing poetry in his journal by the light of a single candle. Sparkbolt had decided to drop out of band this year and concentrate on his writing. It was just as well; the Frankenstein had made almost no progress on his tiny trumpet, the squeakalo.

"Falcon Quinn," said Sparkbolt, looking up from his journal. "Friend."

"Hey, Sparkbolt," said Falcon. He looked around the room. There were cobwebs in all the corners now, and candles sitting atop skulls. Wax from the melting candles drizzled down into the eye sockets. There were some chemicals foaming in beakers, and a large wooden toaster.

"Monster decorate room," said Sparkbolt. He smiled an awkward Frankenstein smile.

"You did," said Falcon, still taking it all in. "Yeah. Love what you've done with the place."

"Monster work on poem," said Sparkbolt.

"Cool. You want to read it to me?"

Sparkbolt sighed. "Poem bad," he said. Then he cleared his throat. "Road Not Taken Destroy!" he read.

Two roads divide in heinous wood.
Sorry could not destroy them both.
Be one monster, there I stood
And groaned and groaned as best I could
And took the road with poison growth.

Two path explode in wood and me—
Me take path less treachery.
That make difference.
Not much though.
Path make flame alive and orange.
Path make—

"Rrrr," groaned Sparkbolt.

"What's that?" said Falcon.

"Orange," growled Sparkbolt. "No rhyme!"

"No," said Falcon. "I guess not." He opened up a small bag of things he'd collected over the summer— books, seashells, a prize he'd won at the Carousel of Disintegration—and arranged them on his desk. "Hey, Sparkbolt," said Falcon. "Does Twisty still have control of Vonda's body?"

"Borange," Sparkbolt muttered. "Forange . . . what?"

"Remember when we were on Monster Island and we found that amulet?"

Sparkbolt groaned softly. A large tarantula was slowly crawling across Falcon's desk. "Amulet bad," he said.

"I was just wondering if Twisty was still, you know . . . stuck."

"Vonda bad," said Sparkbolt. "Twisty stuck good."

"Don't you think we should—talk to somebody about that?" said Falcon. "It's not right for Twisty to take over Vonda's body. Even if Vonda was kind of—you know. Annoying."

"Vonda bad!" said Sparkbolt more angrily. "Her make fun of monster talk."

"I know," said Falcon. "I hate her too. But she doesn't deserve to have Twisty controlling her body for the rest of her life. Does she?"

"Falcon good," said Sparkbolt, turning in his chair to look at his friend. "Falcon care even Vonda. Falcon care enemy!"

"Oh, Vonda's not my enemy," said Falcon.

"Amulet bad," said Sparkbolt. "But good. It both."

"How was it good?" Falcon said.

"Monster turn smoke," said Sparkbolt thoughtfully. "Summer. On beach. Monster stuck in Twisty brain! Before Falcon put amulet Twisty. And Twisty—turn smoke."

Falcon was having a little difficulty following this, but he thought Sparkbolt was talking about the time when Max had, briefly, been stuck in his brain and then later when he had, briefly, been stuck in Twisty's.

"Monster escape Twisty brain," said Sparkbolt. "Escape good. But monster—" Sparkbolt was thinking hard, trying to express an idea that seemed beyond his Frankenstein tongue. "Monster learn Twisty. When monster in Twisty brain. Monster feel sorry Twisty. Her ugly. Hunchback. Vonda slave bad! Her feel bad. Monster not understand bad Twisty feel. Until monster stuck. In brain." He rubbed his head as if even making these words was making his brain hurt. "It teach lesson," said Sparkbolt. "About other heart. Other brain. So amulet bad. But amulet good! Lesson good. Smoke bad."

Falcon listened, thinking carefully about what Sparkbolt was saying.

"Falcon—understand?"

"Falcon understand," said Falcon.

Sparkbolt smiled. "Friend good," he said. "Monster tired. Now sleep."

"Okay," said Falcon. Sparkbolt stood up to put on his Frankenstein pajamas. Then he got into bed and blew out his candle. For a while, there was silence in the boys' room. Falcon turned on his side, but this was no more comfortable than lying on his back. One thing about being an angel: it was hard to sleep comfortably with wings.

"What like?" said Sparkbolt softly.

"What's—what like?"

Sparkbolt groaned. "Have parents."

Falcon didn't know what to tell Sparkbolt. He wished he had more for him.

"I don't know, Sparkbolt," said Falcon. "My father lives up in a tower. My mother's—well, you know. Sometimes I think I might as well have been an orphan."

"Falcon *not* orphan," said Sparkbolt. "Falcon know." He groaned. "Sparkbolt not know. Sparkbolt sewn out of—pieces. Sparkbolt given life by—mad scientist. Scientist—look at baby Sparkbolt. Father—abandon. Sparkbolt—cast out! Alone!"

The Frankenstein moaned in the dark.

Falcon said, "I feel like that sometimes, alone I mean. I think about Megan and Jonny Frankenstein. I miss them a lot."

Sparkbolt groaned again. "Jonny good," he said. "Him like brother."

"Jonny said something to me once kind of like what you just said. About growing up in an orphanage. How bad it was."

"Bad. Jonny right." There was a long silence. "Where Jonny—now?"

"I don't know," said Falcon. "The last time I saw him

he was up in the Tower of Souls with my father. The Crow was going to punish him for being a spy for the guardians. But he let him go when he saw how Jonny had changed."

"Sparkbolt miss Jonny too. Him friend."

"I don't know where he went. The Crow wouldn't let him stay here. And the guardians wouldn't let him come back, I bet. So I don't know what happened to Jonny. He's kind of stuck between worlds, I guess."

"Stuck," said Sparkbolt dramatically. "Between worlds!"

"That's another reason I miss Jonny," said Falcon. "He was the only other person who really knew what it was like not to fit in anywhere."

Sparkbolt growled softly. Then he said, "Falcon Quinn—friend. Falcon Quinn—family. Monster not have family—until come. To Academy. Meet Falcon. Others. Monster finally—have home! Falcon stop worry. Home good."

Falcon nodded. "Home good," he said.

Sparkbolt sighed happily. "Home," he said, his voice growing drowsy. "Love . . . Friend . . ."

A moment later, the Frankenstein was asleep.

Falcon lay in the dark for a while, listening to his roommate breathe his Frankenstein breaths. *Falcon not orphan,* he thought. *Falcon know.*

Sparkbolt began to snore. As he inhaled, he made a

sound like *rrrr*. On the exhale, he made a sound like *eee bee bee bee*. Falcon opened his eyes and walked over to the window. The moon shone down on the campus. There was a harsh sound from the direction of Castle Gruesombe, like *caww—caww-ca-cawww*, and Falcon looked over to see the castle's ravens perched at the top of the broken turret.

He opened the sash. Wind from the ocean, smelling of salt and sand, blew into the room. Sparkbolt muttered in sleep. "Friend," he said. "Friend."

Falcon crept out the window onto the roof of Dustbin Hall. Then he closed the window behind him. He turned to face Castle Grisleigh and spread his wings.

The young angel stepped off the roof. He fell for a few seconds before he was uplifted on a thermal current. He pulsed his wings. Falcon looked down upon the campus, at the ancient buildings and the long stone wall that separated the Upper School from the Lower. There, on top of the gates, was the stone statue of Scratchy Weezums, his mouth frozen open in midscream. Beyond this were the grounds of the Lower School he had first seen last spring—with the cinder-block Wellness Center and the old gymnasium in which he and the others had celebrated the Zombie Jamboree. He saw the four dormitory towers of Castle Grisleigh—the towers of Science, and Blood, and Moonlight, and Aberrations. It was the Tower of

Aberrations that Mrs. Redflint had first brought him to and shown him his dorm room with its coffins and lab equipment, and the chains upon the wall. He smiled as he remembered the night that Lincoln Pugh had arrived. It was funny now, Falcon thought. But it had been scary at the time.

There, in the center of the castle, was the Tower of Souls, lit by what appeared to be the soft light of candles. There was an arched window on each side of the tower, and Falcon flew through one of these and stepped onto the stone floor. The room was full of turning gears and ticking machinery.

"Ah," said the Crow. "It's you." The tall, thin creature was sitting in a chair wearing a jeweler's loupe, holding a tiny gear with a pair of tweezers.

"I couldn't sleep," said Falcon.

"Are you restlessss?" asked the Crow.

"You could say that," said Falcon.

"And what is the sssource of this restlessnesss?"

"There's something I want to ask you," said Falcon, although now he felt more than a little self-conscious.

"Assk," said the Crow. "Very well." He took the magnifying eyepiece from his face. The creature rose from his chair and went over to Falcon. "Assk."

"Why did you and Mom—get married?"

"Why—"

"Why did you get married, in the first place? If you were a demon, and she was a guardian. That's what I don't understand. Why?"

"We—" The Crow looked uncertain. He shrugged his wings. "Thisss . . . was long ago," he said.

"You got married, and you had me. And now you want to murder each other. How is that possible?"

"I don't want to murder her," said the Crow.

"She wants to murder *you*," said Falcon.

"Yess, well, that," said the Crow, "is different."

"What did you do to her?"

"Do?" said the Crow, and now his wings rose angrily in the air again, and a small blue flame ignited above his head. "I? I did nothing to her. She knew what I was. From the very beginning, she knew."

"Did you know that she was their queen? That she was the leader of the creatures whose only purpose is to kill us?"

The Crow lowered his wings, and the blue flame died down slightly. There was a stopwatch that hung from a chain around his neck, and for a moment the Crow looked at it. The hands were not moving. "I notice you said *us*. As if you are one of us."

"You think I'm not?"

"Perhapsss . . . I am mistaken. But I thought that in the wake of your time within the Black Mirror last spring, you had decided to choose your own path. To live as neither monster nor guardian. Or as both."

"I did," said Falcon.

"Then—why are you here, Falcon? If you are not one of us?"

"I—I don't know," said Falcon. "Because—"

"Because here on Shadow Island, you are among those you love. Yess? The Chupakabra. The Sasquatch. You love them not because they are monsters. But for their spirit. Yess?" He nodded, and the flame went out. "It was something like this with your mother, and with me, once. We knew what we were. But we wished to live apart. To defy the rules of the world, with which we disagreed."

"Rules?" said Falcon. "There aren't any rules!"

"Ah," said the Crow. "But in this—you are *mistaken*."

"Mistaken how?"

The Crow looked sad. "The world is not forgiving," he said.

"What do you mean? You had each other. You had me. Why couldn't you just live the lives you wanted?"

The Crow walked over to the window and looked out at the night for a long time. "The world catches us in the end," he said.

Falcon went to his father and took him by the elbow so that the Crow turned from the window and looked his son in the eye. "What happened?" said Falcon. "Why did she change her mind about you?"

"What happened," the Crow repeated softly. "A storm. One morning. In Cold River. There was ice on the lake. I heard something—a voice. I walked out on the ice. There was a hole. I remember looking at the water, thinking how *cold* it must be. That was when I felt her behind me. Pushing me in. The cold of that water, like knives! When I awoke, I was here. In this tower. Back in the world of *monsters* and *demons*. And everything in the world, back in its assigned place."

"But why did she push you in?" said Falcon. "Why?"

"That," said the Crow, "is a question I should like to ask her myself." His wings pulsed softly now, like those of a butterfly just emerging from its cocoon. "I have wondered about this for many years now, from this tower. What it was that made her decide to go back. And live the life I thought she had renounced."

Falcon felt a rising anger. "So you have no idea," he said. "You and Mom were together, and then one day she just decided to kill you. Is that it?"

The Crow nodded. "I sssuppose," he said.

"You suppose," said Falcon.

"It may be that she changed her mind, once—"

"Once what?"

"Once she . . . had a child, Falcon."

"Wait. It's *my* fault?"

"I recall coming back to our trailer one day that winter. She was sitting in a rocking chair. You were six months old, perhaps. She was looking at you with such an expression. Well. You have seen the blue of those eyes. And then she looked from you to me. And her face changed, from that look of love to a look of—something else."

"Didn't you ask her what was wrong? Did you ask her to explain?"

"I did not," said the Crow. "I went outside and stood by the lake and listened to the sound the ice made as the water moved beneath it. A week later—well. That was when I went through."

The Crow went back to his desk and picked up the tweezers again. "And so I stay up here, fixing clocks. I have become very talented at fixing things." The Crow's voice crackled with bitterness and regret. "So, do bring me a clock, Falcon, if you ever have one that is broken."

"That stopwatch around your neck—," said Falcon.

"Begins to tick if I leave the tower," said the Crow. "And measures the time subtracted from your mother's life—and from yours—while I am away." He looked at the stopwatch. "And so I protect her—I protect you both—by remaining here. It is the one thing I can do, to save you both."

"I don't understand why you're being punished," said Falcon. "It was Mom who tried to kill you. Why are you the one sent into exile?"

"Falcon," said the Crow, and his eyes shone. "Don't you see? She is being punished as well."

"How is she being punished? She's their queen! She lives in a castle!"

"The world is full of people who live in castles, Falcon. Most of them are not free."

"She's free. Isn't she?"

The Crow looked at his deformed right hand, with its thin bones protruding through the translucent, leathery skin. "If you return to them," said the Crow softly, "beware of Cygnus. He will tell you he is your friend, that he wishes to serve you, and call you prince. But he despises you most of all, Falcon. Do not trust him."

"What are you talking about? I'm not going back there, all right?"

"So you say. But I suspect, Falcon, that you will not remain here for long either. You said as much yourself, when you looked into the Black Mirror. You chose a separate path."

"I did," said Falcon. "But that doesn't mean I'm joining up with them. With Mom. The guardians are crazy."

"We are *all* crazy, Falcon," said the Crow.

"I'm not," said Falcon.

"No?" said the Crow, looking at his son thoughtfully. "Well. Perhaps not. But life is not easy for those who are not crazy. It is a difficult path, the path—of sanity. Choosing it can drive a creature . . . insane."

Falcon nodded. "I have to get back to Dustbin," he said.

"Indeed," said the Crow. Falcon walked over to the arched window. "Falcon—"

Falcon turned back to face his father.

"I . . . am glad you came, and spoke. I don't suppose I am much . . . of a father."

"Well, I don't have much practice being . . . a son," said Falcon.

The two stared awkwardly at each other for a moment.

"Perhaps we might learn?" said the Crow.

Falcon nodded. "Perhaps," he said, and jumped out the window. His wings spread and he floated across the campus toward Dustbin Hall.

The Crow stood in his window for a long time and, watching the angel descend, felt a heaviness in his heart. He raised his hand to the side of his face. Then he lowered his hand and looked at it, remembering what it had been like, long ago, when he had disguised himself as a human and lived out in the Reality Stream with his wife, away from this world. He had had fingers then.

He thought about the words he had spoken to his son—*The world catches us in the end*—and wondered whether it made any difference whether the world caught him or not. He remembered coming home, that day long ago, and finding Vega in her chair, with their son in her lap, and the expression that had crossed her face when she looked upon her husband.

Didn't you ask her what was wrong? Did you ask her to explain?

The Crow looked through the west window, out at the Sea of Dragons. The moonlight shone upon the waves. He thought about the distant island where his wife lived. He wondered what she looked like now, whether her hair had gone gray.

The Crow raised his suction cup hand again. The blue flame ignited above his head, softly at first and then with greater luminescence. "Vega," he said aloud.

Then he stepped out of the Tower of Souls. The Crow spread his wings and flew west toward the sea.

As he flew, the stopwatch that hung around his neck began to tick.

9

THE PROPERTIES OF SCORPION BLOOD

The school year began to fall into a routine. Sparkbolt and Falcon woke up in their room in Dustbin each morning, headed over to the cafeteria for breakfast, then began the morning's classes: Literature and Fabrications, Mad Science, Mutant History, and First-year Egyptian. After lunch there was Numberology with the moth man, who as always, refused to teach the young monsters any actual math. "It uses the calculators," said the moth man with his silvery voice. "It pushes the buttons. Writes down the answer. Math is pointless. Enough horror in world without math too." The moth man made the students uncomfortable, what with his long dun wings and obsession with lightbulbs, but one thing was true enough: his class was very popular.

In the afternoons, Falcon did homework or watched the Monster Croquet team or practiced the godzooka. He saw a lot less of his friends than he would have liked—both Ankhhoptet and Lincoln Pugh were on the Monster Croquet team, and Sparkbolt was frequently busy with Crackthunder and the other editors of the literary magazine. Even Max and Pearl frequently seemed occupied, and when they weren't, they were with each other. Falcon noted that they had occasionally begun to bicker, particularly over the issue of Pearl's friend *el Boco*, who was the only other Chupakabra at the Academy and with whom Pearl occasionally flew around the Academy grounds speaking Spanish.

One night after dinner, Falcon took a walk by himself along the beach, to look at the ocean and watch the rising moon. He stood there for a while with his wings raised behind his back, feeling the force of the ocean breeze blowing through them. It lifted him off his feet for a moment before gently lowering him back to the sand. He thought about Megan, the wind elemental.

Falcon stood there for a little while, looking at the sea and feeling the wind in his wings. Then, from down the beach, came a pair of voices.

"It's just not fair," roared Max.

"It is not a question of fair!" countered Pearl, buzzing around the Sasquatch's head. "It is a question of freedom! And I am free to choose my companions! As are you yourself, Señor Max!"

"If you like him, you should just say so," said Max. "I'll get out of your way. Quit comin' around."

"Señor," said Pearl. "You cannot be jealous? Of *¡el Boco!* This nada de nada from Argentina!"

"Hey, guys," said Falcon, a little self-consciously.

"Dude," said Max by way of greeting.

"I for one am glad that we have come upon you, Señor Falcon!" said Pearl. "It is a relief. For at this moment I am full of irritation with Señor Max. He has taken some ideas into his head. Ideas I find an affront to my dignity and my freedom!"

"It's about *el Boco*, man," said Max. "The blabbity blabbity blabbity from Argentina. You know, *el Chupakabro*."

"One of my own kind!" said Pearl. "One of my brethren! From whom Señor Max would have me sundered!"

"I'm not tryin' to sunder anything," said Max. "It's just that—you're letting him buzz all around! Talking in Spanish! Which you know I can't understand!"

"Perhaps you should learn the Spanish then!" shouted Pearl. "Perhaps it is you, Señor Max, who should be doing the buzzing!"

"You know, you could learn Spanish, Max," said Falcon. "Might be a handy thing, knowing Spanish."

"Hey, whose side are you on, man?" said Max.

"I'm on both your sides," said Falcon. "I'm saying, maybe you should learn how to say a few things in Spanish. And Pearl, maybe you could be sympathetic to Max feeling a little left out when you're hanging out with *el Boco*?"

"Hey, what are you, Mr. Therapy Dog?" said Max.

"I should sting the both of you for suggesting my relations with *el Boco* are deserving of this reproach!" She buzzed around Falcon and Max with her stinger extended. "Okay, Pearl, put the stinger away," said Max. "You don't have to, like, threaten us."

"I will not be disrespected!" shouted Pearl. "I should sting you just for being Señor Estúpido!"

"I am not Señor Estúpido!" shouted Max. "I am Señor uh—Smarto!"

"Do not raise your voice with me," said Pearl. "For this I cannot stand!"

"I gotta!" shouted Max. "'Cause you're—like—" Max roared louder than Falcon had ever heard before. "YOU'RE HURTING MY FEELINGS!" He raised his hands over his head. "Aaaaagghhhhh!"

Okay, Falcon thought. *That went well.*

"Never have I been so disrespected!" shouted Pearl.

"Honk." Max wiped his tears on his big hairy arm. "I need a tissue."

"I think you're both overreacting," said Falcon. "Why can't you both—"

"Why can you not leave us to our affairs!" shouted Pearl. "Instead of meddling in things that are not yours in which to meddle!"

"I wasn't trying to—" Pearl's harsh words hurt him. She had never yelled at Falcon like this before. "I was just trying to help."

"Hey, man," said Max. "We were fine before you started helping!"

"Okay," said Falcon. "Good. I'll just—head back to the castle."

"Dude," said Max.

"*Señor,*" said Pearl. And then the Chupakabra and the Sasquatch walked down the beach.

So what did I just learn? Falcon thought. He shook his head. *That sometimes, when you try to help people, you wind up making things worse than when you started?*

Falcon walked through the Academy's front gates and then across the campus toward Dustbin. He was just passing Screamer Library when he nearly collided with Mr. Lyons, who was coming around the corner with his nose deep in a book.

"Oh, for heaven's sake, Falcon Quinn," said Mr. Lyons. "I am so sorry. Wasn't looking where I was going." He held up the book. "Sherlock Holmes. 'The Sign of Four.'" He sighed happily. "Never fails to satisfy."

"Mr. Lyons," said Falcon. "Are there any books on angels in Screamer Library?"

"Books on angels?" said Mr. Lyons. "Hmm. Well, there is a nice inventory of celestials written by Zarah Zhumway. A taxonomy of the form—cherubim, tricksters, protectors, demons, and so on. I think that has a chapter on angels, yes."

"I mean more like a guide to—being one," said Falcon.

"A guide," said Mr. Lyons.

"Yeah," said Falcon. "Because a lot of the time, I don't know exactly—" He raised his wings and lowered them. "I don't know what it is I'm supposed to be doing."

"My dear boy," said Mr. Lyons. "I had no idea you were so—uncertain. I thought your path was crystal clear!"

"Not really," said Falcon. "I mean—I know I'm supposed to do good and everything. But sometimes—I don't know how."

"Sometimes doing good requires making a mess of things," said Mr. Lyons. "Doesn't it?"

"I don't understand any of this," said Falcon, his voice rising. "What am I supposed to do? Why aren't there any—" His voice fell now. "Never mind."

"Any what?"

"Directions," said Falcon. "You buy something stupid like—I don't know, a waffle iron, say. They give you a twenty-page booklet on how to make waffles. But when it comes to living your life, there's nothing! You're totally on your own!"

"My dear boy," said Mr. Lyons, purring. "Why would you think you're on your own? The whole world is an instruction book. Start anywhere! Read everything! Here, look—" He gave Falcon the copy of "The Sign of Four." "Start with the Holmes. So much wisdom to be found in Sherlock Holmes. In this story, for instance, he says to Watson: *When you have eliminated the impossible,*

whatever remains, however improbable, *must be the truth.'*
It is a good phrase to bear in mind, if what you intend to
do is solve mysteries."

Falcon took the volume from the librarian. "So I'm a
detective now?" he said.

Mr. Lyons clapped him on the shoulder. "Yes, that's
it, exactly. A detective, solving the crime of life. Well. You
should come to auditions tonight, for the play? *Romeo and
Juliet.* The human translation!" He purred again. "Do
come, Falcon," said the librarian. "I am certain you will
shine."

When Falcon got back to his room in Dustbin Hall, he
found Sparkbolt sitting on his bed, yellow tears rolling
down his green cheeks.

"Sparkbolt," said Falcon. "What happened?"

He groaned sadly. "There."

Lying on Falcon's bed were a number of items that had
been lost by Falcon's friends in the final weeks of the summer. There was Weems's paddleball. There were Lincoln
Pugh's glasses. And there were Destynee's sandals. All of
these things appeared to have been repaired and fixed
recently: the elastic on the paddleball had been freshly
replaced, the glasses shined up, and the sandals repaired.
The Filchers, Falcon thought.

"Where did you find these?" said Falcon. He put down

the volume of Sherlock Holmes that Mr. Lyons had given him.

"Under Falcon bed!" Sparkbolt growled.

"Why were you—"

"Poetry book missing. Monster look for poems. On chair. In sock drawer. Finally, under Falcon bed." He growled again. "There find book. Plus others. Things Falcon steal. And hide. Hide from friend!"

"You think I stole these?" said Falcon. "Is that it?"

"Stealing bad!" shouted Sparkbolt. "Falcon betray friends!"

"But I didn't take these," said Falcon. "I—"

Sparkbolt raised one of his jagged eyebrows. "Things here. Beneath Falcon bed!! Rrrrr! Things stolen!"

"Sparkbolt," said Falcon. "Listen—there's something I never told you about. Because I was supposed to keep it secret."

"Falcon Quinn have many secret!" said Sparkbolt. "Secret from friend! Friend trust!" Two more tears edged over Sparkbolt's eyes and rolled down his cheeks. "Falcon Quinn monster only friend! Sparkbolt travel path—of alone! Alone!"

"Sparkbolt," said Falcon. "Remember that time you found me in the woods, back on Monster Island? I met these creatures—they call themselves the Filchers—a group of elves . . . and a Squonk—"

"Falcon Quinn stole poetry book! Of rhyming poems! Let octopus dog chew! Like bone!" Sparkbolt's face turned angry. "Falcon Quinn steal poems! All Sparkbolt care about, poems! All in world! Except Falcon Quinn! Rrrrr! Betrayal! Dark!" He stood up and moved toward Falcon with his fingers spread, as if to strangle him. Falcon quickly stood up too, and his angel wings lifted from his back. He felt his dark eye heat up, and in an instant a fireball soared out of him, hitting Sparkbolt in the chest. Sparkbolt fell back for a moment, releasing his grip on Falcon, who gasped for air. But Sparkbolt was just further enraged, and he came after Falcon again. Falcon ducked out of the way, but Sparkbolt managed to connect with a hard punch to his face.

Falcon stood there, stunned, his eye and cheek throbbing. "Sparkbolt," said Falcon. "You—"

Sparkbolt went to the bed and gathered all the stolen items, then stormed out the door. Falcon sat down on his bed and held his head in his hands. His face ached where Sparkbolt had slugged him. *This is bad,* Falcon thought. *If I've lost Sparkbolt, I've lost everybody.*

He looked at his feet, and there he saw a small, brown envelope just peeking out from under the bed. He bent down and picked it up and found that his name was written on the front of the envelope in ornate, curling script.

Inside the envelope was a short note:

*Dear Falcon. All well on the Filcher front! The
missus said we ought to give these items to you so that
you can return them to your friends. Normally we
don't give things back, you know, but we thought
that this might help you in the months ahead.
Yours sincerely,
Mr. Grubb.*

"Help," said Falcon out loud. "Yeah. Thanks a lot."
At the bottom of the page, in a different hand, was a
final note.

*Falcon, do remember you are not alone in the world.
If you ever need a place to go where you can count
on a warm reception, you know where to find us. It
would be an honor to have you among our number.
Mr. Sweeny.*

Falcon held the note in his hand for a long time,
thinking about it. He saw the wart-covered Squonk; the
beautiful, distant Clea; the kind, thoughtful face of Mr.
Sweeny. He heard the songs they had played as they ate
their afternoon feast. *The man in the moon says, "Please
keep it down. All the church bells are waking up the dead. A
fool looks better than a headless clown. Send yourself to bed."*
Then he put the letter back in the envelope and headed

out the door and down the hall, toward the play tryouts in Castle Gruesombe. He still hoped that the words of Mr. Lyons—*I am certain you will shine*—might prove true. As he rushed outside, however, he ran directly into Copperhead, who was leaning against the wall, holding a large conch shell to her ear and talking to herself.

"Falcon," she said, surprised at his appearance.

"Copperhead?" he said. "What are you doing? What's that shell for?"

"Nothing, I—"

"Why are you hanging out in front of Dustbin?" he said. "You're not supposed to be over here."

"I am listening—," she said, "to the sea." She held the conch shell toward Falcon's ear. "Can you hear it? The sounds of the ocean? They are so soothing for a mind that is troubled!"

"Is your mind troubled, Copperhead?" said Falcon.

"Not half as troubled as yours, Falcon Quinn."

"Troubled?" said Falcon. "What makes you think I'm troubled?"

"I might have a bag over my head," she said, "but I see things others don't. That black eye of yours, for instance. Who punched you?"

"No one," said Falcon.

"Sparkbolt," she said. "He's turned on you too."

"I don't know what you're talking about."

"Of course you do. Since the attack at that Bludd Club, everyone thinks you're a spy."

"I'm not a spy!" shouted Falcon.

"I know that," said Copperhead.

"You do?"

"Here," said Copperhead, reaching into her purse. "Let me put some scorpion blood on that bruise."

"Some—what?"

"Sssh," said Copperhead, squeezing a little of the ointment onto her fingers and rubbing it onto Falcon's face. "This will heal you, Falcon. Nice thing about scorpion blood. It takes away the pain."

"I can heal my own bruises," said Falcon, and this was, of course, true. His blue eye had the ability to heal all sorts of injuries.

"I know that," said Copperhead. "But don't you ever want somebody else to look out for you? It must be exhausting, always healing yourself."

"I don't mind—*owww!*" Falcon's blue eye suddenly began to sting. "It hurts!"

"Of course it hurts," said Copperhead. "Things hurt when they heal."

10

A BEAM OF RED LIGHT

Falcon and Copperhead entered the auditorium a few minutes later to see that the auditions had already begun. Mr. Lyons was onstage holding a clipboard, and two other students—Squawker, the werechicken, and *el Boco*, the famous goatsucker of Argentina—were doing a scene, reading from scripts. They were pretending to have a sword fight, and at just this moment, *el Boco* pretended to slay Squawker.

"I am hurt," said the werechicken. *"A plague on both your houses! I am sped. Cluck cluck cluck cluck! Is he gone and hath nothing?"*

El Boco looked concerned. "Señor Chicken," he said. "You hurt?"

"Cluck cluck cluck *cluck*," replied Squawker. "A scratch!"

Squawker and the Chupakabro paused and looked up as Falcon and Copperhead entered the room. Everyone turned to look at them, including a whole row of students with the items that Sparkbolt had just returned. There was

Destynee with her sandals, and Lincoln Pugh, once more wearing his rectangular orange glasses. Next to them was Weems, slowly bouncing his paddleball.

Well, thought Falcon, *at least I know things can't get much worse.*

He sat down in a chair in the audience next to another one of the students, a vampire girl about his age. She looked over at him and chuckled softly.

"Well, well," said Merideath. "If it isn't Falcon *Quark.*"

For a moment, Falcon sat there stunned, looking at the vampire girl. Then he began to stutter. "You—you got expelled—," he said. "You're—"

"Yes, Falcon Quinn," she said defiantly. "But I'm back. My father just made *one* phone call. That's all it took!"

Mr. Lyons clapped his hands. "That was nicely done," he said to Squawker and *el Boco.* "Let's see another pair of actors. Ah, Falcon, you're here, excellent. Let's try you out as Romeo."

There was some murmuring at this, a mixture of snickering and growling. Sparkbolt groaned. Quagmire sent up some bubbles that floated in the air and then burst with an unpleasant smell.

"I'll be Juliet," said Merideath, following Falcon up to the stage.

"Ah, Miss Venacava," said Mr. Lyons. "Actually, I think that first I'd like to see—"

"I said I'll be Juliet," insisted Merideath. "My father promised me I could have my way!"

"Miss Venacava," said Mr. Lyons. "You'll audition the same as every other student. The ultimate choice of casting rests with me."

"Oh, I'm going to be in the play," said Merideath. "I don't think you want to find *out* what happens if I don't make the play."

Mr. Lyons growled. "I will cast the students who are most deserving," he said.

"Exactly," said Merideath. "And who's more deserving than me?"

Mr. Lyons growled even louder.

"And please stop that growling. It's so unattractive!"

"Miss Venacava," said Mr. Lyons. "May I remind you that you are addressing a member of the faculty?"

"You're not faculty!" said Merideath contemptuously. "You're just a librarian!"

Mr. Lyons's growl grew rumbly and deep now, and he stepped toward her with a bloodthirsty look. "Perhaps," he said, "if you actually read books, you might hold librarians in somewhat higher regard."

"I'll see that you're fired," said Merideath.

"Yes, well," said Mr. Lyons. "I'll see that you're *eaten*."

"Ah, ah," said a voice, and Falcon looked over to see Count Manson standing in the back of the room. "Temper.

Dewouring the students is perhaps not the best choice for a staff member currently on *probation*."

"Count," said Mr. Lyons. "What are you doing here?"

"Making certain that none of our students suffers the same fate as Captain Hardtack," said Count Manson.

Mr. Lyons growled again. "Act two," he said, handing scripts to Merideath and Falcon. "Scene two."

Merideath scanned the script and wrinkled her nose again. "What version of the play is this? This isn't the original Frankenstein!"

"It's the English translation," said Mr. Lyons. "We're doing a little experiment."

"Okay, now wait," said Merideath. "What's my motivation in this scene?"

"You're a spoiled little rich girl," said Mr. Lyons. "To whom no one has ever said no."

"I beg your pardon?" said Merideath.

"You have asked for your motivation. Here it is. At last you have met someone wholly outside your small, inbred circle, someone unlike anyone you have ever known." He nodded toward Falcon Quinn. "And now you find yourself changed and moved by him. You stand on the balcony of your room. And you say—"

"*O Romeo, Romeo! wherefore art thou Romeo?*" said Merideath.

She had only read one line of the play, but it was already

clear to Falcon that Merideath might be the worst actress in the history of theater. Her voice was flat and uninteresting and dull. *"Deny thy father and refuse thy name; Or, if thou wilt not, be but sworn my love—"* She wrinkled her nose and said in a very whiny, unhappy voice, "This makes no sense!"

"You're doing vonderfully!" said Count Manson. "You seem so sveet—and wulnerable!"

Falcon looked out at the audience. The vampires were sitting there, openmouthed and agape at the wonder of Merideath's performance. Max looked at Pearl, who was sitting next to him, and the two of them exchanged gazes that suggested that either or both of them were about to vomit.

"Try a little farther down—Falcon, *'Lady, by yonder—'"*

Falcon cleared his throat. *"Lady, by yonder blessed moon I swear,"* he said. *"That tips with silver all these fruit-tree tops—"*

Merideath moved closer to Falcon. He could see her long vampire teeth now. She said, *"The inconstant moon, that monthly changes in her circled orb, Lest that thy love prove likewise variable."*

The theater was suddenly very quiet. Falcon felt his hearts pounding. He whispered, *"What shall I swear by?"*

"Louder, Mr. Quinn," said Mr. Lyons.

"What," he said, looking deep into Merideath's black, liquid eyes. *"What shall I swear by?"*

"Sweet, good night," she said. *"This bud of love, by summer's ripening breath, May prove a beauteous flower when next we meet!"* She moved close to Falcon, and she put one hand on his cheek. Her mouth opened wide, and Falcon could see those long, shining canine teeth coming closer to him. He could feel the place on his neck where she would bite him, any moment now, could imagine the rush of his blood into her mouth.

"Very nice," said Mr. Lyons, putting one hand on Merideath's shoulder and pulling her away from Falcon. She staggered backward, her mouth still open, as if she had forgotten for a moment where she was.

"And now others may try their hand at this part!" said Pearl, buzzing around Max's head. "The auditions shall continue!"

"I don't think it vill be necessary to cast anyone else," said Count Manson. "You've got your Juliet. Haven't you?"

Mr. Lyons made a soft, muffled growl. "Yes," he said. "I suppose so. But perhaps we might let the others have a chance—just to—to demonstrate how superior Miss Venacava's performance is!"

"You have your Juliet," said the count a little more forcefully.

"Ah," said Mr. Lyons. "Well, let's try out some other Romeos, then."

"Dude!" shouted Max. "I want to try it! I would be an

awesome Romeo. Guy."

"I said I want him," said Merideath, pointing a long finger at Falcon.

"I thought you didn't like him," said Max.

"I *do* want him," said Merideath, her lips parting once more and her long canines glistening in the stage lights. *"As my victim!"*

"She vants him," said Count Manson conclusively.

"Dude," said Max, leaping to his feet. "This is *bogus.* How come she gets to push everybody around? She sucks!"

"What did you say?" said Merideath. Her fan club turned around to face him, their faces shocked.

"I said—" Max was suddenly embarrassed by the attention that had fallen upon him. "I don't know. It's just not fair, is all. I can, like—sit down now."

"You should not be afraid of speaking the truth!" said Pearl, buzzing toward the stage now. "Truly her talents leave much to be desired! For this—this—creature to dictate terms to the rest of us is an injustice that shall not go unavenged! What Señor Max has spoken must not be unsaid! We must fight for justice! For equality! For our lives!"

"Pearl," said Max in a hoarse voice. "You gotta let this go, man."

"I shall not let this go!" shouted Pearl. "I do not suffer injustice!"

"That vill be enough," said Count Manson.

"And who are you, to arrive from nowhere and tell the director of the play what he may do, and what he may not do?!"

"I am vun of the senior faculty members," said Count Manson. "Mr. Lyons is not faculty. He is only—*staff.* I am the authority in this room. And those who disrespect me, Miss Picchu, vill be squashed like—ah yes. Like a mosquito! Like wermin!"

Max shook his head. "Dude," he said.

"Mosquito!" shouted Pearl, enraged. *"Mosquito!"* She flew toward Count Manson. "Prepare to feel the poison of *¡la Chupakabra!"* she shouted. "The famous goatsucker of Peru!"

But Count Manson just raised one hand, and Pearl suddenly bounced off what seemed like an invisible wall in space. She fell to the floor, still buzzing, as Count Manson yawned wearily. "And you should prepare to feel the utter indifference of Count Manson. The wampire from Transylwania."

"Pearl," shouted Max, jumping to his feet. He ran to the aisle of the theater, where the Chupakabra lay buzzing upon the floor. "She's hurt!" he said, looking at Count Manson angrily.

"Of course she's hurt," said the count. "She ran directly into the force of my *vill!"*

Mr. Lyons rushed to Pearl's side. A dark violet liquid was seeping from her mouth. "Mr. Quinn, I believe we could use your healing eye here. As quickly as possible."

"Yes, sir," said Falcon. He began to walk toward Pearl and Mr. Lyons, and then he remembered—*I have wings*—and spread them. In one second he flew off the stage, over the rows of seats, and then landed in the aisle.

"Please focus your beam on her neck," said Mr. Lyons. "There is a great deal of blood."

"You stupid idiot," roared Max, heading toward Count Manson. "You hurt her! You seriously hurt her! You should—"

But Count Manson raised his hand again and Max bumped against the force of the count's will, just as Pearl had before him. It felt like an invisible wall. "You're not being fair!" Max roared.

"Fair," said the count dispassionately. "*Fairness* is not vun of my considerations vhen I am considering the velfare of wampires!"

Falcon was concentrating on Pearl's wounds. His light began to shine upon her. As he focused, however, he noted something strange about the light. It wasn't coming out blue, as it usually did. It was coming out red.

Pearl screamed softly, and now more blood rushed out of her mouth. Her eyes fluttered open for a moment and looked into Falcon's. "Stop," she said. "*¡Señor!* You are— killing me—"

"Falcon?" said Max, rushing back to Pearl's side.

"What's happening, Mr. Quinn?" said Mr. Lyons. "I said the blue light. The healing light."

"This is the healing light," said Falcon, confused. His light faltered as he lost concentration, and went out.

"I am—," Pearl whispered. "I am *slain*."

Then her head fell against the floor once more, and her wings, which had been buzzing intermittently, suddenly stopped.

"What do you mean, 'slain'?" said Max.

"Pity," said Count Manson.

Mr. Lyons was down on his knees, looking at Pearl with a grave expression.

"What's wrong with her?" said Falcon.

"Oh no," said Mr. Lyons. His dark eyes seemed especially moist.

"Mr. Lyons," said Falcon. "Should I shine my healing light on her again?"

"Healing light?" said Merideath, who had rushed up to join them. "You *killed* her with that weapon of yours! That's no healing light! That's a death ray!"

"I was trying to save her!"

"What do you mean, exactly, when you say—'slain,'" said Max, holding Pearl's hand. "Pearl. Wake up. Come on. I'll get you some—sandwiches."

"Falcon Quinn killed her!" said Merideath again, pointing at him. "You all saw it!"

"He did," said Picador, standing up. "He used his eye thing on her and wasted her!"

"It's what you did to my sister," said Dahlia Crofton, her voice catching.

"And the Sasquatches," said Maeve, "Peeler and Woody!"

The crowd of young monsters began to stagger toward him now, anger and vengeance in their eyes. Falcon began to walk backward, and as he walked, he looked at the faces of the many monsters he knew, some of whom he had counted among his friends. But now he saw only hate-filled strangers.

"That's enough," said Mr. Lyons to the students. "Back to your seats, all of you!"

But the mob paid no heed. "Traitor!" said Merideath.

"Mr. Quinn," said Mr. Lyons. "I might suggest leaving this area with all due speed."

"But you saw," said Falcon. "You saw what happened—"

But Mr. Lyons transformed into his full lion self at this moment and roared at him.

Picador the minotaur shouted, "Destroy Falcon Quinn! Destroy!" The others took up the chant. "*Traitor! Enemy! Destroy!*"

The last thing Falcon saw, before spreading his wings and flying away, was Max kneeling by Pearl's body. He looked at Falcon, his eyes full of tears. "Dude?" he said.

Falcon beat his wings twice and sailed over their heads. He flew out a window and ascended to the Tower of Souls.

The young monsters yelled and screamed and pointed in the direction in which Falcon had flown. "After him!" shouted Merideath. "Don't let him escape!"

They grabbed torches from the wall and raced after him. Mr. Lyons rubbed Pearl's tiny body with his large lion paw. His eyes closed, and he licked her face with his lion tongue. A soft blue light surrounded Pearl's body.

"She was the bravest person I ever knew," said Max. "She was—"

A faint, weak voice said, "I was—*la Chupakabra*. The famous—goatsucker of—"

"Dude," said Max. "You're alive!"

Mr. Lyons licked her face again, and Pearl sat up. "Dude," said Max. "What did you just do?"

Mr. Lyons transformed back into human form. "Max," he said. "Take her to the Wellness Center. She will survive. Do you think you could carry Miss Picchu for me?"

"I would carry her *anyplace*," said Max, slowly picking Pearl up in his arms. "But how did you—"

"Go," said Mr. Lyons.

Max rushed out of the auditorium, holding the Chupakabra in his arms. "Where is our friend Falcon?" said Pearl to Max. "We have to—"

"Falcon's in trouble, man," said Max. "After what he did."

"What did he do?" said Pearl.

"He's the one who fried you, man," said Max. "He's the one who—"

"*Señor,*" rasped Pearl. "Falcon Quinn—is our sworn friend. He has done me no harm. We have pledged—with our lives—to defend him. . . ."

From down the hall, they heard an angry roar from the mob.

"Listen," said Max. "About that."

Pearl's eyes rolled back in her head. "Sweet—prince—" she said. "Sweet—Good—night—!"

Falcon flew through the eastern window of the Tower of Souls. His ears filled with the ticking of the clockworks.

"Dad—," he said. "I'm in trouble!"

"He's not here, Falcon," said a voice, and he turned to see a shadowy form hiding behind the golden frame of the Black Mirror.

"Who's there?" said Falcon, squinting in the dark.

"A friend," said the voice, and he could tell that it was a woman speaking. It was a voice he knew from somewhere.

"I'm kind of short on friends right now," said Falcon. "Maybe you could give me a hint?"

"It's me," said Copperhead, stepping into a small pool

of moonlight cast onto the floor through the west window. Falcon could hear the snakes hissing softly beneath the burlap bag that covered her head.

"You," said Falcon. "What are you doing here?"

"Waiting for you," said Copperhead. "I knew you'd come up here. Once they turned on you. As I knew they would."

"Where's my father?" said Falcon. "Do you know what's happened to him?"

"I was going to ask you the same question," said Copperhead.

"I don't understand."

"Don't you?" said Copperhead. "I think you do. I think you and I have understood each other from the beginning."

"You," said Falcon. "That stuff you put on my eye. That wasn't—"

"Honestly, Falcon," said Copperhead. "Scorpion blood? You're so gullible. What I rubbed into your eye was an ointment specifically designed to alter the effects of that blue eye of yours. To change it from a healing eye to a *killing* one, and without you even knowing! I must say it was far more effective than I expected."

"Why would you want to hurt my friends?" said Falcon. "What's wrong with you?"

"Your friends," she said, shaking her head sadly.

"Whenever you use that word, I just feel sorry for you." She inched toward him.

"Listen—," said Falcon. "I don't know what you think I'm—"

"I know exactly what you think," said Copperhead. "Because we're two of a kind, you and me—aren't we? Two creatures that have no place. At least—not *here*." She reached up to her head and pulled off the burlap bag that concealed her face.

Falcon tried to cover his eyes, but it was too late. All at once he found himself looking directly upon the face of the Gorgon.

Except that, as Falcon now discovered, Copperhead was no Gorgon. She was, in fact, a beautiful young woman with soft black hair and piercing blue eyes. He recognized the color of those eyes. They were guardian blue.

"You're—a *guardian*," said Falcon, stunned. "You're not a monster at all."

Copperhead nodded. "Neither are you, Falcon Quinn."

"But the snakes—I heard them hissing—I—"

"Hsssss," said Copperhead, hissing through her teeth. "Monsters are so easy to deceive. You put a bag on your head and hiss like a snake, and everyone concludes you're a Gorgon. And you stick Quagmire inside somebody's god-zooka, everyone assumes he did it on purpose!"

"Y-you," sputtered Falcon. "What are you *doing* here?"

"Keeping an eye on you, of course," said Copperhead. "Hoping that you'll come to your senses. About who you are. About where you belong."

Below them, a large crowd of monsters was now storming into Castle Grisleigh, bearing torches and pitchforks and axes and swords. Falcon could hear their angry voices calling his name.

"They'll be here soon," said Copperhead. "What are you going to do?"

"I don't know, Copperhead," said Falcon. "I'm out of ideas."

"My name isn't Copperhead," said the girl. "It's Creeper."

"And you're a guardian?"

Creeper nodded. "Like you."

Falcon looked around the Tower of Souls in dismay. "Where's my father?" he shouted. "He's supposed to be here!"

"He is," said Creeper. "So why *would* he abandon you, at your time of need?"

"I have no idea!"

"Really?" said Creeper. "I should think it'd be obvious."

"Why?"

"Because he's a monster, Falcon. Like all such creatures, he has no loyalty, or faith, or love. Not even for his own son!"

"What am I supposed to do?" shouted Falcon. "I can't fight them all by myself!"

"What *will* you do?" said Creeper. "It's a very good question."

The sounds of the approaching monsters were growing louder now. Light from the flickering torches reflected from the trapdoor in the middle of the floor.

"Good luck, Falcon," said Creeper, placing the burlap bag back on her head.

Merideath was the first one to emerge through the trapdoor. She was followed by Mr. Hake, Count Manson, and Mrs. Redflint. The Tower of Souls filled with angry creatures—vampires and zombies and Frankensteins, dark elves and banshees and boiling pools of slime.

"Wait," said Falcon. "Everybody calm down! There's been a mistake!"

"Miss Copperhead," said Mrs. Redflint. "Are you all right?"

"I'm fine," said Creeper, rushing to Mrs. Redflint's side. "He captured me! Took me prisoner! He said he was going to throw me out of the tower window!" Creeper's voice dissolved into tears.

"She's lying!" said Falcon. "She's a guardian!"

Mr. Hake shook his head. "This is making me unhappy-happy!"

"Pull the bag off her head, if you want proof! She's a guardian!"

"Pull the bag off her head so we'll all turn to stone," said Picador. "That's your plan?"

"Don't let him hurt me!" sobbed Creeper. "Please!"

"There, there, dear," said Mrs. Redflint, pressing the girl to her bosom. "You're all right now."

"She's not a Gorgon!" said Falcon.

"Oh please," said Count Manson. "Must ve listen to this?"

"I'm sorry, Falcon," said Mrs. Redflint. "But you've left us no choice."

Mr. Hake reached toward Falcon with his slithery tentacles.

But Falcon beat his angel wings and rose up in the air. He took one last swoop over their heads, then sailed through the northern window of the Tower of Souls and out into the open air.

The monsters shouted as Falcon flew off. "And so," said Count Manson. "Ve bid farewell to Falcon Qvinn."

"Farewell?" said Mrs. Redflint. "You honestly think we've seen the last of him? I fear the next time we see Falcon Quinn, he will be at the head of an army of his kind, bent on our destruction!"

"Then ve should prepare," said the count. "Perhaps, should he return, ve vill be ready for him. Ready for them all!"

For a while the monsters stood there, observing Falcon's retreat, as he flew, silhouetted by the bright yellow moon. Then he grew smaller and smaller as his receding form reached the shores of Shadow Island and flew out above the sea.

Creeper sobbed piteously. "He said he was my friend! He said we were two of a kind!"

"Dear, dear," said Mrs. Redflint. "You've had such an ordeal, Copperhead. But you're going to be fine now. It's over, for now. You're going to be fine."

"You're right," said Creeper. "I *am* going to be just fine among my *friends*."

11

A Little Black Rain Cloud

Falcon flew above the Sea of Dragons, the waves below him flickering faintly with moonlight. As he flew, the awful images of the last several days careened through his mind. None, however, was so terrible as the one of Pearl lying in a pool of blood. In his mind he heard the voices of his friends, chanting, *Traitor! Enemy! Destroy!*

As he thought of these things, he felt his two hearts pounding. He remembered asking Copperhead, *What are you* doing *here?* And her reply, *Keeping an eye on you, of course. Hoping that you'll come to your senses. About who you are. About where you belong.*

For the first time he felt his guardian heart beating more strongly than his monster one.

The sea beneath him was calm. Falcon felt a warm thermal current passing beneath his wings, and for a moment he stopped flapping them and just rose on the thermal. It was very beautiful out here above the ocean in the bright moonlight.

He thought of Mr. Sweeny, sitting on a stump on

Monster Island, smoking his pipe, as Mrs. Grubb made an enormous feast. The Squonk played with his caged bird. Clea ate a cherry. Fascia hammered away at her shoes. Willa the Wisp twinkled and shone, indicating the approach of a stranger.

Hey, Falcon thought. *I'm no stranger.*

When that time comes, remember us. You will always find yourself welcome among those who live apart.

Falcon flew toward Monster Island as the waves beneath him rolled and swelled. A little while later, he saw the silhouettes of the closed-down rides illuminated by moonlight. Soon his feet were touching the sand by the ocean, and he bent over, winded, pulsing his wings. The skies were slowly growing lighter as sunrise approached.

He'd landed at the very spot where just a few weeks earlier he'd enjoyed the Monster Beach party with his friends. To his left was the fire pit where Mortia had played "I Wish They All Could Be Zombie Mutants" on her guitar; in front of him was the place by the ocean where Lumpp had dug up the amulet.

He looked down the beach and saw a small misshapen sphere bobbing in the waves. There was a voice. *No,* Falcon thought. *It couldn't be.*

"My, my, what's this?" said Quimby, the floating head. He rose toward Falcon now. "Falcon Quinn, all alone on Monster Island during the off-season! That can't be right!"

"Quimby," said Falcon. The bald, blubbery face looked Falcon in the eyes.

"*Would you like to ride,*" sang Quimby, rising and falling on the breeze. A thin necktie, like a string, hung down from his round, blobby face. "*In my beautiful balloon? Way up in the air in my beautiful balloon?*" Thank you, Las Vegas, thank you!

"I thought you blew away," said Falcon. The last he had seen of Quimby, the fortune-telling head, he had been floating on the breeze above Castle Grisleigh.

"So did I!" said Quimby. "And yet, here we are, blown back to Monster Island." He began to sing. "*I'm just a little black rain cloud, hovering over the honey tree. I'm just a—* Well. Whatever. Say, Falcon, get me! I'm Quimby the Pooh!"

Falcon nodded dejectedly. "Hilarious."

"Heavens to Murgatroyd, someone's wearing his Mr. Sad Face. What happened? Your little monster friends turned on you? Ran you out of town on a flaming pie?"

"Something like that."

"Ah. And now you're here, figuring you'll join the Filchers."

"I thought the Filchers were a secret," said Falcon. "I thought they lived outside of things."

"And so they do. But remember, I'm a fortune-teller, Falcon. It's my business to know secrets. And speaking of fortunes, *yours* is not hard to tell, oh no, not with an expression like that. It's as plain as the nose on your face."

"Yeah?" said Falcon. "What's my fortune?"

"I already gave you your fortune—remember? *Falcon Quinn gets torn in half. Makes his choice, and starts to laugh.*" Quimby's head began to inflate, and as it inflated, the balloon slowly rose. "I do think that's an impressive bit of work. Don't you? I have to admit—it's given me a bit of a swollen head!" Quimby laughed at his hilarious joke.

"But I did make my choice," said Falcon. "Last spring."

"This choice of yours, what was it again?" said Quimby. "Remind me. All this helium plays havoc with my short-term memory."

"I decided—when I was in the Black Mirror. That I didn't have to choose between monsters or guardians. That I could choose my own path."

"Well, that sounds very sensible. So why . . ." Quimby stretched his face so that it was long and tubelike, the kind of balloon you'd use to make balloon animals. "Why the loooong face?"

"I don't know," said Falcon. "I mean, I want to choose my own path and everything. I just don't know what it is."

"Doesn't know what it is, he says," said Quimby, astonished. "Doesn't know what it is!" He stretched himself back into a sphere. "My, my. Say, look at those highly fashionable wings you've got! I imagine those came out right after you made your big decision?" Quimby nodded thoughtfully. "It seems to me as if you've learned *something*, Falcon. Otherwise, those wings would still be in storage. It looks to me as if you're right on track!"

"Being chased out of school by my friends, with pitchforks and torches?" said Falcon. "That sounds like the right track to you?"

"Did they *really* use pitchforks and torches?" asked Quimby, shaking his head. "How terribly cliché!"

Falcon looked at the ground and sighed.

"You won't find it here," said Quimby.

"What?"

"That amulet. Your friend the octopus retriever went and buried it again."

"How do you know about that?"

"I made it, Falcon. The crimson madstone. Which turns things to vapor. Did you read the runes? I had great fun engraving those! They translate as: *To seek to know another's pain, first spend some time inside his brain.*"

"Wait, *you* made the amulet, Quimby? When was this?"

"Oh, yah yah yah sure! I made a dozen of those things. Each one created a different color mist. This is back before I got my head cut off, of course, back when I had a little fortune-telling shack, right here on the midway on Monster Island. Oh, they were a lot of fun. The umber madstone gave the gift of laughter. The emerald erased the memory of pain. The turquoise granted the gift of flight. There was a particularly lethal one called the indigo madstone that could shoot a blast of ice and snow! They used to be all the rage! Popular at parties and hootenannies and the like."

"When—did you get your head cut off?" said Falcon.

"Oh, years ago. Your daddy did it, you know. He was very, very cross with me."

"Wait—," said Falcon. "My *father* cut your head off? Put you in that jar we found you in?"

"He certainly did. Pickled me. As punishment."

"Punishment for what?"

Quimby let some air out and floated toward the ground again. "For telling his fortune." He sighed—an irritating squeaking sound, like someone stretching the nozzle of a deflating balloon. "I must tell you, some people *can't handle the truth.*"

"What truth was this?"

"Eoghan Quinn, while still a teen,
Falls in love with the guardian queen."

"You predicted he'd fall in love with my mom?" said Falcon.

"You know, it's funny you should mention old Eoghan—or the *Crow*, as I suppose everyone calls him now. I just saw him last week. Here on Monster Island.

That stopwatch thing he wears around his neck was ticking *very* loudly. So annoying."

"He was here?" For a single second, Falcon's spirits
rose. "Where is he now?"

"Oh, he just stopped in to fix a little mistake of his, I
think. Then he took off again."

"What mistake is this?" said Falcon.

"Oh, he had to turn that mockingbird back into
a—ahh—ahhh—" Quimby wrinkled his nose, as if antic-
ipating a sneeze. "Ahhh—ahh—" He looked at Falcon,
unsatisfied. "Don't you hate that when you feel a sneeze
coming on, and then it doesn't come? So annoying."

"The Squonk had a bird in a cage," said Falcon. "You're
saying my father came to—"

"Yes, of course," said Quimby. "But you know the
Squonk, he couldn't stand keeping anything caged up.
So your friend the Squonk let his mockingbird out of the
cage. Your daddy found it and turned it back into that
angry boy, what's his name—Jahh—ahhh—"

Quimby wrinkled his nose and yelled, "Ahh-choo!"
And, just like a balloon releasing all of its air, the head
suddenly shot off across the sky with a hissing, blubbering
squeal.

And just like that, Falcon Quinn was completely
alone. For an instant he stood still, looking in the direction Quimby had flown, listening to the sound of the

ocean crash on the beach.

"Jaah—," said Falcon.

"Jonny Frankenstein," said a voice, and Falcon slowly turned.

There, standing by the edge of the forest that led to the beach, was Jonny. He looked wan and tired, his blond hair tousled and his black clothes torn. "Jonny," said Falcon. "What are you doing here?"

"You heard Quimby," said Jonny. "Your father turned me into a mockingbird last spring, as punishment. Last week he came here, turned me back. Guess he had second thoughts."

"Punishment," said Falcon. "Punishment for what?"

Jonny sighed. "Same as it ever was," he said.

Behind Jonny, a group of guardian warriors slowly emerged from the woods. There was a group of bowmen, their arrows threaded in their bowstrings and pointing directly at Falcon's hearts.

There was a sudden sound like *phoo*, and Falcon felt a dart prick his neck. The world around him began to spin.

"What did I tell you, the day we met," said Jonny Frankenstein sadly. "I'm just a piece of junk."

III

GUARDIAN ISLAND

12

GUARDIAN JUNIOR HIGH

The towers of Paragon Castle were the first structures on Guardian Island to be struck by the rays of the sun rising up over the Sea of Dragons. The castle—an enormous collection of parapets and flying buttresses and elaborately constructed ramparts—stood on the shoulders of Paragon Mountain, upon which the Hidden City was built. Bright banners and flags fluttered from wires strung from the Tower of Rectitude to the Pinnacle of Virtues.

At the top of Paragon Mountain, above the Hidden City, was a large windmill. Its blue sails spun in the morning breeze.

Falcon opened his eyes in a white room. He was in a large brass bed. He was not entirely sure where he was, but the crisp sheets and the sparkling sunlight gave him the sense that, for the first time in days, he might be in no immediate danger. It was an odd feeling.

He sat up, stretched his wings, and yawned. Then he lowered his wings again and swung his feet out of the bed and placed them on the floor. Falcon walked across a thick

Persian rug to a pair of balcony doors, slowly opened them, and stepped outside. Below him, in the Hidden City, he saw guardians in mail shirts and leather breastplates. There were children in the street playing a game with a bat and a ball. An older woman sold roses from a cart.

"Oh, you're up," said a voice, and Falcon turned to see a man standing in the doorway to his room holding a silver platter. "Sorry to intrude, young sir, but they thought you might be wanting breakfast." The man, who wore a bow tie and white gloves, bowed slightly. "Is it all right for me to enter?"

"What?" said Falcon. "Where am I?"

"The castle, of course. We've got strawberries and cream, Belgian waffles with maple syrup, and a rasher of bacon. Fresh orange juice. A slice of melon. Will that be all right for you? Or—?"

"That's fine," said Falcon, although at that moment he was thinking about his first meal at the Academy for Monsters. *Great big gobs of greasy, grimy gopher guts. Mutilated monkey meat. Little dirty birdies' feet.* "Uh, thanks."

"No need to be thanking me, young sir," said the man, lowering the tray. He looked at Falcon carefully, as if inspecting him for damage. "You've been asleep quite some time. Two days, I think."

"Who are you?" said Falcon. "How did I get here? All

I remember is talking to Jonny Frankenstein. We were surrounded by guardians. I remember the sound of the ocean—"

"I am Mr. Drudge," said the man. "Your servant. As for Jonny, he himself was captured moments before you. They used him as bait, I believe. In order to give you the old dipsy-doodle, sir!"

"The dipsy-doodle—?"

"Poison dart," said Mr. Drudge. "Blowgun."

"So—you knocked me out," said Falcon. "And hauled me back here."

"Well, not me personally, sir. But yes, I'm afraid that's the general outline."

"You people never give up, do you?" said Falcon. "It's just all blowguns and crossbows with you."

"Well, sir," said Mr. Drudge. "We *are* trying to keep the peace. The price of liberty, you know, is sometimes measured in blowguns and poison darts!"

"I want to see my mother," said Falcon. "I want to talk to her right away!"

"Well, there's time for all that, young sir," said Mr. Drudge. "For now, let's have you enjoy your meal. Then you can change into the uniform I've left for you in the closet here and we'll begin your training. I'm afraid it's rather a full day, but then just because you are the prince is no reason to expect special treatment. No, no reason at all!"

"Training?" said Falcon. "What training?"

"Well, the school day starts at nine."

"School?" said Falcon. "What school is this?"

"Well, what do you think?" said Mr. Drudge. "Guardian Junior High."

Falcon's mother watched her son from a high window in the queen's chamber as he and Mr. Drudge walked down the cobblestone path toward Guardian Junior High. She smiled. "He's giving Mr. Drudge an earful, from the looks of it," said Vega.

Tippy, her tiny dog, stared down at the street below and watched as Falcon disappeared around a far curve. The dog had ratty, oily hair and a pink bow on his head.

"I don't like him," said Tippy.

"Who? Mr. Drudge? Or my son?"

"Anybody," muttered the dog.

Vega sighed. "You'll stop the complaining now, or I'll put you in the crate."

The dog growled, then lay down on the floor.

Vega sipped her tea. "I hope this was the right thing to do," she said. "Bringing him back."

"I thought you said he would come of his own free will," said the dog. "To rescue the girl in the windmill. The wind elemental! Wasn't that the plan?"

"It was," said Vega. "But Megan Crofton is so young,

and much weaker than I thought. There won't be much of her to rescue, even if he does figure out she's up there."

"What about the father?" asked Tippy. "Cygnus says the father's left the Academy."

"He has," said Vega. "He's at large in the world again."

"What's he doing? Where's he going?"

"He's coming here, I believe."

"Here? Why?"

"Why else?" said Vega. "To win me back, of course."

"To win you—" The dog looked nauseated. "Why would he do that?"

"Because he thinks that Falcon's coming-of-age has changed—the nature of our history. And our future."

Tippy scratched one ear with his hind leg. "Cygnus has never forgiven you for taking up with Eoghan Quinn, has he?"

There was a long pause before the queen replied. She watched her son walk down a cobblestone street in the city below her, on his way to Guardian Junior High. For just an instant, Falcon stopped in his tracks and looked back up at Paragon Castle.

"He has not," she said.

First she swirled up and then over and then down again. She tried to think how it was she had come to be in the sails of the turning windmill, but there was so little of her left now it was hard to think, and when she could think, all she could think about was how she was going over and then up and then down again. Sometimes she dreamed, but sleeping was different, invisible. She dreamed of rushing through piles of dead leaves, of rotating in a tiny cyclone on a city street, of shaking the windows in an abandoned house, of extinguishing a candle in a dark room.

Pieces of Megan Crofton's past life came to her now and again, but it was hard with this constant spinning to know what things had happened and in what order. She was fairly sure that some of the things she remembered from her past were things that had never occurred. Other things she felt to be true in her heart, but since she had lost her form it was impossible to say, with any certainty, where her heart was.

Once, though, she had been a young girl, living in Cold River, Maine, with her older sisters, Maeve and Dahlia. Maeve, the oldest, had red hair and a hot temper. Dahlia, the middle, was drawn to lakes and rivers, adored the rain. Then her sisters had died, and Megan was alone with her crazy mother. *It should have been you,* her mom had said. *I wish it had been you!*

She whirled around and around. *Oh, Mother,* Megan thought. *I wish it had been me too.*

She wanted to call out the name of her friend—that boy with a name like some kind of bird, or color. . . . What *was* his name? In the dark and endless swirling, words too were fading. It was hard now to remember his face, or even the reason why he would care about her fate.

First she swirled up and then over and then down and over and then up again. Then she went down.

Falcon and Mr. Drudge walked through the narrow cobblestone streets of the Hidden City. There were shops selling knives and swords and flails. There were stone cottages with dark windows. Everything was very clean. The sun shone down.

Falcon paused to look up at Paragon Castle. On the mountain above the castle was an old windmill.

"What is it, dear boy?" said Mr. Drudge. "Are you feeling a little—under the weather?"

Falcon looked at the blue sails swirling around and around. "It's nothing," he said.

"I hope you're not having a delayed reaction from that blowgun poison," said Mr. Drudge. "It can have unpleasant side effects. You must promise me not to operate any heavy machinery!"

"What's with that windmill?" he asked.

"Oh, that's been up there for years. It used to be all in ruins, but they fixed it up nicely last spring. I think it's rather charming, to be quite honest. The way those sails go right around. Always raises my spirits." Mr. Drudge gently pulled Falcon onward. "Let's keep moving, shall we? A shame to be late on your first day."

Falcon nodded and took a step forward, but now his eyes fell upon the harbor below them. There were several guardian warships covered with cannons and catapults. Slightly farther offshore was a small, homely boat. "Hey," Falcon said. "The *Destynee II*. My friend Weems made that." He paused. "Uh—ex-friend. I guess."

"Ah yes, the *Destynee II*," said Mr. Drudge. "Your mother's been quite insistent on preserving it, right where it came to anchor. She says that craft has historic value. Marking the place of your first return to higher civilization, Prince Falcon." He paused. "Of course, there are others who feel differently. Who feel that a craft of monstrous origin ought rightly to be sunk. To maintain the dignity of our harbor. It is a matter of some debate, I don't mind saying."

Falcon gave the *Destynee II* one last look before following Mr. Drudge on through the city.

Soon they came to the open front door of a large, dilapidated building that reminded him of Cold River Middle School, except that it was covered with blue and tan camouflage stripes.

"Very well then, sir," said Mr. Drudge. "You are to report to room one-eleven and present yourself to Miss Bloodstone. She's your homeroom teacher, and she's also the instructor for Monstrosity."

"Look," said Falcon. "I don't think this is such a good idea."

"What?" said Mr. Drudge. "Getting yourself an education?"

"I just got here," said Falcon. "Why can't I talk to my mother first? There are a lot of questions I need answers to, all right?"

"I'm sure your mother will come to see you when she can," said Mr. Drudge. "The business of government consumes her time! In the interim, school will help you learn the answers."

Falcon sighed. "Look, the last time I was here, I got locked up in a tower. My friends got killed. I'm not just going to—"

"I know, I know," said Mr. Drudge. "Everyone regrets that. Still, you have to admit that you know more about these so-called friends of yours than you did then." The bell in the tower had stopped pealing now. "We grow, with time, do we not? We come to understand things in a new way as we get older?"

"I don't understand *anything*," said Falcon.

"Yes, I see," said Mr. Drudge. "Perhaps this is why schooling might be helpful? Perhaps?"

Falcon sighed. "Fine," he said.

"Ah," said Mr. Drudge. "Just one more thing." He

pulled an eye patch from his pocket and affixed it over Falcon's left eye. There we go. Now you're all set."

"I have to wear this?"

"Well, I don't suppose you *have* to, but it would be sensible, wouldn't it? To keep that dark eye covered? Just in case you feel the urge to—ah—you know. Burn things."

Falcon was going to protest but then just nodded. "Fine," he said.

"Off you go then. Remember—your schoolmates have been waiting for you. You are their hero. At last you have found a place where you belong."

"Listen, you're crazy if you think I belong here, okay?" said Falcon. "I don't belong *anywhere*."

Then Falcon turned his back on Mr. Drudge and walked down the hall.

Mr. Drudge stood at the threshold for a long time, watching the angel walk alone on the shiny, waxed tiles of Guardian Junior High.

13
GO, ASSASSINS, GO!

The walls of Guardian Junior High were hung with pennants that said GO, ASSASSINS, GO! In a glass case were trophies honoring the various triumphs of the school's teams. On a wall beyond the trophy case were framed photos of notable alumni. There was a photo of a woman named Francis Ruthmeyer Sponge and beneath her portrait a plaque that said KILLS: ELEVEN BANSHEES, FORTY-SEVEN LEPRECHAUNS, SIXTY-ONE OTHERS. Next to that was a photo of a young man with a wide tie. Beneath him was the legend ROBERT HOOVER JOHNSTON. SIXTEEN VAMPIRES. R.I.P. In smaller letters, beneath this, it read HE GAVE HIS LIFE SO THAT OTHERS COULD GIVE THEIRS.

Next to the portrait was a door marked 111. Falcon felt his black eye burning softly in its socket.

He opened the door.

There were twenty students sitting cross-legged in a circle on the floor. A young woman with a ponytail was leading them in a song.

I'd like to be under the sea!
And be an octopus's guardian in the shade.
We would defend our mollusk friend,
And be an octopus's guardian in the shade.

I'd ask my friends to count to three
Then kill the octopus's enemies with me!

I'd like to be under the sea!
And be an octopus's guardian in the shade.

The young woman looked up. "Oh, hi, Falcon!" She smiled. "Look everyone, Prince Falcon's here!'

The other children, all wearing their identical camou-flaged uniforms, smiled as one. Then they started a kind of welcoming chant that reminded Falcon of one of those songs that waiters in a chain restaurant sing for a customer's birthday.

We welcome you, Prince Falcon,
    we're glad you come to slay!
We'll smash the brains of zombies,
    and then it's time to play!
Hey!

"Very good, class," said the teacher. "Falcon, my name is Miss Bloodstone. We're just finishing up morning sing-along. Why don't we all get settled and listen to Cadet Chandler's oral report? Does that sound like fun?"

"Fun?" said Falcon uncertainly.

"He's got wings," said one of the young guardians suspiciously.

"Yes, Cadet Snick, he's an angel."

"Angels aren't monsters?" said Snick. He was a beefy young man with a square jaw.

"Angels are *celestials*," said Miss Bloodstone.

"There are so many kinds of creatures," said a very small boy with orange hair and large, circular glasses. "It makes my brain hurt!"

On the walls, Falcon noticed, were posters of famous monster slayers in history. There were paintings of Teddy Roosevelt and Elvis Presley. On bulletin boards there were pinned-up clippings from newspapers and magazines. Letters made from colorful construction paper spelled out MONSTER SLAYINGS IN THE NEWS. There was a story about the death of Gerald Ford.

"Tell you what," said Miss Bloodstone. "Let's all sit down at our desks and listen to your report, Cadet Chandler. That will make our brains stop hurting."

The young guardians headed to their desks. The boy called Snick took one more look at Falcon, then shook his head. "You don't fool me," he said.

"Fool you?" said Falcon to Snick. "About what?"

Snick shook his head. "I know who your father is,"

he said. "Everybody does."

"Are we all in our seats?" said Miss Bloodstone. Falcon turned away from Snick and sat at a free desk. At the front of the room, the young, orange-haired boy was now standing and holding a group of index cards. He was shaking.

"Cadet Chandler, your report is on zombie slaying, correct?"

"Yuh-yuh-yuh-yes, Miss Bloodstone," said Chandler.

"You may begin. And please, Cadet Chandler. There is no reason to be nervous. We are all friends here." She looked at the class with her wholesome, sparkling eyes. Something about her reminded Falcon of someone else he had known, but he couldn't pin it down. "Aren't we?"

Snick laughed to himself. A few of the others looked at him.

"Friends," said Chandler, glancing at Falcon. "Uh. How to Kill Zombies. A Report." The boy was so overwhelmed that his knees began to knock together. "Um. Zombies are bad for you and bad for me. So killing them is important for everyone. Zombies can be killed by lots of different methods. Some of them include putting them in a wood chipper, for instance, or running over them with a steamroller. Putting them in a microwave works especially if the zombie is small and has some metal on him. Or lighting them on fire. The important thing is to destroy the zombie brain. If the brain is not destroyed, the zombie will come back at you and be mad. And that would be a bad thing for you and a bad thing for me. So destroy the brain and the zombie will die. This is the end of my report on how to kill zombies. Thank you."

"Thank *you*, Cadet Chandler," said Miss Bloodstone. Chandler was about to sit down when the teacher added, "Are there any questions?"

"Questions?" said Chandler, more anxious than ever.

"I don't understand what makes someone a zombie," said a very pale girl at the back of the room. "Is it an infection you get, like mono?"

"Cadet Chandler?" said the teacher. "Can you tell Cadet Portia what causes zombieism?"

Chandler's eyes opened wide. For a moment he looked like he was going to have a heart attack. Then he dropped all his index cards on the floor. He bent over to pick them up, but now his cards were all in the wrong order. Some were upside-down.

"Tell us the cause," said Miss Bloodstone more forcefully. "I presume you researched that? Did you not?" There was the soft hint of anger in her voice.

"Uh," he said. "Is it because—they didn't obey the rules?" His voice broke as if he was about to cry.

"Hmm," said Miss Bloodstone. "I'm not sure that's right. Does anyone else have an idea where zombies come from?" She looked around the room and pointed at a thin girl. "Cadet Femur? Can you tell us what causes zombies?"

"Is it," said Cadet Femur, "because they ate too much?"

"No, no," said Miss Bloodstone, her voice sounding exasperated. "Ah, Cadet de Celestina. Tell us."

A small, proud girl sitting in the row next to Falcon stood up. "I—Chenobia de Celestina—the monster slayer of Paragon Mountain!—shall tell you of the origin of the zombie creatures! Their kind was first invented by the sorcerers of voodoo, in the mysterious regions of the Caribbean and the Congo! It is these sorcerers who created a mysterious compound that reanimates the dead and enables them to walk among us! From these creatures come others of the zombie kind, with their staggering and their decaying that I—Chenobia de Celestina, the monster slayer of Paragon Mountain!—find highly distasteful! The zombie virus is thus spread from creature to creature, usually through the biting of the flesh with the teeth of undeadness! It is this that causes the zombies to walk! But it is we—the monster slayers!—who shall put an end to them and restore the world to justice! To this we pledge our sacred honor!"

Chenobia de Celestina sat down. Falcon looked at her with his mouth open.

"Is a Frankenstein a zombie?" asked Cadet Femur. "They're dead things brought back to life, aren't they?"

"A Frankenstein is not technically a zombie," said Miss

Bloodstone. "Although their components are similar. But Frankensteins are easy to kill, compared to zombies. First, you frighten them with fire. Then—"

The door to the classroom swung open, and a girl walked in. It was the same girl Falcon had seen at the Bludd Club, the one who looked exactly like Megan. "Ah, Cadet Gyra," said Miss Bloodstone. "How nice to see you. We were just discussing the methods for killing Frankensteins. Oh, and Prince Falcon has joined us. Cadet Falcon, this is Gyra, our class's Teaching Assassin."

"Falcon and I have met before," said Gyra. "On Monster Island, when Cygnus and the colonel attempted to bring him home." She sighed. "I'm glad you're here at last."

"Uh," said Falcon uncertainly. "Hello?"

"So have you ever killed a Frankenstein?" said Snick.

"I have," said Gyra. "On a field trip to California last year. They have lots of them there."

"Tell the fledglings how you killed this Frankenstein," said Miss Bloodstone.

"Frankensteins are easy," said Gyra, and as she spoke, again Falcon was struck by how similar she was to Megan. He still wasn't certain whether she was some other girl entirely or whether Megan herself had been brainwashed by her captors. She looked at Falcon for a moment and smiled the smallest of grins. "You scare them with fire. Then you break their hearts."

"I!" shouted Chenobia de Celestina. "Find this hard to believe! That a monster could be destroyed by confusing their affections!"

"Oh, I can believe it," said Chandler. Tears were now hanging on his eyelashes.

"But that's their weakness, the Frankensteins," said Gyra. "Their need for love. Remember, they're not born, they're *fried*. Reanimated with a bolt of lightning. So they never have a childhood. That makes them highly vulnerable—all they want is someone to love them. Which, on account of their being sewn out of dead bodies, nobody does. It's easy to kill them. You just make them love you, then dump them. It's a cinch."

"I don't know how to break anybody's heart," said Chandler sadly.

"Can't you just blast 'em with a flamethrower?" said Snick. "That's what I'd do!"

"What did I just say?" said Gyra, and she snuck another look at Falcon. "*You break their hearts.*"

"So informative," said Miss Bloodstone. "Any other questions?"

"I!" shouted Chenobia de Celestina. "Would like to inquire about the nature of banshees! How may they best be dispatched, so that the humans whom we protect may be kept safe?"

"Anyone?" said Miss Bloodstone. She looked at the

girl called Gyra. "Well, let us ask our T.A. once more. Thoughts on banshee slaying?"

"Banshees feed on your tears," said Gyra. "They scream in order to make you cry. So it's easy enough. You just train yourself not to cry."

"You train yourself?" said Chandler, still crying. "Not to cry?"

"Good luck, Chandler," teased Snick.

"What about mummies?" said Cadet Femur.

"Destroy their treasure," said Gyra. "Remove the soul from the body. Then burn the tomb."

"Werecreatures?"

"This is a method well-known to all!" said Chenobia de Celestina. "The creature must be executed, with a bullet of silver."

"Silver anything works, actually," said Gyra. "Bullets, swords, stakes. It's all good. Just make sure it's real silver, though. Stainless steel or pewter isn't going to do the trick. I heard some sad stories where guardians went in to kill some werewolves with a pewter butter knife." She shook her head. "Didn't end well."

"Any other questions," said Miss Bloodstone, "before Cadet Gyra has to go? We should move on to our next report."

"I got a question," said Snick, casting a glance over at Falcon. "How would you kill him?"

There was a moment's horrified silence before Chenobia

de Celestina spoke. *"¡Señor!"* she said. "Surely you would not suggest that the son of our queen—Prince Falcon!—should be exterminated like a monster of the wild! This is a suggestion of dishonor, and shame, which I—the famous monster slayer of Paragon Mountain!—cannot endure!"

"I don't mean him," said Snick. "I just mean angels in general." He smiled a mean smile. "It'd be a good thing to know."

"Cadet Gyra?" said Miss Bloodstone.

Gyra looked uncertain. "I don't know," she said. "I've never killed an angel." She shrugged. "Break its heart, maybe? Like a Frankenstein?" She cast a glance at Falcon. "I think it would take longer, though."

"Interesting," said Miss Bloodstone. "But not quite correct. You see, fledglings, that even our T.A. has things to learn." Gyra blushed slightly at this. Miss Bloodstone looked at Falcon. "To kill an angel, my young cadets, you need *qeres*. The infamous embalming perfume of the Egyptians."

"Qeres?" said Snick. "I never heard of that."

"That is because it is so rare," said Miss Bloodstone. "But mummies often have some stored with their treasure, in tiny golden bottles with stoppers. I believe General Cygnus, in fact, procured some in a raid he performed in Cairo several years ago."

"And what does one do with this fragrance?" said

Chenobia de Celestina. "Does one poison the angel with it?"

"No," said Miss Bloodstone. "One would coat the blade of a knife or a sword with it and then stab the angel through the heart." She looked frightened. "But it is a terrible thing to kill a celestial. Against the guardian code, and a thing for which the Watcher provides no forgiveness! Those who break the code must stay with the Watcher on the Island of Nightmares. They do not wake up."

There was a long, awkward pause.

"Still a good thing to know," said Snick. "In case you knew an angel who went off the reservation." He looked over at Falcon. "What about you, Prince? You think you might go haywire, if things didn't go your way?"

They all looked at Falcon. He felt his dark eye growing warm. "I'm not going haywire," he said.

"There now," said Miss Bloodstone. "Time for our next report. Cadet Chandler, you may be seated. Cadet Femur, you're up. Your report is on killing leprechauns, I believe."

"Yes, Miss Bloodstone," said Cadet Femur. Gyra nodded to the class and headed for the door.

"Can you say 'Have a nice day, Gyra' to our T.A.?" said Miss Bloodstone.

"Have a nice day, Gyra!" said the students as Gyra left the room.

Then the thin girl made her way to the front of the

class and cleared her throat. "There are two ways to kill leprechauns," she began. "The first is to stare them in the eyes until they blink. This is difficult, because they almost never blink, and if *you* blink first, they disappear. The second—"

"Dude," said a soft, whispered voice. Falcon glanced to his left.

There was a huge, hairy cadet. He was eating a baloney sandwich. He handed half of it to Falcon.

"Go on," said the young guardian. "Have some baloney." Falcon took the baloney sandwich from the boy. The cadet smiled and stuffed his half into his mouth. Falcon took a bite of the sandwich. It wasn't bad at all.

The boy smiled happily. "Baloney," he said.

When the bell rang, the young guardians all stood and marched neatly out the door and down the long, waxy corridors to the cafeteria. There Falcon stood in a line to receive a platter loaded with salad and meat loaf and chocolate milk. He took his platter out to the dining hall and stood for a moment looking at all the tables filled with beings he did not know. A few cadets looked over at Falcon, then glanced at each other and laughed. He sat at the nearest empty table.

"Can I sit here?" said a voice, and Falcon looked up to see Jonny Frankenstein holding a tray full of salad.

"Sure," said Falcon, and sighed. "Why not?"

Jonny sat down. It had been a long time since Falcon had gotten a good look at him; his brief encounter with Jonny on Monster Island seemed like a dream to him now. In some ways, Jonny didn't look all that different than he had last spring when he'd showed up at the Academy with his electric guitar and a duffel bag full of comic books. He still had those bright blue eyes and the head full of raggedy blond hair. The two bolts on his neck seemed a little rusty now, however, and there was a look of anger about Jonny's eyes that seemed to have deepened since the spring.

"Guess you don't wanna talk to me," said Jonny. He shrugged. "I told you I was a piece of junk."

"Yeah, you always say that," said Falcon.

"It's true."

"I don't even know what you are," said Falcon. "A monster? A guardian? What?"

"I could ask you the same question," said Jonny.

"You know what I am," said Falcon. "I'm their prince."

Jonny ate a forkful of pickled beets. "How's that workin' out so far?"

"Explain this to me," said Falcon. "If you're a Frankenstein, how come they let you stay here?"

"I told you last spring. Weren't you listening? I grew up in an orphanage. They adopted me."

"Who?"

"Colonel Hemingway. He thought it would be funny, raising a Frankenstein to be a guardian. It was part of some bet he had with Cygnus. The colonel said that if they raised me as a guardian, I'd become a guardian. Cygnus said it wouldn't work, that you couldn't make a guardian out of a monster no matter what kind of education I got. Ten pieces of silver they wagered on me."

"So who won the bet?"

Jonny looked discouraged. "Bet's not over yet," he said.

They ate their lunches in silence for a while. "I see they got you wearin' an eye patch," said Jonny. "That's real jaunty."

"The eye patch was Mr. Drudge's idea," said Falcon.

"Heard they're comfortable," said Jonny.

"Yeah," said Falcon. "You should wear one, maybe."

Jonny laughed to himself. "So have you made up your mind yet?"

"About what?"

"About whether you're going to trust me."

"Of course I'm not going to trust you," said Falcon. "You're a—a piece of junk."

"Well, good," said Jonny. "At least we've got that straightened out. If I was you, I wouldn't trust me either."

"I guess we have a lot in common. We both hate you."

"Hey, guys," said a loud, happy voice. "Can I eat with you? I'm totally starved." They looked up to see the large,

hairy guy who'd given Falcon half of his baloney sandwich standing there with a tray heaped high with salad.
Gobs of shiny, lumpy blue cheese dressing were slathered
over the top.

"And I—Chenobia de Celestina!—the famous monster slayer of Paragon Mountain!—shall join your table as
well. Let us begin our midday feast in the spirit of mutual
friendship and welcome!"

"Dude," said the hairy guy. "I'm Sam."

"It is an honor to be seated with you, Prince Falcon,
an honor! Please do me the honor of calling me by the
name of Celeste! It is the name used by those—whom I
am sworn to defend!"

"Hello, Celeste," said Falcon.

"Hey, electricity dude," said Sam to Jonny. "What's
happening?"

"You know each other?" said Falcon.

"Prince Falcon, the community of young guardians is
small but intimate!" said Celeste. "All of us are familiar
with one another, even those whose character we find in
question!"

"She means me," said Jonny.

"Dude," said Sam, digging into his salad. "Jonny's
outta the doghouse, man. He helped Cygnus rescue Falcon
and bring him to us so he can be prince and stuff!" Sam
smiled. "Jonny's awesome!"

"Perhaps it is as you say," said Celeste. "And Señor Frankenstein should be forgiven his past indiscretions! Indeed, he has proved himself of value to our sworn goals of justice and purity!"

Falcon shook his head and laughed.

"What's so funny, dude?" said Sam.

"Nothing," said Falcon.

"Surely it is not nothing that causes you to assume the sounds of mirth!" said Celeste.

"Really, it's nothing," said Falcon. "You just remind me of some friends of mine, back at the Academy."

Celeste dropped her fork. "What is this?" she said. "You are comparing ourselves to—to—these demons and villains? Surely my ears have mistaken me!"

"Falcon—," said Jonny.

"I'm not saying you're monsters," said Falcon. "I'm just saying you remind me of them, a little. You and Sam. You're a lot like two of my friends. . . ." A trace of sadness flickered over Falcon's features as he remembered Pearl's death and the way Max had looked at him as he cradled her body in his arms.

"I shall not remain here and be insulted," said Celeste. "I—the famous monster destroyer of Paragon Mountain!—shall not suffer myself to be compared to all that I most despise! Good day, Prince Falcon! Good day!" The girl picked up her tray and stormed away from them.

"Dude," said Sam, shaking his head. "You oughta watch

your mouth, okay?" Grabbing his tray, Sam stood up and hurried after his friend. "Celeste!" he called. "Wait up!"

Falcon watched them go, then looked at Jonny. "That's so weird. They're exactly like Max and Pearl. Don't you think?"

"Of course they are," said Jonny. "Every monster's got a guardian who's his opposite. Just like Miss Bloodstone is the opposite of Mrs. Redflint. And that girl Gyra is the opposite of Megan."

"I thought she was Megan at first," said Falcon.

"Her?" said Jonny. "Nope. She looks like her, but she's no Megan. Gyra's pretty hard core about all the guardian stuff. You oughta watch your step around her."

"So where do you think Megan is now?" asked Falcon.

Jonny looked at his tray. "I don't know. I was hoping she got away from this place, blew away on some breeze. But sometimes I get this weird feeling. Like she's not really gone at all."

"You think . . . they have her somewhere? You think she's their prisoner?"

"Sometimes. But how could they hold her? How would *you* keep the wind hostage?"

"So you think she got away."

"Yeah, except . . . if she did get out of here . . . why hasn't she come to find me? And let me know she was okay?"

"Or me," Falcon said tersely.

"Yeah, sure," said Jonny. "Either of us."

Falcon looked around the cafeteria and saw other guardians whose features or mannerisms reminded him of monsters he had known. There was Cadet Femur, picking at her salad, who reminded him of Bonesy; to her left was a group of self-satisfied mean girls who could easily have been the cousins of Merideath and the other vampires. His eye moved around the room, taking in all the young guardians. Each one reminded him of a friend he had lost—Mortia, and Ankh-hoptet, and Lincoln Pugh, and Weems.

"So who are *our* opposites?" said Falcon.

"We don't have opposites," said Jonny. "That's why we don't fit in anyplace, you and me. The only place we belong is out *there*." He nodded toward the window.

Through the panes of glass, Falcon could just make out the Sea of Dragons crashing endlessly upon the shore.

"So where does that leave us?" said Falcon.

"Where do you think?" said Jonny. "We're finding Megan. Then we're breaking out."

"Great," said Falcon. "Another plan to get us killed."

"What can I tell ya, Falcon?" said Jonny. "I've *always* got a plan."

14

THE VALLEY OF DEATH

At the end of that day, Falcon returned to his room in Paragon Castle, carrying an extremely heavy backpack and overwhelmed with homework assignments. In addition to Miss Bloodstone's class, Monstrosity, there was another titled Weapons and Implements, another on the History of Virtue, and a fourth called Battle Strategy. In addition to these, the colonel taught the Literature of Mayhem, which was devoted to short stories and poems all about destroying things. Once a week, according to a schedule Mr. Drudge had given him, there was something called Field Research, which would meet for the first time the next day. And finally, as always, there was math. Unlike the moth man's class back at the Academy, however, at Guardian Junior High they actually had to do the problems instead of just work them out on a calculator.

Falcon sat down at a large desk in the chamber that had been prepared for him and started in on the reading for the Literature of Mayhem. The first item in his textbook was a poem by Lord Tennyson:

Half a league, half a league,
*   Half a league onward,*
All in the valley of Death
*   Rode the six hundred.*

A shadow crept over his right shoulder, and Falcon turned to see his mother standing behind him. She wore a white dress, and her long, white hair fell nearly to her waist.

"Ah, the 'Charge of the Light Brigade'!" said Vega. "A classic!"

"Mom!" said Falcon. He stood and took a step toward her, then hesitated. He didn't exactly want to rush forward into the arms of a woman who had imprisoned him up in a tower when last they'd met.

"Oh, I know you're cross with me," said Vega. "I wouldn't blame you if you wanted to blast me with one of your fireballs. I let you down, Falcon. I'm so sorry."

"Let me down?" Falcon said. "That's what you call killing my friends? Turning Peeler and Woody into stars, turning Pearl and Max into crystal music?" He shook his head. "Yeah, I guess you could say you *let me down.*"

"Falcon," said Vega, kneeling on the floor before him. "I made a mistake. I expected too much of you, all at once."

Falcon smirked. "I think you expected too little of me, actually," he said.

"Maybe you're right," said Vega. "I don't know—I guess everything I've done has been a disaster. As far as you're concerned, I mean."

Falcon mostly agreed with her; everything she'd done *had* been a disaster, starting with trying to kill his father and then abandoning him when he was only a child. But now, with his mother before him, he was unable to feel angry; as he looked at her, all he could feel was pity.

"Remember last spring?" asked Vega. "When I played the piano for you, in the cottage by the sea? Since you left, I've thought about what our lives would have been like if we'd just stayed there, in the cottage, instead of—"

"Instead of starting up with the war again. Instead of hurting my friends."

"Yes," said Vega. "Instead of that. But now you know, maybe a little better, what they're really like. Creeper has informed us of what they did to you at the Academy. I'm so sorry, Falcon. You did not deserve that after the loyalty you showed to them."

Falcon was just about to defend the monsters back at the Academy but stopped himself. She was right. He *had* deserved better, after the sacrifices he had made.

"I am sorry the world is the way it is," said Vega. "I remember how hard it was for me when I realized what the world is like. I was older than you are when I came to understand. Still, it broke my heart. I don't think I've ever been the same."

"What do you mean, what the world is like? You mean that there are monsters in it? That was a surprise to you?"

"Oh, I knew that monsters walked the earth—I'd gone to Guardian Elementary School, of course. But I didn't want to be a guardian, Falcon, any more than you did. I didn't want to devote my whole life to all this—destruction and strife."

"So why did you?" said Falcon. "Why not try to get along with monsters?"

"Because I found what you found, Falcon, when you tried the same thing. They come for you. They suck your blood. They take your life. They are relentless, and terrible, and dark."

Falcon thought back to his last night on Shadow Island, up in the Tower of Souls. He saw all of those angry monsters coming for him, shouting, *Traitor! Enemy! Destroy!*

"In a way," said Vega, "it is unfortunate that you befriended so many of these creatures when they were young, before they came into their full powers. Because you learned to love them, just as I thought I loved your father."

"Is that why you pushed him through the ice?" said Falcon. "Because he was so terrible?"

Vega gasped softly and looked at her son with shock. "I never tried to hurt your father," she said. "I tried to protect him!"

"You tried to protect him by murdering him?"

"I never touched him," said Vega. "It was Cygnus who snuck up behind him and pushed him through."

"What?"

Vega nodded sadly. "That was when they came for me—Mortlock and Miss Bloodstone and the others. They captured and tied me, while Cygnus went out to destroy the Crow. I pleaded for them not to do it. I begged them!"

"But if you'd left their world, why wouldn't they just leave the two of you alone? You weren't doing anybody any harm, were you?"

"I was doing Cygnus harm," said Vega.

"How were you doing Cygnus harm?" said Falcon. But even as he asked this question, he began to suspect he knew the answer.

Vega cleared her throat. "He did not take my defection well. Because we were close once. He brought me back here, in hopes I would . . . well. In this he was mistaken. I have given my heart away once. I will never do so again."

Falcon looked at his mother and saw in her face a flicker of what she might have looked like when she was young. "You don't want to be queen," he said, "do you?"

"But I am," said Vega. "And so here I stay. You really only get one chance in life to resist your nature, Falcon. My chance is done."

"Well, I'm not like you," said Falcon. "I won't be like you."

Vega waved her hand through the air. "I suppose we will see. You will make your choices, as best you can, between this life and the other."

"What happens if I don't choose a side?" said Falcon. "What if I just want to live . . . apart?"

"And live alone, you mean? Why would you choose to be a hermit? To live in isolation and exile?"

"Because I don't want to spend my life trying to kill things, Mother," said Falcon. "Because life is better than death."

Vega opened her mouth, then shut it. She sighed. "I used to think that," she said. "When I was young."

The next day, on his way to Guardian Junior High, Falcon ran into Sam. He was chewing on a piece of beef jerky. "Hey, man," he said. "I got some jerky. You like jerky? It's excellent."

"I'm partial to jerky," said Falcon.

"Man," said Sam, handing Falcon a piece. "Who *isn't*?"

A platoon of men and women in uniforms marched by, each of them playing a drum. There were military snares and djembes and deep tom-toms, making a jubilant, celebratory noise. The warrior-musicians had large bows and quivers of long, steel-tipped arrows strapped to their sides.

Although the guardians kept their faces forward, many of them followed Falcon with their eyes.

"So what do you play?" said Sam.

"Play?" said Falcon.

"Yeah. You a drummer? You must be, the way you're checking out the pounders."

"Pounders?"

"Yeah, that's what they call the drummers. They can be pretty intense, once they get into a groove."

"I play godzooka," said Falcon.

Sam wrinkled his nose. "Hey, man," he said. "I wouldn't be, like, talking about monster instruments, okay? You might give people the wrong impression."

"What do you play?" said Falcon.

"Clarinet," said Sam.

"I used to play tuba," said Falcon. "Back in Maine."

"Weird," said Sam. "I keep forgetting you were born in the Reality Stream. What was that like, anyway? Was it wacky?"

"Sometimes," said Falcon. "I lived in a little town called Cold River. Maine's a pretty great place to live. Except that it's winter five months of the year. That can make you a little stir-crazy."

"Winter," said Sam. "I read about winter. Is it true that when the snow comes down, it doesn't come down straight?"

"What do you mean?"

"I saw this video. When the snow fell, it was like, all wavery."

Falcon nodded. "Yeah, it wavers, I guess."

"I have always found the merits of snow more than a little overrated," said a voice, and they turned to see Cygnus walking behind them.

"Juh—General Cygnus, sir," said Sam, saluting the man awkwardly.

"At ease, Cadet," said Cygnus. He nodded to Falcon. "Good morning, Prince. I hope you'll forgive my eaves-dropping. I remember seeing snow when I visited Maine. I was among the party that was sent to bring back your mother. As you know, she had a rather rebellious youth. Before she accepted her fate." He smiled. "I remember how disappointed I was by snow, the first time I saw it. It is true, Cadet Samit, that it is beautiful when it falls. And then when it lies upon the ground, sparkling and pristine, there is something almost miraculous about it, as if the world itself has begun to shine." His face darkened. "But then creatures begin to walk upon it. Dirtying and befoul-ing it. Ruining it! I remember one morning, looking out a window at a field of perfect snow—not far from your town of Cold River, Falcon. I watched that field all morn-ing. And then these *creatures*—idiots—tromped across it, destroying its beauty. Leaving behind their ugly, careless footprints." He sighed. "We found out later they were a group of Sasquatches in disguise. I caught up with them later that day and solved that problem. They left no more footprints." He shook his head. "But there are so many monsters in the world. Tromping through the world and wrecking its purity. Sometimes I fear we can never destroy them all." He looked lost in thought for a moment more. Then he looked up. "But we shall try, won't we, gentlemen? Yes. We will try. Because how else will we bring about a perfect world? How?"

"By killing monsters and stuff, sir," said Sam nervously.

Cygnus looked very carefully at Falcon, and his eyes narrowed for an instant. "Indeed," he said, and nodded. Then he walked past. Sam and Falcon watched him merge into the crowd on the street ahead.

"Okaayyy," said Sam. "That was weird."

"I've walked across a field of snow," said Falcon.

"Dude," said Sam. "Better not tell the general."

"Running around in snow is fun, actually. I never thought I was wrecking the purity of anything."

"It'd be cool to see it someday," said Sam. "Don't they have, like, lobsters and junk up there too?"

"Yeah," said Falcon. "Lobster's a big thing in Maine."

"Snow, and lobsters, and moose! That'd be so awesome. It'd make it easier to—you know. Do the other stuff."

"What other stuff?"

"Dude. You know. Kill all the monsters."

Falcon shook his head. "I don't know how many monsters there are in Maine."

"Oh, they got 'em, all right," said Sam. "They showed us a chart. Maine's a very high-density area for monsters. I think it's second only to Texas. Course, in Maine it's like, werecreatures and vampires, and in Texas it's mostly zombies, but still. If I got sent up there, I'd have to do a lot of slaying." He sighed. "It'd be better if they sent me to, like, Ireland, or England. I'd rather get rid of a bunch of leprechauns or elves or something that's not, you know, all bloodthirsty or dead, or whatever. Actually, I'd rather be sent someplace with no monsters at all. Like Idaho."

"Why?" said Falcon.

"To be honest?" said Sam. "Monsters kind of creep me out. What's it like, being surrounded by them all day? Weren't you afraid?" He got another piece of beef jerky out of his pocket.

"You get used to them," said Falcon. "Most of the time, I mean. Then, other times—I don't know, it's like people turn on you, and then you feel like you don't know them."

"Dude," said Sam. "That's exactly how I feel about some of the guardians." He looked around nervously. "Don't tell anyone, though, okay? But it's like everybody's your friend, until the time comes when—you know. They're all . . . not."

Falcon looked over at Sam. "What would you be, if you could be something other than a guardian?"

Sam's eyes danced with excitement. "Someday," he said, "I don't know how—but somehow I'd like to own a *diner*." He looked at Falcon. "What would you be if you weren't an angel?"

"I don't know," said Falcon. "I don't think about it anymore."

"Tell you what," said Sam. "We ever get out of here? You could work at my diner, making pies. 'Cause if I have a diner, it's totally going to have awesome pies."

"You really think that's going to happen?" said Falcon. "Us getting out of here, and you starting a diner?"

"Sure, why not," said Sam. "You gotta dream of *something*."

15

FLAILING

The next day, the young guardians had Field Research, which was held in something called the Temple of Honor. Falcon had breakfast in his room—a platter of eggs Benedict brought by Mr. Drudge—and then headed toward the main stairs of Paragon Castle to get to class. Sam and Celeste were waiting for him in the main hallway.

"Hey, Prince Falcon," said Sam.

"Good day, *Señor*!" said Celeste.

"We thought we'd, like, show you where the Temple of Honor is. It's kind of a walk from here."

"Indeed," said Celeste. "It is a treacherous journey, full of twisting alleys and corners of blindness!"

"Thanks," said Falcon. "That's nice of you."

"*Señor*," said Celeste. "I have decided, in my mercy, to offer you forgiveness for your rudeness of the other day. I am certain you meant no offense."

"Plus," said Sam, "I told her you like jerky."

They had almost reached the main door of the castle when Falcon saw a strange, blue light flickering from a room just off of the main stairwell. "Hey," he said, "what's that?"

Before them was a stone chamber lit by a strange blue glow. The light was coming from a dozen computer monitors in an otherwise lightless stone chamber. At each computer terminal was a small, emaciated guardian boy with enormous round eyes. The boys' hair was thinning, like that of middle-aged men. None of them looked up as Sam and Celeste and Falcon stood on the threshold.

"Intruder detected," said one of the boys. "Intruder— oh no! Now look what you did! I was just about to level up!"

"Dude," said Sam. "Who are you? What is this place?"

The boy looked at them. "Scanning life-forms," he said.

Celeste looked around the room. "These young gentlemen," she said, "would appear to be playing a most complicated series of electronic games! Upon their computers they play! With diligence and speed!"

"We're the Snoids," said the boy, walking to a small refrigerator and pulling out a soda, which he then drank. "We're fighting Smaulgtrons."

"Dude," said Sam. "I've played that game. Infernal Darkness II. It's awesome!"

"Smaulgtrons are evil," said the Snoid.

"But I am confused," said Celeste. "You are guardians!

Why do you not join the others of our kind in learning how to destroy the world of monsters!"

"We *are* destroying monsters," said the Snoid, dumbfounded. "That's all we do, all day, is battle!"

"I've never seen any of you guys in the cafeteria or the classrooms," said Sam.

"We never leave the game room!" said the Snoid. "We have to get to the next *level*!"

A red light began to flash, and there was a clanging sound at one of the Snoids' terminals. "Level four thousand," he said.

"Dude," said Sam.

"But surely playing video games all day becomes exhausting, even for virtuosos of the form such as yourselves!" said Celeste.

The Snoid opened up a large bag of crunchy snacks that were an orange color not found in nature. On the front of the bag were the words CHEESE DINKLES. "I don't understand what she just said."

"She means, don't you ever get tired of playing video games all day? Don't you want to, like, go outside?"

"Ha, ha," said the Snoid. "Funny."

"Hey," said Sam. "Can I have some of those Cheese Dinkles?"

The Snoid held the bag toward Sam, who dug his hand in.

"But it seems as if you are imprisoned here," said Celeste. "Imprisoned by your own fun! Can this be true?'

The Snoid looked confused. "We are fighting Smaulgtrons. Destroying them gives you points. The points can be redeemed for items at the online store. The items make it possible to fight the Smaulgtrons on the higher levels! That gives you more points!"

"Dude," said Sam. "Why don't you come with us? We're going to Field Research class in the Temple of Honor!"

"Sorry," he said. "I'm in the middle of a battle."

"But surely you can simply save the game, where you are," said Celeste. "And return to it at a later time."

"This is a cut scene," said the Snoid. "Can't save now. Oh look—it's the princess! We have to save the princess."

"How do you save the princess?"

"By killing her father. The Ruler of the Smaulgtrons."

"What happens when you rescue her?" said Falcon. "Do you marry her?"

"Ha, ha," said the Snoid. "Funny."

"I fail to see the humor in this," said Celeste.

"The princess cannot be saved," said the Snoid. "Because then the game will end."

"But then your work would be complete!" said Celeste. "Enabling you to venture out of your cave and explore the wide world!"

"Ha, ha," said the Snoid, and started typing even faster.

"You have to go now. Gotta kill more Smaulgtrons."

"This is a curious place," said Celeste, looking around the room at the entranced, hypnotized boys. "It is as if they have all been enslaved by their own amusement!"

The Snoid's computer began to ding, and the red light flashed again. "Huh huh huh," said the Snoid. "Level four thousand and one." He smiled, and Falcon and his friends saw that he had no teeth. "Now I can buy a *shield*."

They hurried through the twisting streets of the Hidden City. Celeste was right—the Temple of Honor was not easy to find. When they arrived, however, Falcon saw that it was a magnificent stone building with large pillars and a domed roof. Inside, the temple was a large, curving chamber. There was a circular hole in the center of the dome over their heads that let in a large column of light. Around the outside perimeter of the room were statues of various guardian heroes battling an assortment of monsters. There was a strong man cutting the head from a Frankenstein. There was a virtuous-looking woman impaling a stake through the heart of a vampire. A man with a thick book stood with his eyes closed and his hand extended as a mummy was driven back by the force of his will. "All right, kiddies," said a good-looking man wearing leather armor. He had a shock of wild, black hair and eyes of guardian blue. "This here is Field Research. Me, my name is Mortlock. Why don't you all get yourselves some weapons outta the armory over there, and we'll see if we can't chop somebody up."

There was a moment of silence, and then Chandler started to cry. "Chuh-chop somebody up?" he said.

A wicked smile crept across Mortlock's face. Falcon noticed that the man had a scar that sliced down the right side of his neck, from just below his ear to the top of his collarbone. "Better hurry," he said. "Could be you."

The young guardians scurried toward the armory, hauling out flails and flamethrowers and morningstars and bazookas. Jonny Frankenstein had a dagger. Falcon and Sam got broadswords.

"I don't have a weapon," said Chandler, his voice rising in panic. Behind him, the armory was empty. "There aren't enough weapons to go around."

"Hey, kid," said Mortlock. "Who says you got no weapon?"

"What?" said Chandler, looking around. "I don't see any—"

"You got your *brain*, kid," said Mortlock. "Most important weapon of all."

"Hey, yeah!" said Chandler. "I got my—"

"You don't use your brain," said Mortlock, "weapons are useless. You see this?" He pointed to the scar on his neck. "I got *this* because I didn't use my brain."

He smiled. "Smarter now."

There was an awkward moment of silence. Then Mortlock said, "Course, having the right weapon helps too." He held up a club with a thick round head. "Take this, for instance. The smashing jigger," he said. "What would you use this for?"

"Fighting something close at hand," said Gyra.

"Yeah," said Mortlock. "Good. But not just anything. Like, let's say you're up against a ghoul. You gonna use a smashing jigger on a ghoul?"

"Yeah," said Snick. "Why not?"

Mortlock smiled again. "Anybody want to tell Snick here why not?"

"The Crystal Scream," said Gyra. "A ghoul's going to use the Crystal Scream on you."

"Score one for the T.A.," said Mortlock. "You all know what the Crystal Scream is?" He looked at the class. "Cadet Gyra. Tell them what the Crystal Scream is."

"It's a high-pitched blast of aural energy," said Gyra again. "Fine tuned to resonate at the pitch at which the subject's eardrums vibrate, usually around eight hundred hertz."

"Bingo," said Mortlock. "So what happens to—well, let's say it's ol' Cadet Chandler here. What happens when he tries to attack a ghoul using a smashing jigger?"

Chandler looked frightened. "I'm attacking?"

There was an awkward silence for a moment. Then Jonny Frankenstein said, "His brain explodes."

"Yeah," said Mortlock. "Pretty much."

Everyone laughed except Chandler, whose lower lip thrust forward.

"But all I wanted was to be brave," said Chandler, his voice trembling. "My mommy tells me I'm the bravest of them all!"

"If we have to hear any more about your mommy," said Snick, "I'll use a smashing jigger on you, Chandler!"

"Who said that?" said Mortlock, the muscles in his jaw tightening.

"Me," said Snick.

"There's no dishonor in defending your parents, Cadet Snick," said Mortlock. "That's how I got this." He pointed to his scar again. His face was still dark and angry. "Banshees," he said.

There was silence in the class. Then Gyra looked skeptical. "What?" said Mortlock.

"I thought banshees screamed."

"Oh, they scream all right," said Mortlock.

"So—how did you get a scar? From a scream?"

"The scar is from my own mother," said Mortlock. "Who was carried off by banshees during the attack. She was clinging to me. While I had to stand there, stunned from the effects of the banshee scream. Because I did not know how to fight them. Because I had not yet learned how not to cry."

There was a long pause. The Temple of Honor was very quiet.

"Smarter now," said Mortlock.

After Field Research ended for the day, Falcon and Jonny Frankenstein walked through the streets of the Hidden City toward Paragon Castle. Through the windows of the stone houses they saw families gathered around tables for supper, men reading books in soft chairs, women playing guitars and fiddles.

"Must be nice," said Jonny, walking at Falcon's side. "All that."

"What?"

"Having a family."

"That's what I keep hearing," said Falcon.

"How about that guy today? Mortlock."

"What about him?"

"No wonder he hates monsters," said Jonny. "His mother got carried off by banshees."

"Remember that banshee girl at the Academy, Elaine Screamish?" asked Falcon. "I can't see her carrying off anybody."

"Not yet," said Jonny. "But the guardians are right. Once she gets a little older, Screamy will be pretty deadly."

They heard a pair of footsteps behind them, and Falcon turned to see Gyra running toward them.

"Hey, Falcon," she said. "You okay?" Her eyes fell on Jonny Frankenstein, and her expression seemed colder.

"Catch up with you later, Falcon," said Jonny.

"Yeah," said Falcon. "I'll—"

But Jonny just turned his back and walked up the hill toward Paragon Castle.

Falcon turned to Gyra. "What's that all about? You and Jonny don't get along?"

Gyra shrugged. "I don't trust him." She wrinkled her nose. "Why? Do you?"

"I don't know," said Falcon. "We got some things in common, I guess."

"Like what?" said Gyra.

"Well, we're both orphans," said Falcon. "Or—whatever. I used to *think* I was an orphan, anyway."

They walked up the hilly street. Falcon looked up at Paragon Castle, its many towers and ramparts glowing in the sunset. Flags fluttered in the breeze.

"You shouldn't," said Gyra, giving him a hard look. "You got all kinds of family."

"Yeah, I guess," said Falcon. She reminded him so much of Megan he felt a little bit dizzy. He remembered the moment last spring when he and Megan had stood up in the Tower of Souls, next to the giant clock face, and looked out at the Sea of Dragons.

"What's wrong with your eye, Falcon?" said Gyra.

"What?"

"That eye patch. Did you get hurt?"

"No," said Falcon. "I'm fine. Mr. Drudge thought I should keep my dark eye covered."

"Really?" said Gyra. She reached toward his face and slowly pulled off the eye patch. "I don't see why."

"He thought—I might hurt somebody with it."

Gyra looked deeply into Falcon's black eye. "But you wouldn't," she said. "Would you?"

"Gyra!" shouted a voice from a stone house.

Gyra turned, and there was her mother, wearing an apron.

Her glance fell upon her daughter and Falcon Quinn, and for a moment there was a look of uncertainty on her face. "Come on, honey," she said. "It's dinnertime!"

Gyra turned back to Falcon. Her face seemed strangely flushed. "I gotta go," she said.

16

CREATIVE WRITING FOR ASSASSINS

Several days later, the young guardians were sitting in Colonel Hemingway's class, Literature of Mayhem. As in all of the colonel's classes so far, the story under discussion was one of the colonel's own. This one was called "The Harpies of Gettysburg."

"There we were, in the attic of a building right in the town square," he said. "Our hearts pounding, my brother, Mycroft, and I climbed the stairs—cautiously! Cautiously! When, all at once, from behind us, there came a hideous scream!"

From the back of the room came a small, sad whimper.

"What's all this?" asked the colonel. "Cadet Chandler? Come, come, now! Let's show a little backbone!"

"My mommy says your stories promote witchcraft!" said Chandler miserably.

"Yeah," said Snick. "But your mommy said that about *The Velveteen Rabbit* too."

"*The Velveteen Rabbit does* promote witchcraft!" Chandler looked frightened.

"Come now, lad," said the colonel. "Show some spine! I remember back in eighty-three, when I was stalking the madwoman of Chicago. Well, there we were, stepping in—"

"Colonel," said Gyra, "will the students ever get a chance to write stories of their own? Instead of just listening to yours all the time?"

"I'd like to do some writing," Jonny Frankenstein said. Snick looked over at Jonny and laughed derisively.

"Yeah, that'd be some great stuff to read," said Snick. "Poems about a bunch of nasty guts all held together with duct tape."

"Curious," said the colonel. "Any other fledglings with an interest in yarn spinning?"

"I've written some poems," said Gyra softly.

"I say," said the colonel. "Extraordinary collection of talent! Bully!"

At this moment, the bell rang, and all of the students leaped to their feet and rushed toward the door. Falcon and Gyra and Jonny were the last ones remaining, and as they packed up their things, the colonel sat in his chair stroking his mustache.

"Well, then!" said the colonel. "About this creative-writing business. Might be good fun. Would you three like to convene a small workshop? We could specialize in poems about monster killing! Sonnets about zombie destroying and the like!"

Gyra looked at Jonny. "Does he have to come?" she said.

"Oh, the more the merrier," said the colonel. "First meeting tonight. Seven, in my chambers? I'll show you some of my trophies from my collection as well. Some remarkable specimens, if I do say so."

"You don't want me to come, Gyra?" said Jonny with a grin.

"Jonny Frankenstein," said Gyra. "I don't care if you live or die."

The colonel smiled happily. "It's all settled then! Good show!"

Falcon was just beginning to wonder what the colonel meant by "specimens" when the bell for the next class rang and he found himself running down the hallway, late for the History of Virtue.

Falcon wasn't quite certain what to expect that night when he arrived at the colonel's residence, which was a tower of Paragon Castle called the Turret of Adventure. The old man, however, opened the door to reveal Jonny Frankenstein and Gyra in the heart of a wood-paneled study, sitting in chairs covered with elephant hide. Gyra had her bullwhip coiled on her right hip. The stuffed heads of various monsters lined the walls. Colonel Hemingway wore a silken robe and puffed on a large meerschaum pipe.

"Grand to see you, old chap, come in, come in. Bully!"

"Hey, Falcon," said Jonny.

"Hey, Jonny," said Falcon. He nodded at Gyra. "Hi."

"Hi, Falcon," she said.

"Now here's a fascinating specimen," said the colonel, pointing at a stuffed head of a ferocious beast. "The Chimera of Philadelphia. Ah, look at him, fledglings! Quite a ferocious chap in his day!" Falcon looked at the chimera, and as he looked, a long line of slobber fell from the creature's lips and dripped onto the floor. The chimera followed Falcon with its eyes, sniffed the air, and then roared.

"It's alive!" said Falcon.

"After a fashion," said the colonel, chuckling. "But he's harmless enough. Without his goat body and dragon tail, he's more meow than roar, I should say." He laughed loudly. "Jolly good!"

Falcon looked around the room and saw that many of the other trophy heads were watching them, their eyes shining. On a far wall was a large case with a wide variety of elephant guns and machetes. Beneath these were traps and elixirs and binoculars.

"Ah, now here—look at these two!" said the colonel, moving along to the next trophy. "A gargoyle—and his wife!" Mounted on the wall was the head of a man wearing a beret. Right next to him was the head of a woman with high cheekbones. "Good evening, old boy! How are we this evening?"

"*Bonjour,*" said the gargoyle.

"The LaFleurs," said the colonel. "Bagged them near Marseille, I believe."

"*Je n'ai jamais aimé mon mari,*" said the woman.

"What did she say?"

"Can't say," said the colonel. "Never did learn French, you know."

"*Il nous faut sortir d'ici!*"

"Bully!" said the colonel. He ushered Falcon over to a wing chair next to Jonny Frankenstein and Gyra. "Well, let's get started. Best place to begin is at the beginning, don't you know. Analyzing the structure of dramatic action."

"Do I need all that stuff?" said Gyra. "Just to write poems?"

"I should say so," said the colonel. "A poem can't just begin anyplace, you know!"

There was a deep, gonging bell, and a far door swung open, which Falcon at first thought—and hoped—was the arrival of another guest. Then he saw a servant enter the room, a man wearing white gloves and carrying a large platter, upon which were four plates covered with silver domes.

The servant had no head.

"Ah—Quimby," said the colonel. "There's a good man. Just put those down on the table here, and we'll serve ourselves. Right!"

"Quimby," said Falcon. "Wait. His name is Quimby?"

The servant put the platter down, bowed slightly, and then turned and walked back toward the door through which he had entered. The creature's ability to sense its surroundings seemed somewhat limited, however; it had to pause for a moment to feel around for the door with its gloved hands. Then at last the headless body exited, the door swinging closed behind it. The colonel removed the silver dome from his plate. "Ah!" he said enthusiastically. "Buffalo wings! Bully! Be careful, fledglings! They're spicy!"

"Colonel," said Falcon. "I used to *know* somebody named Quimby! He was the spirit of the crystal back in my dorm room at the Academy. Before he got loose, anyhow."

At the mention of the Academy for Monsters, Gyra looked at Falcon uncomfortably. She shook her head.

"What?" said Falcon.

"Nothing," said Gyra.

"Ah, Quimby," said the colonel, biting into a wing. "Big, lurching, headless chap."

Jonny picked up a buffalo wing. In his hands was a

large, sinewy thing covered with sauce. "Wait. What's this?"

"A buffalo wing, my good man!" said the colonel. "Made from the dangerous flying buffalo of northern-most Saskatoon! Bagged these bison myself, last autumn. Had Quimby put them in the smokehouse for me!"

Jonny smiled. "Buffalo wings," he muttered.

"You've fought a lot of monsters, Colonel," said Gyra.

"As shall you, Cadet Gyra," said the colonel. "You're the most promising student we've had in a generation!"

"Is there anything that's escaped you?" said Jonny, cautiously biting into a wing. "Anything you wanted to capture but couldn't?"

"What's that? Well, there are a few I've never encoun-tered. But I'll get them yet, I trust! One thing you can depend on—there are always more monsters!"

"How'd you capture that chimera?" asked Gyra, look-ing at the head of the creature mounted on the wall.

"Well, it had three heads when I found it. Froze one, hypnotized the second. And this one I just chopped off clean."

The chimera growled.

"And the gargoyles?"

"Very difficult. Had to slip a Mickey Finn into their Beaujolais!"

"*Le salaud!*" muttered the gargoyle.

His wife shook her head. *"J'allais demander le divorce!"* she said. *"A cause de ses ronflements!"*

"I say," said the colonel. "Sometimes I *do* wonder what they're on about!"

"What about a wind elemental?" said Jonny. Gyra looked at him suspiciously.

"Ah, now. The elementals are tricky. Tricky, indeed. Too dangerous to be kept inside, even once they're captured. Some are easier than others. A fire elemental you can douse with an enchanted hose, and you're all done. A water elemental's tougher. Those you have to boil, and then capture the steam. I remember one water elemental we captured back in seventy-nine, I think it was. Seventy-nine or seventy-eight. In any case, there we were, boiling the elemental when the steam re-formed in midair, taking on the form of a ferocious steam dragon. Well! For a moment I feared the worst. But then, I cleverly grabbed a teabag and—"

"That's fascinating," said Jonny. He cast an urgent glance at Falcon. "But you were going to tell us about wind elementals, weren't you?"

"Why do you want to know so much about wind elementals, Jonny?" said Gyra.

"Well, they're fascinating, don't you know," said the colonel. "Of course, a wind elemental's a much easier prospect than the other kinds. You trap it in a wind sock, or a windmill, with entangling yarn, or entangling sails, or what have you. Quite simple, really. You just trap it, let it tire itself out, and then it just fades. Doesn't make much of a trophy, of course, being invisible and all that. But satisfying, yes! We just caught one last spring, if I recall. That girl from the Academy, what was her name? Kept the sails of the old windmill up on the mountain going for weeks and weeks. Still up there, I believe! Probably spun all to pieces by now!" He chuckled. "Bully!"

"Megan?" said Falcon. "Megan Crofton? She's trapped in the sails of that windmill?"

"Quite," said the colonel. "But she's—"

"Falcon," said Gyra, a tone of warning in her voice.

"Now then, fledglings," continued the colonel. "We ought to get to work on the matter at hand—our workshop for assassin poets! Why don't we begin by analyzing the proper elements of a limerick? Bully! Now, your first line should always begin with the phrase 'There once was a—'"

"Colonel," said Jonny, "before you go any further, may I just, um—shake your hand, sir? It really is an honor to be chosen for this workshop. And I want to thank you for giving me this opportunity. A lot of other teachers wouldn't give someone like me a chance like this."

"What are you doing?" said Gyra.

"I'm expressing my admiration," said Jonny, getting to his feet.

"Well, now," said the colonel, visibly pleased by the

flattery. "You know the faculty has followed your progress, my boy, with great interest."

"Thank you, sir," said Jonny, extending his hand. "This class has me really—*charged up.*"

"Colonel," said Gyra, growing more alarmed. "Don't let him—!"

"Bully!" said the colonel, taking Jonny's hand. "Bu—"

Jonny's eyes rolled back in his head, and forking bolts of electricity consumed the colonel. The old man was entwined with flashing, twisting light as Jonny shocked him with his alternating current. When Jonny let go of the colonel's hand, the man fell limply onto the leather sofa.

"What did you do?" said Gyra, pulling out her bullwhip.

"Jonny," said Falcon. "You toasted him."

"Yeah, I don't know," said Jonny. "He was kind of boring me."

"Do you electrocute all your teachers when you're bored?"

Jonny smiled. "If I can."

"I'm placing you under guardian arrest!" Gyra said. "For attacking a member of the faculty! Put your hands behind your backs, both of you!"

"What if we don't?" said Jonny.

"I said put your hands behind your backs!"

"I got plenty of voltage left for you too, Gyra," said

Jonny. "If that's what you want."

She cracked the whip in the air. "Try it, Jonny," she said. "Go on."

"Gyra," said Falcon. "Megan Crofton is my friend. We have to save her."

"I don't have to do anything," said Gyra. "Except turn the both of you in."

From Jonny came the sound of electricity softly crackling. "Stand back, Falcon," he said.

"Don't hurt her," said Falcon.

Jonny looked at Falcon curiously. "Whose side are you on?" he said.

"Gyra," said Falcon. "Remember when we were talking about what it was like to have a family, that day after Field Research? Megan was *my* family, back in Cold River. I can't leave her here. I can't."

"She's a monster," said Gyra. The whip trembled in her hand.

"Gyra," said Falcon. "You don't have to stay here. There's more to life than just killing zombies."

"Falcon," said Jonny. "Come on. I gotta zap her."

"Wait," said Falcon. He looked at Gyra again as an expression of uncertainty crossed her face. "Gyra. Remember on Monster Island, when you tried to get me to come with you? You said I could have a better life. Remember?"

"Yeah," said Gyra. "I remember."

"Well, that's what I'm offering you," said Falcon. "If you come with us."

"Come with you," said Gyra slowly.

"She's not coming with us, okay?" said Jonny. Small blue flashes of electricity crackled across his palms.

"Come on, Gyra," said Falcon. He held out his hand. "Join us."

Gyra looked at Falcon, standing there with his hand outstretched, and then at Jonny, humming and sparking with voltage.

"I can't," she said. She rolled up her bullwhip. "I'm a guardian, okay? I have to protect my friends, just like you have to protect yours."

"That's it, I'm zapping her," said Jonny.

"Don't," said Falcon. "It's all right." He turned to Gyra. "Give us a ten-minute head start?"

"What?"

"Ten minutes."

Gyra thought it over. "Five," she said.

Jonny raised his hands to blast Gyra with electricity. But Falcon's hands went to his temple, and he pulled off the eye patch that covered his dark eye and threw the eye patch on the floor.

"If you touch her, Jonny," said Falcon, "I'll shoot you with a fireball. I swear, I'll do it!"

Now it was Jonny's turn to think things over. He sighed. "Fine," he said, lowering his hands, although it was clear he wasn't happy about it. "Whatever you say, boss."

Falcon looked at the colonel. "How long's he out for?"

"Couple hours, I think," said Jonny.

"Well, all right then," said Falcon. "Let's get out of here. We got a windmill to stop."

Jonny nodded. "Course, they'll come after us once she tells Cygnus what we're doing." He glanced at Gyra again. "You *are* going to tell them what we're doing, aren't you?"

"Probably," said Gyra.

"So what's your plan, Falcon?" said Jonny. "They aren't going to like us setting Megan free. Matter of fact, I think it's gonna tick 'em off in a big way."

"Let's get back to Monster Island," said Falcon. "Join up with the Filchers. Live with them."

"The Filchers?" said Gyra. "Who are the Filchers?"

"Let's keep that our secret, okay?" said Jonny.

"Let's go," said Falcon.

"Wait," said Jonny. "How are we going get to Monster Island?"

"We sail," said Falcon. "On Weems's boat, you know, the *Destynee II*. It's still sitting in the harbor. I saw it my first morning, when Mr. Drudge was walking me to school."

"Listen to you," said Jonny. "You are devious, aren't you?"

"You'll never get away with this," said Gyra. "You know that, right?"

Jonny and Falcon went over to the open window. "Climb on my back, Jonny," said Falcon.

"Ride 'em, cowboy," said Jonny.

"Gyra," said Falcon. "Look out for Sam and Celeste, okay?"

"You look out for yourself, Falcon Quinn," said Gyra.

Falcon stepped out of the tower, spreading his wings. He and Jonny soared above the Hidden City.

Gyra watched them fly. Then she turned away from the window and went into the hallway. She coiled up her bullwhip and fastened it to her belt. She looked at her watch. *Five minutes, Falcon,* she thought. Then she would have to wake Cygnus.

She remembered walking back from the Temple of Honor with Falcon. *Would it be so wrong,* Gyra thought, *just to let them go? What would be the harm, if Falcon and Megan got to live their own lives, in peace?*

"Why, Gyra," said a voice.

Gyra looked up to see Vega standing there in her long, white gown. Tippy was at her side, growling.

"What are you doing up?"

17

THE WINDMILL

Falcon flew toward the top of Paragon Mountain.

"Ow," said Falcon.

"What? Am I too heavy for you?"

"No. But you're leaking current or something. I'm getting a shock from you. Can't you turn off the juice?"

"Sorry," said Jonny. "I got a short."

"Yeah, well, it's really unpleasant."

"Speaking of crossed wires . . ."

"What?"

"You and Gyra," said Jonny. "You know that relationship is really sick?"

"Sick? What do you mean, sick?"

"Come on. The only reason you wouldn't let me zap her is because she looks like Megan. Admit it."

"You know, you don't have to shock everybody with your electricity," said Falcon "just because you can."

"You're going to wish I'd zapped her," said Jonny. "Trust me."

"Since when have I ever trusted you?"

The windmill was before them now, and Falcon swept down and lowered Jonny onto the ground. The windmill seemed much larger now that they were up close to it. The blue sails slashed through the air like blades on the propeller of a giant ship. There was a high-pitched, almost inaudible wailing, like the voice of someone crying out from a dream.

"Megan?" said Falcon.

There was no reply. Falcon stepped a little closer to the windmill, but Jonny pulled him back. "Careful," said Jonny as a heavy wooden sail whirled past, only inches from Falcon's head.

Falcon looked into the heart of the rotating blades. Something gray and luminous flickered there. For a single second Falcon thought he saw Megan's face. He spread his wings, flew toward the blades, and tried to grab on to the whirling translucent form. But one of the slashing sails crashed into his shoulder with a merciless *whump*, and Falcon tumbled through the air and crashed.

"Are you all right?" said Jonny as he helped Falcon back onto to his feet.

"That *hurt*," said Falcon. He didn't appear to have broken any bones, but he felt shaken, and his shoulder ached.

"Okay," said Jonny. "So what's our plan B?"

Falcon rubbed his shoulder and thought. "There must be a brake of some kind. Maybe inside this—what do you call it, the *engine house*, where all the gears are. If I can turn on the brake, do you think you could catch her?"

"Catch her?"

"If she falls once the blades stop."

"You're sure *you* don't want to catch her?" said Jonny.

"I'll stop the windmill, you catch her," said Falcon. "Just don't shock her, okay? I don't care whether you've got crossed wires or not."

"All right," said Jonny. "I'll play catch. Just be careful in there, Falcon. Okay?" He looked up at the old engine house. "This place gives me the creeps."

"I'll be careful," Falcon said, and flew over to the far side of the windmill, giving the spinning sails a wide berth. There was a wooden door on one side of the old stone building, and there was a loud creak as Falcon swung it open and flew inside.

The interior of the windmill was dark. As his eyes adjusted, Falcon saw the shadows of large, intermeshing gears. On the floor were some old grain sacks, and on the side of the sacks was written 100% RAW GUARDIAN BARLEY.

Around the perimeter of the room, at about knee level, was a slowly spinning grindstone, a huge circular stone with a hole in the middle. It passed beneath a heavy stone roller on the far side of the engine house, where the grain had once been crushed into flour.

There was a large glassless window in the wall above the grindstone, and dim moonlight slanted in. A small set of rickety, circular stairs curled around the outer wall and up to a platform high over Falcon's head. Next to another set of spinning gears by the platform were two red levers. One was marked REVERSE, the other, STOP.

There we go, Falcon thought. He rushed up the stairs, passing the window as he made his way up. Outside, the blades of the windmill swirled past, and through their swiftly moving forms he could see Jonny, who had his arms raised and his fingers spread. He yelled, "Stand back!" A moment later, there was a forking flash of lightning from Jonny's hands.

Jonny looked up at the windmill. "Better hurry," he called to Falcon. "We got company."

Falcon ran the rest of the way up the stairs. The rumbling of the rusted gears and cogs here in the center of the windmill was deafening. Falcon reached forward and grabbed the brake lever. The iron was cold in his hands.

From outside he heard Jonny cry out again. The inside of the engine house was illuminated by flickers of lightning.

He was just about to pull back on the brake when he felt a sudden blast of frozen wind, like an ice storm in the heart of winter back in Cold River. The air around him turned into a freezing mist, and crystals of ice ran up his arms. As the cold crept beneath his skin and into his hearts, Falcon began to lose consciousness. His wings froze, and Falcon toppled off the platform like a dead thing. As he hit the floor, the ice that had encased him shattered, sending fragments of crystals and tiny broken icicles skittering in every direction.

"You know what I don't understand," said a voice. Falcon looked up, and there was Vega in her long, white dress, carrying a scepter. "Why is it so important to you to free the wind elemental? Why would you even *care* what happens to her?"

"Ow," said Falcon, crawling forward and slowly staggering back onto his feet. "You—froze me."

"I am sorry about that, dear, but I had to stop you from making a mistake."

"You think rescuing Megan is a mistake?"

"Oh, of course it's a mistake," said Vega. "I just don't see why you don't leave her whirling around in the blades? It's not such a bad place for a wind elemental, really, the sails of a windmill. It's like keeping a hamster in a cage."

"She's not a hamster, Mom. She's my friend."

"Ugh, there is that tedious word again." Vega ran her fingers through her long, white hair. "Such a low bar you seem to set for friendship. Honestly, it seems as if all a person has to do to win your unending loyalty, Falcon, is to *stab you in the back*. Just as your friend Gyra did now."

"What did you do to Jonny?" said Falcon, looking back toward the door.

"Now, don't you worry. He's keeping nice and fresh in the deep freeze. We can reheat him later, if you want."

Falcon's dark eye grew hot. "Just because you've given up," he said, "doesn't mean I have to."

"Given up?" said Vega. "You think I've given up? No, Falcon. I am fighting."

"Fighting what?"

"Why, Falcon. Fighting to protect the innocent, of course. To keep them from being pulled into the monsters' world of darkness and horror—as I was!"

"What did Megan ever do to you?"

"Nothing yet," said Vega. "That's why we keep her imprisoned. Preventing cyclones, and hurricanes, and all the other trouble her kind are responsible for. Can't you see, Falcon? Keeping her in the windmill helps people. It saves lives!"

"Megan won't do any of that," said Falcon. "I know her!"

"You *used* to know her," said Vega compassionately. "Before she came into her powers. You'll find her changed now."

"I'm going to pull that brake, Mom," said Falcon. "I don't care what you say. I'm pulling it."

Vega looked over her shoulder at the long, spiraling

staircase that led up to the brake lever by the great wheel. "Well, you'll have to get past me first, won't you?"

Vega lifted her hand and pointed a scepter at him. There was a blue jewel in it that was surrounded by ice crystals. Something about it seemed strangely familiar to Falcon.

"Wait—," he said. "That's—"

"The indigo madstone," said Vega. "For freezing things that have grown too hot. Like your passions, Falcon." Vega pointed the scepter at his hearts. "Let her go, Son," she said. "Forget her. You'll feel more complete when you let go of these attachments. After all, she's just a little breeze. You can't even see her."

"I don't have to see her," said Falcon, and shot a fireball out of his eye. It hurtled toward Vega. Just as it was about to hit her, however, a black figure stepped between Falcon and his mother and caught the fireball. Rubbing his hands together, the black creature extinguished the flame, then let the ashes fall from his fingers.

The Crow nodded. "I'll take it from here, Son."

Vega looked unsurprised. "Well," she said. "Here we are. The monster and child reunion."

"Dad!" said Falcon. "I was—"

"Why don't you go up those stairs," said the Crow, "and pull that brake while your mother and I have . . . a little talk?"

"We have nothing to say to each other," said Vega.

"Vega," said the Crow, his great wings quivering. "You don't mean that."

"Don't I?" said Vega, raising the scepter and shooting a blast of frozen crystals at him.

For a moment the Crow's face was covered in ice, and he stood still like a marble statue. Then the crystals shattered and fell to the floor. A small blue flame flickered above the Crow's head.

"This was not the conversation I imagined," he said, and stepped toward Vega once more.

"Mom," said Falcon. "Dad."

"Not now, Son," said Vega. "Your father and I are killing each other." She raised her scepter again, and a spear shaped like a long icicle flew through the air toward the Crow. He caught it with one hand, looked at it dispassionately, and then broke it over his knee like a stick. The Crow dropped the pieces onto the floor and his fire went out.

Falcon looked up the stairs at the windmill's emergency brake. "I'm pulling that lever," he said.

"Really?" said Vega, blocking the way. "And then what?"

"And then I'm getting out of here. Leaving you behind. Leaving you *both* behind."

"But then where will you go?" said the Crow. "Do you really think there is somewhere in the world where you will not have to choose between us?" The flame atop his head relit itself once more with a *woosh*.

Falcon looked at his father, then his mother. He pulsed his wings and flew toward the platform at the top of the stairs.

"Stop," said Vega, and shot him with another blast from the scepter, coating Falcon's wings with ice. This time he crashed onto the grindstone that rotated around the outer perimeter of the engine house. He tried to move, but his wings were frozen to the stone. Falcon slowly rotated toward the crushing stone rollers.

The Crow moved toward Vega once again. "You cannot freeze me," he said, "without also freezing yourself." He moved toward her once again, and now Vega backed away from him, slowly ascending the stairs.

"I don't even know what that means," she said.

"Yes you do," said the Crow.

"Dad," said Falcon. He had rotated almost halfway around the circular grindstone toward the crushing rollers now. "I could use a little help here."

"Just a moment, Son," said the Crow.

"Dad!"

Vega and the Crow kept climbing the stairs.

"Explain this theory of yours to me, Eoghan," she said.

"We are linked, Vega," said the Crow. "The connection we share is not our curse. It is our gift."

"Mom! Dad!" Falcon shouted again. He was almost to the stone rollers now. He could hear the grinding, scraping sound as the two granite faces rumbled against each other.

Vega and the Crow had reached the top of the stairs. Vega shot another iceball at her husband, and the Crow caught it in his hand. He held it up so she could see the ice turn to water and run through his fingers. "Do you truly not remember?" he said. "The winters in Cold River? The fires that I built?"

"That's done," said Vega softly. "I've put that out of my mind."

"I can help put it back in your mind," said the Crow, and reached toward her with his suction-cup hand, slowly placing its tendrils against her cheek. For a moment Vega looked hesitant. She looked at Falcon and then back at the Crow. Then she pulled on the lever behind her marked REVERSE, and there was a grinding, groaning sound from the gears. Falcon stopped just a few inches from the roller. The windmill was still, for a single instant.

After this fleeting pause, the giant wheel began to spin in the other direction, and Falcon found himself slowly rotating around the perimeter once more, back toward the *other* side of the crushing rollers.

The Crow's eyelids drooped. "Remember," he said.

"I—," said Vega. "I can't—"

"Remember," he said again. For a moment longer, a

look of tenderness remained on Vega's face.

Then she slapped his hand away. "Get that away from me," she said, and raised the indigo madstone once more. Ice crystals flew through the air, and the Crow spread his wings and flew to the left and right in order to avoid the blast. The fire atop his head flickered brightly now, like an industrial flame.

"So it's going to be like this, then?" he said.

"Tell me," said Vega, "what other way could it be?" She held one of her arms out to the side and blasted a thin sheet of ice between her body and her wrist, making a delicate, crystalline wing. She put the madstone in the other hand and did the same thing on the other side. Vega looked at her husband with contempt, then stepped off the staircase. She flapped her shining ice wings and soared through the air, firing off balls of ice and snow as she descended.

Falcon had spun halfway around the mill's rotating grindstone, still struggling to get his frozen wings free. He called out for help, but his parents were more focused on hurting each other than on saving their son.

He watched as his mother and father flew through the air above him, taking part in a strange aerial battle—Vega on her wings of ice, blasting her husband with snow crystals and hail, and the Crow, sweeping around her on his black wings, returning her attack with balls of fire. Around and around the turning gears of the windmill they flew as fire and ice rained down into the darkness.

The Crow reached up and put his deformed hand in the flame that roared above his head. With a flick of his wrist, he sent a flying disk of fire through the air, just missing Vega. He threw a volley of these burning, spinning disks at her, but Vega was too fast. They exploded against the walls of the engine house like fireworks. Ashes and embers drifted toward the floor.

Vega sent a huge blast of ice toward the Crow's feet, encasing them. This dragged the Crow down toward one of the spinning vertical gears, and his right foot, covered by a giant ice block, got jammed in the gear's teeth. He managed to free himself just before the gear meshed with another, and the cracking ice flew through the air in a rain of shattered crystals. Vega swept in, ready for the kill.

But the Crow just threw his head back and made a piercing, *kawww* sound, like the screaming of a bird. Vega paused in midair and held her ears.

Falcon was nearing the rollers of the grindstone. He had managed to get one of his wings free, but there wasn't going to be enough time to free the other one before he was dragged beneath the crushing round stone.

The air filled with the sound of hundreds of flapping wings. There were sharp, harsh cries from the throats of many strange birds. Through the open window, a murder of crows swept into the engine house, encircling Vega.

There were hundreds of them—hooded crows and jack-daws and carrion crows and forest ravens and rooks. The vast murder of crows descended upon Vega's body, their wings fluttering, their sharp black beaks pecking, their harsh voices filling the air with avian screams. Somewhere in the midst of all those furious, angry wings was a flash of white hair, the fabric of a white dress being torn to pieces.

The Crow flew up to the high platform and pulled on the lever marked STOP, and a set of metal teeth scraped against the gears, bringing the windmill to a halt. Falcon stopped just inches before the crushing rollers. His wings finally free, he hopped onto the floor. There, in the center of the engine house floor, was the murder of crows, screaming and swarming over the guardian queen.

"Mom?" said Falcon.

Then the Crow gave another earsplitting *kawwww*, and the birds all flew up in the air once more. They circled around the Crow, like a pack of dogs cavorting with their master, before flying out the window. In a moment, the windmill was silent, except for the sound of the crows *kawww*ing as they all flew off into the night.

"Falcon," said his mother, and he went over to her. Vega, weak and dazed, had a multitude of peck-marks on her arms and cheeks.

"What did you do to her?" said Falcon to his father.

"I tried to show her—," said the Crow. "That I loved her."

"That you—?" In spite of his father saving his life, it was all Falcon could do not to blast the Crow with one of his fireballs. "Did anyone ever tell you, *ever*, that you and Mom have the strangest marriage in the world?"

The Crow kneeled and ran his fingers through Vega's white hair. Then he glanced at his son. The flame atop his head went out. "Go," he said.

"Let me heal her," said Falcon. "I can use my light."

"This is beyond your power, Falcon," said the Crow. From around his neck, the stopwatch was ticking loudly.

"I can heal the pecks of a bunch of birds," said Falcon.

"Falcon," said the Crow. "Those were not birds. Those were the souls of the lost. They are under my command."

"Lost—?"

"There is no time to explain. I must take her to one who can heal her, both her body and her soul. I will take her to the Watcher."

"Dad—," said Falcon.

"Go!" shouted the Crow. "There is nothing more you can do. There are others coming for you, guardians from the city, below. They are coming."

"But—"

"Go!" shouted the Crow again. Falcon watched as his father gathered Vega into his arms and slowly got to his feet. The Crow pulsed his wings and flew up to the circular window in the windmill's wall.

Then he flew out into the night and was gone.

Falcon ran to the door in time to catch a last glimpse of the Crow, who held Vega as they soared out toward the dark ocean. He went outside and was just about to run to the other side of the windmill to see what had happened to Jonny when a small creature suddenly blocked his path. He stood before him, growling and snarling.

"Now I've got you, Falcon Quinn," said Tippy, the tiny dog. He opened his mouth, baring his awful fangs.

"Oh, for god's sake" said Falcon.

"And now you will meet your doom, Falcon Quinn! For I shall bite you at last, bite you with the poison fangs!"

"Listen—," said Falcon.

"I will not listen!" snapped Tippy. "Now I will destroy you, with the terrible venom of—"

But Tippy never got a chance to finish this sentence, for at this exact second a huge carrion crow swept down and grabbed the dog with its black talons and carried him off into the night. The last Falcon saw of the dog, he was still howling as he disappeared over the horizon. There was a last, distant *kaww*, and then Tippy and the crow were gone without a trace.

He heard a soft cry to his right and turned to see Jonny Frankenstein, completely coated in ice, standing like a statue below the now-motionless sails of the wind-mill. Megan Crofton, a translucent, glowing ghost, lay in Jonny's frozen arms, moaning softly.

She smiled weakly. "Falcon," she said. "Look! Jonny saved me!"

IV

THE ISLAND OF NIGHTMARES

18

A Rhyme for Orange

Sparkbolt sat in his room, a quill pen in his hand. "'Porridge,'" he murmured. "'Forage.' 'Door hinge.'" He scowled, then sighed. "Rrrrr. Poem belong dead," he said.

"Dude," said a voice, and Sparkbolt jumped.

"Rrrrrr!" he shouted, nearly falling out of his chair. "Not sneak up on monster. Monster jumpy!"

"You do the homework for Redflint's class?" said Max.

"What homework?" said Sparkbolt.

"You know, this whole chapter about scare tactics? About, like—the right way to frighten somebody?"

"Monster not want to scare anybody," said Sparkbolt. "Monster want—*to be loved!*"

"Yeah, okay," muttered Max. "Good luck with that."

"It so wrong to want—to want *love?*"

Max licked his lips. "Yeah, okay. But like, if we get attacked or something, we're supposed to know how to scare people. It's part of the whole monster code, you know? I mean—well, you were in class. Weren't you?"

"Monster not paying attention," Sparkbolt moaned. "Heart—hurt."

"Heart hurt because . . ."

"Because Falcon!" shouted Sparkbolt. "Rrrr!"

"Yeah, well," said Max. "You should hear Pearl on this subject. She's convinced we're all wrong about Falcon. That it was all some big mistake."

"Pearl—," said Sparkbolt. "Good?"

"Oh yeah," said Max. "They let her out this morning. She's fine. You know how Chupakabras are. They heal fast."

"Mistake," said Sparkbolt. "Mistake how?"

"I don't know," said Max. "But she's pretty hard core about it."

"How Sasquatch?" asked Sparkbolt. "Sasquatch—hard core?"

Max looked pained. "I don't know, man. I want to be. But I saw him—my buddy!—blast Pearl with that eye thing of his. That was the worst! If anything had happened to her, I'd have—I'd have—" Max lowered his head.

"Sasquatch doubt," said Sparkbolt.

"I guess, yeah. I mean, you found all that stolen stuff under Falcon's bed. That's pretty bad."

"Bad," said Sparkbolt.

"What was that whole story he gave you about the Flippers or whatever? I mean, that *is* kind of sketchy, isn't it?"

"Filchers," said Sparkbolt. "Elves and Squonk."

"Right," said Max. "I mean, you gotta admit that

that's way out there, don't you? There being—Squonks and stuff?"

"World . . . contain . . . *Sasquatch.* Why not Squonk?"

"Well, of course, the world contains you and me, man. We're here!"

Sparkbolt waved his arms around. "Monster not talk more," he growled. "Monster angry!"

"Okay, change the subject," said Max. "Whatcha doin', anyway? Workin' on another poem?" He bent down and picked up one of the pieces of paper that was lying on the floor. "*Art of losing not hard master! Burn down house, make big disaster!* Hey, Sparkbolt, that's a good one."

"Poems," said Sparkbolt. "Belong dead."

"Hey, what's this one?" said Max, picking up another piece of paper. This one was not crumpled into a ball, and lay partly concealed beneath Falcon's bed. "'*Dear Falcon,*'" Max read. "'*All well on the Filcher front! The missus said we ought to give these*—' Hey, what's this, your imitation of a letter from those Filcher dudes? Look at the wacky runes you drew, man! This handwriting is all—elvish and junk!"

"Rrrr?" said Sparkbolt, confused. He grabbed the letter out of Max's hand and read through the rest. "Rrr," he said again. "Monster not write."

"Don't be modest, man," said Max. "It's totally convincing."

"Monster not write!" Sparkbolt shouted, shaking

the letter in his hand. "Not monster handwriting! This letter—from Filchers!"

"Wait," said Max. "The—Filchers? I thought you said—"

"Filchers *real*," said Sparkbolt. "Falcon—telling truth. Monster—betray friend! RRRRRRR!"

"Dude, it's not your fault," said Max.

"Falcon Quinn . . . join Filchers," moaned Sparkbolt. "Falcon Quinn leave to join—outcasts." He murmured. "*Knew* him not guardian. *Knew* him not false. Falcon Quinn good!" Then his voice fell. "Sparkbolt—*bad*. *Sparkbolt false!*"

"We gotta find him, man," said Max. "Let him know we believe him."

"It too late," said Sparkbolt. "Falcon vanish. Join Filchers. Him Squonk friend. Gone. Forever!"

"You can't think that way," said Max. "You gotta believe in good—stuff!"

"Stuff bad," said Sparkbolt, sitting down at his desk. "Sasquatch leave."

"It's okay, man," said Max. "I don't have to—"

"Sasquatch LEAVE!" shouted Sparkbolt. "Monster write *dark* poem now."

"Okay, man. Well, this isn't over. I'm going to talk to Pearl and everybody about it. We'll come up with something—"

"Up with nothing," said Sparkbolt. "You go. Down! Down with things."

"Boy, somebody ate a bunch a grouchy pills," muttered Max as he headed out into the hall. Sparkbolt listened to the Sasquatch's footsteps as they receded. Then he dipped his quill into the inkwell.

The feather tip of Sparkbolt's quill brushed against his nose, but the Frankenstein did not notice. He dipped his quill into the inkwell again and wrote line after line filled with words for which there were no rhymes.

Then Sparkbolt put his quill down on the page. "Down—bad," he said as if having a sudden insight. "Up—good."

He stood up and went out into the hall. "Sasquatch?" he called. "Sasquatch come *back*." He began to lurch down the hallway, his arms trembling before him.

Out on the main quad in front of Castle Gruesombe, young monsters were playing croquet as Mrs. Redflint sat on a high chair judging the match. Pearl, Ankh-hoptet, and Copperhead watched as Squawker lined up his shot. The werechicken's head bobbed back and forth as he concentrated. He shouted *"Brawwk"* as he swung his mallet through the air. His yellow ball moved an inch or two. The others sighed quietly.

"Croquet is not among the werechicken's talents,"

muttered Weems, who sat in a lawn chair observing the game and drinking iced tea. To his left, in other chairs, were Twisty, Destynee, Lincoln Pugh, and the heavy metal elves, Serj and Ozzie. On the ground near the elves was the bubbling pool of glup named Quagmire.

"Squawker," said Serj, laughing. "You're a total drumstick!"

"Hey, Squawker," said Ozzie. "Are you original recipe or extra crispy?"

"There will be no demeaning of the students," said Mrs. Redflint. "That is my responsibility. Miss Ankh-hoptet. You're up."

Ankh-hoptet's ball was just shy of the center wicket, and Squawker's ball was placed in a vulnerable position on the far side.

"I *hate* Monster Croquet," said Copperhead. Her voice was muffled by the burlap bag on her head and the hissing of her snakes.

"Silence!" said Pearl. "The mummy prepares to strike!"

Ankh-hoptet's mallet head made contact with the ball, making a satisfying whacking sound. The ball began to glow and then rolled forward slowly, curving through the wicket and knocking into Squawker's ball.

"Cluck cluck cluck *cluck*!" said Squawker.

"And now," said Ankh-hoptet, placing her bandaged foot upon the werechicken's black ball. "I shall send thee away!"

"*BRRAWWK!*" shouted Squawker with even more anger. His face turned darker and darker—first red, then purple. All at once, an egg plopped out of his pants leg and rolled onto the ground.

"Hey," said Ozzie. "Squawker laid an egg!"

"But—," said Pearl. "This is astounding! It is not biologically possible!"

"Eeeew," said Destynee. "That's disgusting."

"*Brawwk!*" said Squawker. "Giant enchanted slug! *More* disgusting!"

"At least I didn't lay an egg in my pants," said Destynee.

"Our mollusk friend has made a reasonable point, I believe!" said Pearl. "For indeed—during the time I have known her, never—never!—has she filled her own pants with the eggs of poultry!"

"Children, *please*," said Mrs. Redflint in a tired voice.

"Mrs. Redflint," called Max as he and Sparkbolt came running across the croquet field. "Mrs. Redflint!" In his hand, Max was waving a piece of paper. Sparkbolt was growling and snarling. "We found this! In Sparkbolt's room! You gotta read this! You gotta!"

"*¡Señor!*" said Pearl reprovingly. "We are attempting to concentrate on the game before us!"

"Rrrrrr!" shouted Sparkbolt. "Falcon Quinn true! Sparkbolt false!"

"Gentlemen, please," said Mrs. Redflint. "These histrionics are uncalled for."

"These histrionics are *totally* called for!" shouted Max, his voice breaking. "Because I hurt my best friend's feelings! I hurt him totally *bad*! *Honk!*"

Sparkbolt joined in as Max wept. "Rrrrrr!" he shouted. The two of them stood there wailing.

Squawker picked up the egg he had laid. "Cluck cluck cluck *cluck*!" he said, astonished.

"Let me see this," said Mrs. Redflint, looking at the piece of paper. "Good heavens, it's in a semi-cursed elvish script. Who taught you boys to write in accursive?"

"Us not write!" explained Sparkbolt. "Filchers write— to Falcon Quinn, friend! Falcon tell truth—about Squonk! Him innocent!"

"He wasn't innocent!" said Ozzie. "He tried to fry the Chupakabra! With his eye thing. Remember?"

"He did," said Copperhead. Her snakes hissed softly beneath her burlap bag. "No one should forget that! He did not belong!"

"Yeah," said Serj. "He was a traitor! The Chupakabra almost kicked the bucket, thanks to him!"

"I have said before that I felt this was a mistake," said Pearl. "I do not see why others cannot forgive Señor Quinn if I—his alleged victim!—have already done so myself!"

"Falcon Quinn," said Squawker. "Cluck cluck cluck *cluck*!"

On the ground before the spectators, Quagmire began to bubble.

Ankh-hoptet swung her mallet against the ball trapped beneath her own bandaged foot, and Squawker's black ball was instantly airborne. The mummy must have roqueted the ball harder than she intended, however, for the were-chicken's ball traveled over their heads, sailed across the croquet field, and smashed through a stained-glass window in Castle Gruesombe.

"Uh-oh," said Max.

"*Brawk buck buck!*" shouted Squawker. "Not fair! Not fair! *Bwuuuk!*" In a fit of rage he threw his egg at Ankh-hoptet. It cracked against the mummy's face. Yolk dripped down onto her bandages.

"Thou . . . thou hast *yolked* the blessed wrappings!" said Ankh-hoptet, astonished.

Lincoln Pugh roared angrily at Squawker.

Squawker, meanwhile, was staring at the castle, where Count Manson was now looking out the broken window with a furious expression. "Vhat wulgar willain!" he shouted. "Vhat wulgar willain has vrecked my vestern vindow?"

Max shook his head. "Uh-oh," he said.

Squawker stepped toward Ankh-hoptet and pecked her. Lincoln Pugh roared and picked Squawker up and threw him through the air. The mummy and the chicken both fell backward, arms windmilling, and they collided into Copperhead, who was standing just behind them. Ankh-hoptet, Squawker, and Copperhead all rolled onto the ground in a heap, and as they rolled, the burlap bag that had covered Copperhead's face fell off.

Copperhead looked around for her bag, but Ankh-hoptet was sitting on it. The others looked in astonishment at the girl with the pale skin and shocking blue eyes.

"*Rawk,*" said Squawker. "Not a Gorgon! Not a Gorgon!"

Mrs. Redflint rushed forward to look at the unmasked girl. "Good heavens! Who *are* you? What are you doing here?"

"I'm *laughing* at you," said Creeper. "That's what I'm doing! I'm laughing at *all* of you!"

"I see no reason for laughter," said Mrs. Redflint. Smoke began to curl out of her nostrils.

"Oh, but if only you hated you as much as I do," said Creeper, "then you would find everything amusing, *everything*! It is my greatest source of joy—my hatred for *you*!"

Shortly thereafter, Creeper was brought before the members of the faculty of the Academy for Monsters, wearing heavy chains and a self-satisfied smile. Her eyes glowed guardian blue.

"Right beneath our noses, all this time," said Willow. "It's unbelievable!"

"Ve must admit," said Count Manson. "Ve have been drifting. Living in a vorld of dreams!"

"I like dreams," said Mr. Hake. "I dream about sausages!"

"I would like to suggest that the young monsters who apprehended her receive a commendation," said Mrs. Redflint. "They were very brave!"

"Vere there any wampires among this wirtuous party?" said Count Manson.

"No, Count," said Mrs. Redflint. "Just the croquet team. The vampires were all playing polo."

"Then I do not think that medals are called for!" said Count Manson.

Creeper shook her head and laughed.

"What's so funny?" said Mr. Hake. "I like jokes!"

"You are," said Creeper. "I hate you so much, you *all* make me laugh!"

"Shaddap," said Mr. Shale.

"What do you mean, '*drifting*,' Count?" said Willow Wordswaste-Phinney. "You said we've been drifting. I think we've been doing well enough!"

"Yes, vell, you vould," said Count Manson. "I am sure that all the fans of *wiolins and vater lilies* have been *overjoyed* at the state the school has been in. But vhile ve drifted, under the direction of this heartsick *willain*, the school has become overrun with these—" The count shuddered. "*Special needs* students. The—Chupakabras. And the Sasquatches. And the—others."

"Those are some of our best students," said Willow. "The heart of the student body!"

"I suppose that depends on how you define *best*," said Count Manson thoughtfully. "I for vun vould like to think of us as continuing a noble tradition of scholars! From vun generation to the next. Rather than as some sort of—vorkhouse! Vhere ve take upon ourselves the vurms and wermin of the vorld."

"Oh, *shaddap*," said Mr. Shale. "Whenever I have a vampire as a student, you know what I think? I think, *so what*!"

Mr. Largo's enormous ears began to vibrate. "What is that?" said the music teacher. "What is that sound?"

The other teachers looked at him, confused. "I don't hear anything," said Mr. Hake. "Except the sound of happy!"

"The sea," said Mr. Largo. "There is the sound of waves and seagulls in this room."

There was a pause as they all listened. But there was nothing to hear.

"Charming," said Count Manson. "Now ve have a member of the faculty who hallucinates the sound of ocean vaves!"

Mr. Largo looked around the room, his large ears

pulsing. Then his gaze fell upon Creeper. "Why—it's coming from *you*," he said. He stood up and went over to the girl.

The music teacher reached into Creeper's pocket and pulled out a conch shell.

"A sea stone!" Mrs. Redflint shouted. "Of course. How else could she have been communicating with the guardian command?"

"I thought I put it on vibrate," muttered Creeper.

"Go on," said the moth man. "It answers."

"I'm not going to—"

"Oh, I do think the moth man is right in this," said Mrs. Redflint. She blasted a huge cloud of fire at the guardian girl. Creeper screamed. "You really should answer the call and let us share your conversation. Oh— and do refrain from letting them know we are listening, won't you? Unless you wish to be toasted like a marshmallow? That's a good girl."

Creeper held her conch shell to her ear. "I hate you," she said.

"As you have made clear," said Mrs. Redflint. "Now answer the call. And do be a dear and put it on speakershell."

Creeper glowered, but she held the conch shell to her ear. "Hello?" she said.

"Creeper," said Cygnus's voice, echoing into the room

through the shell, along with the sound of waves and wind. "We've had—an incident."

"An incident," said Creeper, gritting her teeth.

"Yes. The Quinn boy has escaped. He and that Jonny Frankenstein have managed to free the wind elemental. They're making for Monster Island. We're sending a party after them, so they won't get far. Has there been any sign of the Crow there? Has the demon returned to his tower?"

Creeper did not reply at first. Mrs. Redflint blew a glowing red smoke ring at her. "No," she said. "There has been no sign of the headmaster."

The sound of crashing waves and howling wind filled the room for a moment.

"Ah—," said Cygnus. "You're breaking up a little. Can you say that again?"

"I said there's no sign of the Crow. He left weeks ago."

"Are you all right?" said Cygnus. "Your voice sounds—*curious*."

"It's just the connection," said Creeper. "I'm down to one bar here."

There was a long pause. "The war has begun," said Cygnus. "We will recapture Falcon Quinn. And destroy Monster Island. And then take Shadow Island, and the Aca—"

The conch shell shuddered, and then there was the sound of waves and seagulls once more. Then it fell silent.

"Call dropped," said Creeper.

"Thank you, dear," said Mrs. Redflint. "Mr. Hake, I wonder if you might escort our guest to the dungeon now. Oh, and leave that sea stone. We might be able to turn it to our advantage."

"The dungeon?" said Creeper, laughing. "I'm not afraid of your stupid dungeon!"

"Ah," said Mrs. Redflint. "But you should be."

Mr. Hake wrapped his tentacles around her and dragged Creeper down the hallway.

Count Manson went to a corner cabinet and brought out a large map of the Sea of Dragons and the many islands of the Bermuda Triangle, and laid it out on the conference table.

"Ve vill sail out to meet them," said Count Manson.

"And do what?" said Willow. "Start a war?"

"The var has already begun, Villow," said the count. "Ve vill defend ourselves. Let the enemy know the time of drift is at an end." He turned to the dragon lady. "Mrs. Redflint, can you summon the pirates? Ve vill need transport back to Monster Island!"

"The pirates?" said Mrs. Redflint. "Hm. Count, I am slightly concerned that we may find ourselves on the pirates' bad side after Mr. Lyons devoured their captain. And I *do* hate to be on the bad side of a pirate!"

"The librarian," said Count Manson. "Yes. Perhaps

they'll be persuaded if ve promise them a reward. Vhat is the term? *Booty?* I trust ve still have gold in the treasury. Mr. Pupae?"

"It has gold," said the moth man.

"Good, vell, let us promise them gold, in great measure! And also—let us deliver the librarian unto them. They can make him valk the plank."

"Wait—we're going to just *give* them Mr. Lyons?" said Willow. "Hand them one of our own?"

"He is not vun of *my* own," said the count.

"It makes sacrifices," said the moth man.

"But—Mr. Lyons—," said Willow. "To just hand him over to them?"

"Yes. Vell. He might have considered these consequences before dewouring their captain," said the count.

"He was only trying to defend our students," said Willow. "Isn't that what we are all pledged to do?"

"Ve vill defend our students," said Count Manson. "By having them join their instructors in this battle." He smiled. "Indeed! Let us have these *creatures* vith us—the vuns who unmasked the traitor. These—croquet players." Count Manson laughed softly.

"Those are almost all first-year students," said Willow. "They haven't been trained to fight guardians!"

"But you vere all so wery eager to defend their right to be students at our Academy!" said the count. "Let them show their vorth, if they are so walorous!"

"You're cruel," said Willow.

"Miss Vordsvaste," said Count Manson. "The *vurld* is cruel."

"Mrs. Redflint," said Willow. "Do you agree with this? To just sending the first-year students off on a suicide mission?"

"Well, I do think you are all wrong if you underestimate the strength of that group," said Mrs. Redflint. "They have a remarkable sense of pluck."

"Pluck," said Mr. Largo. "They'll need more than pluck to survive a battle with the guardian command."

"Mr. Largo," said Mrs. Redflint. "You may be wrong. It is possible that, in this situation, pluck will make all the difference."

"At last it begins," said Count Manson. "Ve go to var! VAR!"

Mr. Shale shook his head. "*Shaddap,*" he said.

19

HOWEVER IMPROBABLE

The coffin ship sailed slowly to the east. Falcon stood at the bow of the *Destynee II* looking into the rising sun. Over his head, the main sail luffed. The bow of the ship moved slowly through the waves. On the horizon before them was Monster Island. Falcon could see the silhouette of the buildings on Hematoma Boulevard, the towering flume ride of Plasma Falls, the burned-out remnants of the Bludd Club. Summer seemed like a long time ago.

He had flown to the *Destynee II*, still at anchor in the harbor by the queen's beach, with both Jonny and Megan in his arms. There were angry, shouting voices in the streets of the Hidden City as he passed over the spires of Paragon Castle. Guardian warriors shot at him with arrows and spears but missed. Below him he saw the streets of the city, the Temple of Honor, and Guardian Junior High. He felt a strange pang.

Young voices called out to him. He looked down, and there were Sam, and Snick, and Celeste, and Chandler. They were looking at him, holding their weapons in their hands.

Gyra stood a little apart from the others. The wind blew her blond hair over her shoulders. "Falcon," she called.

He expected his guardian friends to attack, but they just watched as he flew over their heads and out above the forest that surrounded the Hidden City. A moment later he crossed over the queen's beach and landed on the *Destynee II*. It took a few minutes to melt Jonny Frankenstein, but once the boy was defrosted, he grabbed the tiller of the coffin ship and off they went. Now they were out on the Sea of Dragons again, sailing to the east. Megan lay on the deck, her eyes closed.

"Falcon," said Jonny. "She's fading. You're sure you don't want to try your healing eye on her?"

"I told you," Falcon snapped. "Weren't you listening? The last time I used it, I killed one of my best friends."

"I thought you said that guardian girl—Creeper—had put something in your eye that turned it poison. It has to have worn off by now, Falcon. Don't you think?"

"I said I don't want to use it!" shouted Falcon. "If I hurt Megan too, I'd—"

Megan flickered. Then she slowly faded back in, although she was dimmer than she'd been before.

"She's not going to last," said Jonny. "We have to get her some help."

"Yeah," said Falcon. "Where do you suggest? Back to Guardian Island? Where they kept her in a windmill's blades for the last six months? Or maybe on Shadow Island, where all my friends think I killed Pearl, where they came after me with torches and pitchforks?"

"Hey, don't yell at me, Falcon," said Jonny. "I'm just saying. She needs help."

"Jonny—," moaned Megan. "Thank you—for saving me."

"Hey," said Jonny. "Falcon was the one who saved you."

"Falcon," said Megan, her eyes opening.

"I'm here," said Falcon.

"Heal me," said Megan. "Please?" She blinked out, then came back a moment later. She was becoming something indistinct and blurry.

"I can't," said Falcon. "I don't trust my eye."

"Falcon," said Megan with a voice like a wind through a graveyard. "Heal me. . . ."

Falcon looked at Jonny, then back at Megan. He searched for Megan's hand, which was not easy since she kept blowing all around. Then he found what felt like fingers, and he held them fast, and concentrated. A blue light began to shine from his right eye, and it fell upon her. Megan disappeared entirely again and then slowly began to take form. She looked at Falcon, seeming to see him clearly for the first time. "Falcon—," she said. "You *are* here."

Falcon continued to focus his healing light upon her.

"Yeah," he said. "We're all together. You're safe."

"I dreamed I was spinning," she said. "I dreamed I was—"

Then, just like that, Megan blinked out entirely. There was a forceful breeze against his face, and against Jonny's, and then the gust was gone.

Jonny and Falcon looked at each other for a long moment. "Megan?" said Falcon.

They looked around the deck. "Megan?" said Jonny.

"I knew it," said Falcon. "I knew it!" He glanced angrily at Jonny. "Now she's gone! I never should have let you talk me into it!"

Falcon raised his hands over his head, preparing to yell at the top of his lungs. But then something about the mainsail caught his attention. It was bursting with wind.

"Falcon," said Jonny. "I think she's all right. Look at the sail."

"Megan?" said Falcon. Seagulls circled around the mast.

"You see," said Jonny. "You *did* heal her."

"Heal her," said Falcon. "She's invisible, Jonny! How can she be healed when she's invisible?"

"She is what she's supposed to be," said Jonny. "She's the wind."

"Great," said Falcon. "So healing her means—we never see her again?"

Jonny shrugged. "She is what she is," he said.

"Yeah?" said Falcon. "And what are we?"

"You?" said Jonny. "You're an angel. And I'm a piece of junk."

Falcon shook his head. "I think I must be the lousiest angel there ever was."

"Yeah, well," said Jonny, his eyes flashing. "I'm a pretty excellent piece of junk."

Falcon was just about to reply to this when he spotted something on the horizon. There behind them was a guardian warship, belching black smoke.

"Falcon," said Jonny. "We've got company."

Falcon was just about to tell Jonny that he was already aware of the approaching guardians, but Jonny was looking the other way, to the horizon ahead of them. Falcon was fairly certain of what he would see as he turned to look. There on the northern coast of Monster Island, approaching from the opposite direction, was the pirate ship *Cutthroat*. It was flying the Jolly Roger.

"Guardians behind us," Jonny said. "Monsters ahead of us."

Falcon saw the flash of a cannon on the deck of the guardian warship. It was drawing closer now. They heard a whistling over their heads. A moment later, a *boom* came over the water. A large explosion rocked the waves beside the pirate ship.

"Okay," said Jonny. "This is bad."

"You think?" said Falcon.

"No way we're going to be able to find the Filchers now. Fighting like this is what they hate most."

Another volley from the guardians soared over their heads and crashed into the water near the *Cutthroat*. They could hear the sound of zombies' and vampires' voices on the wind now, shouting in anger, calling out for revenge.

Falcon looked from one ship to the other, then back at the silhouette of the abandoned rides on Monster Island. For some reason he thought of Mr. Lyons. What had happened to that copy of Sherlock Holmes the librarian had given him? He pictured the volume sitting by his old bed in Dustbin Hall, unopened and unread.

"Okay," Falcon said. "We can't join the monsters. We can't join the guardians. We won't be able to find the Filchers."

"Sounds like we're outta choices," said Jonny.

The memory of Mr. Lyons, however, had not left Falcon's heart. Now he remembered running into the librarian on the beach back at the Academy, that day he'd tried to stop Max and Pearl from fighting and had failed. What was that line Mr. Lyons had quoted to him from Sherlock Holmes? *When you have eliminated the impossible, whatever remains,* however improbable, *must be the truth. "It is a good phrase to bear in mind,"* Mr. Lyons had said, *"if what you intend to do is solve mysteries.*"

"Falcon," said Jonny as more artillery fire burst over their heads. "We're trapped."

Falcon looked at Jonny, still lost in thought. Then he spread his wings.

"Okay," he said. "I just thought of something."

20

THE SINKING OF THE CUTTHROAT

A fireball sailed through the air and crashed into the topsails of the *Cutthroat*, setting the studsail boom and futtock shrouds aflame.

"Ve are sinking!" said Count Manson, enraged. "*Sinking!*"

"Aye," said Captain Deadbeard. "That we are. Down to the bottom. To Peter Tork's locker!"

"It vas my understanding," said Count Manson, "that you could outvit these guardian wessels! But perhaps—I vas misinformed?"

"Captain Deadbeard," said Mrs. Redflint, coming over to the place where the captain, his first mate, and the count now stood. "We must abandon ship!"

"Mrs. Redflint," said Count Manson. "You panic so easily!"

A fireball landed near the aft of the ship, igniting the decking quite near to the place where a large wooden cage was placed. There in the cage was Mr. Lyons, who was watching the progress of the battle with an expression of strange calm.

"It's no good, Count," said Mrs. Redflint. "We should get the students to shore and continue the battle there. It looks to me as if our adversaries are already doing just this."

"Vhat?" said Count Manson.

"They are seizing the harbor and the high ground. In order to hold Monster Island against us, should our ship founder and we seek shelter there!"

Students were now pouring out of the hatch that led from the lower decks. The vampires came first, wearing expressions of outrage and disdain. Other monsters, wearing life jackets, came out the hatch after them—Destynee and Weems, Lincoln Pugh and Ankh-hoptet, Max and Pearl, and many more.

"Count Manson, I'm wet!" whined Merideath.

"Indeed, old man," said Reeves Pennypacker Waldow-Sherrod Binswanger III. "Highly unusual procedures, aren't they?!"

"All the fires are making me hot!" said Muffy. "I'm sweating! I hate sweating!"

"Dude," said Max.

"Now is not the time for announcing our discomfort!" shouted Pearl. "Now is the time for battle!"

"Captain Deadbeard," said Mrs. Redflint. "We are awaiting your orders."

The captain held his spyglass to his eye and looked out

upon the raging sea battle. The guardian warship appeared to be just as damaged as the monsters', and it was steaming in its damaged state toward Monster Island in order to seize control of the harbor. As Captain Deadbeard watched, a fierce volley of hurtling fire slammed against the *Cutthroat*'s starboard side, ripping open holes in the hull and feeding the growing conflagration. Pirates and monsters alike were hurled toward the sea as the *Cutthroat* began to founder.

Captain Deadbeard grabbed on to one of the ratlines on the mainmast's shroud to keep from falling overboard. *"Argh,"* he sighed. "'Tis as I feared." He turned to his first mate. "Give the order, Mr. Snarg. Abandon ship. Deploy the lifeboats. Men and grown-ups first!"

"Abandon ship!" shouted Snarg. *"Yargh yargh targh!"*

"Abandon ship?" said Reeves Pennypacker Waldow-Sherrod Binswanger III. "Is that really necessary, old chap?"

But with this, a cresting wave washed over the ship and hauled Reeves Pennypacker Waldow-Sherrod Binswanger III into the sea.

"Reevey!" shouted Muffy.

"My father's going to hear about this!" shouted Merideath. "You can be certain of that!"

"There will be nothing for him to hear," said Mrs. Redflint. "If first you should perish."

Merideath thought it over. "Into the lifeboats!" she shouted. "I get to go first!"

The pirate crew moved the monsters, both students and teachers, toward the lifeboats. The first boat contained Dr. Cortex, Count Manson, and Mr. Largo, as well as the male vampire students. Merideath was about to climb aboard when Snarg said, "Men and grown-ups first! Men and grown-ups first!"

Mrs. Redflint, standing at his side, however, suddenly engulfed the first mate in flames. "Ow!" he shouted.

"I'm sure you'll agree to reconsider this policy," she said.

"*Argh,*" said Snarg.

Merideath and the Crofton sisters climbed aboard, along with Mortia and Bonesy, Crackthunder and Stinkfinger, Snort and Picador and Twisty. Two pirate crewmen cut the lines with their sabers, and the lifeboat fell into the sea.

"Okay," said Max. "My turn!"

Lincoln Pugh, in giant bear form, held the hand of Ankh-hoptet and growled. A cyborg named Robotron Three Thousand waved his arms around, his bubble-dome blinking on and off.

"Rrrr," growled Sparkbolt.

"You students are next," said Mrs. Redflint, pointing to the next lifeboat. "Make for the shore of Monster

Island. Mr. Hake will meet you there. After you make landfall, you should prepare yourselves for battle. Use all that you have learned."

"Battle?" said Max nervously.

"I shall prepare the poison of deadliness!" shouted Pearl. "I shall use it upon any who would dare to assault those to whom I am sworn."

They climbed into the next lifeboat, along with Owen Fitzhugh, the abominable snowman; Elaine Screamish, the banshee; and Quagmire, the bubbling puddle of glup.

"Honk," said Max.

"Mr. Parsons," said Mrs. Redflint. "Whatever is the matter?"

Max looked ashamed. "I'm afraid," he said.

"Dear boy," said Mrs. Redflint. "Do you think that courage means never being afraid? If so, you are mistaken. No, courage is just the ability to be gruesome under pressure. I do believe you can be gruesome, Mr. Parsons. Can you not?"

Max nodded. "I can be gruesome," he said.

"So can we all!" said Pearl, buzzing in the air above the Sasquatch's shoulder.

"Good luck," said Mrs. Redflint, her eyes shining. Then she blasted the ropes with her fiery breath, severing them. The lifeboat plunged into the waves.

Back on the *Cutthroat*'s main deck, Destynee was

hopping from one foot to another. "Mrs. Redflint," she said. "The salt water . . . I'm dissolving!" The dragon lady looked down at Destynee's feet, where the cold ocean water was indeed beginning to melt the feet of the young enchanted slug.

"Dear, dear," said Mrs. Redflint. "Let's get you into a lifeboat, spit spot." She turned to Snarg. "Can you see that she's taken care of, please?" Another wave crashed over the side, splattering part of Destynee's face. It began to dissolve where the salt water touched her.

"Destynee," said Weems, his eyes aglow. "You look so—so—scrumptious!"

"Shut up!" said Destynee.

"Into the lifeboat with ye," said Snarg, ushering Destynee and Weems into a boat that also contained Mr. Shale, Ozzie and Serj, Ankh-hoptet, and Robotron Three Thousand. The cyborg's lights were blinking on and off in the face of the crashing waves. "Danger!" he noted, waving his reticulated arms around. "Danger!"

"Therma," shouted Mr. Shale to Mrs. Redflint. "Get in the boat already."

"Yes, yes," she said. But she was looking toward the bow at Mr. Lyons. "Captain. I do hope you'll allow me to set free the librarian? I'm sure you don't want him to drown in his cage?"

"He is our *prisoner*," said the captain. "He will go

down with the ship, to avenge his murder of Captain Hardtack."

"Sir," said Mrs. Redflint. "You cannot just let him die!"

"These were the *terms*," said the captain.

Mrs. Redflint took one last look at Mr. Lyons, then turned angrily toward the captain. "You're a savage," she said.

"Aye," said the captain with a cruel smile.

"What's happening?" said Destynee to Mrs. Redflint as she came back to the lifeboat. The main deck was now full of water. The *Cutthroat* would not last much longer. Flames consumed the masts and sails, and pieces of the ruined ship rained down all around them.

"I'm sorry, Miss Bloodflough," said Mrs. Redflint. "We cannot help Mr. Lyons any longer."

"But we can't just let him die!" said Destynee, tears gathering in her eyes. The salt water from the tears began to hiss and sizzle against her slug skin.

"It is out of our hands," said Mrs. Redflint. "We made a promise. A most terrible promise."

"We have to help him!" shouted Destynee. She jumped out of the lifeboat and sloshed in the direction of the foredeck toward Mr. Lyons's cage. As she did, steam rose from her rapidly dissolving feet.

"Miss Bloodflough," said the librarian as Destynee drew near. "You must board the lifeboat now. We are sinking." He was waist deep in water now.

"We have to set you free!" said Destynee, pulling on the bars of his cage. The giant slug was now half dissolved, an unpleasant amalgam of skin and slime, but she didn't seem to care. "We can't just let you die!"

"Destynee," said Weems, catching up with her. "Please! You're melting."

"Miss Bloodflough," said Mr. Lyons gently. "You are very kind to worry about me. But I assure you I will be fine." He smiled, and his deep brown eyes shone. In one hand he held a leather-bound book.

"How can you possibly be *fine?*" shouted Destynee.

"Destynee," said Weems. "It's now or never. We're going down. Plus you're melting. Melting! *Melting!*"

"But—"

"Oh, don't worry about me," said Mr. Lyons, holding up his book. "*Oliver Twist.* Remember, you are really never in danger as long as you have a very good book."

"You're going to drown!" shouted Destynee. "Don't you understand?"

"Miss Bloodflough," said Mr. Lyons. He reached through the bars of his cage and squeezed her arm. The librarian closed his eyes for a moment, and then he released her. Destynee looked down to see that the half of her body that had dissolved in the salt water was now restored. A soft blue mist rose from her body.

"What did you do?" said Destynee. "I'm not dissolving anymore!"

"Will you give Falcon Quinn a message for me? I believe you will see him very soon."

"A message?" said Destynee.

Weems shook his head. "Always Falcon Quinn."

A wave crashed across the sinking deck, lifting them all off their feet for a moment.

"We have to go now," said Weems. "Please, Destynee."

"What message?" said Destynee to Mr. Lyons. "Tell me!"

"Tell him that I will be waiting for him." He purred softly.

"But how will you possibly meet Falcon?" said Destynee. "If you're—"

"My dear, sweet child," said Mr. Lyons with a soft smile. "No cage can hold me."

21
THE MUSIC OF THE SQUONK

"Careful now," said the colonel, as he led the party of fledglings down Hematoma Boulevard. "Our prey is cunning, don't you know? Highly deceptive!"

"Dude," said Sam. "I don't see any prey."

"Exactly," said the colonel. "Naked to the invisible eye, as it were!"

"I've got nothing on the DCS," said Gyra, checking a small, handheld electronic device.

"DCS?" said the colonel. "I say, I'm not familiar with this weapon! Quite irregular!"

"The Disgusting Creatures System," said Gyra. "It finds monsters, using satellites."

"By George," said the colonel. "That is clever! Bully!"

"My mommy says the Earth is going to be destroyed by asteroids," said Chandler. "Afterward, all the good people will float through space eating hot dogs!"

"If I hear one more word about your mommy," said Snick, "I'm going to—"

The DCS in Gyra's hand began to beep.

"Colonel," she said. "The monsters have fled the *Cutthroat* and are coming ashore."

"Bully!" said the colonel. "All right, then, take cover. Wait until I give the signal, and then we'll bear down upon them with all our fury!"

"I'm going to use my sword," said Chandler.

"You stay in back," said Snick. "Let the real soldiers here do the actual killing."

The DCS began to beep with more urgency.

"Dude," said Sam. "Doesn't that thing have a mute on it? It's going to give us away. And then they'll, like— capture us. And suck our blood and junk!"

"Nobody's sucking my blood," said Gyra, but she turned off the DCS's sound.

The six of them took up hiding places on either side of Hematoma Boulevard—Gyra and Sam by the Five Cent Kandy Korner, Chandler and Celeste and Snick by the Olde Tyme Nickelodeon Theatre, and the colonel himself at the House of Wacks. The colonel raised his gun and pointed it down the long, deserted street.

Time seemed to freeze as they waited for their adversaries to appear. For a long time the street was silent. Then they heard footsteps. The steps grew louder as their enemies approached. Snick tightened his hand upon his sword. Gyra looked at the DCS; a blinking red dot on its map was moving directly toward them.

Sam looked over Gyra's shoulder, observing the progress of the impending dot. His stomach growled.

"Steady," whispered the colonel, looking at the young guardians. "Steady!"

The dot on the DCS arrived at the exact center of the map. The device's screen began to blink red. All the guardians looked down the long street as the footsteps grew louder and louder.

"I say!" the colonel shouted suddenly, moving all at once to the center of the street. "Who goes there?! Stand and deliver! You're surrounded!"

"Surrounded?" said a voice.

"Bully!" said the colonel. "Show yourself!"

"Hi there!" shouted Peanut Trunkanelli, running toward them, trumpeting his tiny trunk. "My name's Peanut! You can be my new friend!"

The colonel's face turned ghastly pale as the tiny elephant boy came skipping toward them. "Augggh!" he shouted, dropping his gun in the street. *An elephant! Run for your lives! Aagggggguuugggghhh!"*

"Dude," said Sam.

The colonel turned and began to run as fast as his old legs would carry him, away from the elephant boy. But Peanut pursued the colonel. A moment later, they both disappeared around the far side of the Five Cent Kandy Korner.

Next a gargantuan werebear came snarling down the street. It let loose an ear-rattling roar, then bounded toward Chandler, who screamed and ran toward the Antigravity Bumper Cars. Lincoln Pugh—for, of course, the giant werebear was he—roared again and chased after Chandler.

"Hey, Celeste," said Sam, "what weapon works on a werebear? I think I was asleep when we covered werebears."

"A silver sword is most effective," said Celeste, looking at Chandler's weapon lying in the middle of the street. "In fact this very weapon would have been most useful to our friend had he not dropped it in his fear!"

All at once the lights blinked on in the Antigravity Bumper Cars. The cars started moving across the shiny floor, and an antique steam calliope began to play "Take Me Out to the Ball Game." Lincoln Pugh paused, confused by the sudden light and the noise, and as he stood still, Chandler jumped into one of the bumper cars and drove away in it. Being trapped in the ride, of course, he couldn't get very far, but due to the properties of the gravity-defying bumper cars, he was able to drive up first onto the walls and then onto the ceiling, just out of the werebear's reach. Lincoln Pugh reached over his head with his sharp claws, roaring in anger and frustration.

Now other rides on Hematoma Boulevard were springing to life, lights and music coming on all around them. "Dude," said Sam. "Who's flicking on the power? Everything's all alive and—glowy!"

"I don't know," said Gyra, looking around in confusion.

Lincoln Pugh, still pursuing Chandler, climbed into one of the antigravity cars and drove it across the slick floor, up the wall, and onto the ceiling. The werebear slammed into Chandler's bumper with full force, knocking both of them backward. Lincoln Pugh roared in bloodthirsty anger.

"Let us engage this night bear!" cried Celeste. "We shall make him regret that he has raised his hands against our comrade and our friend!"

"Let's go," said Gyra, and ran toward the bumper cars.

"Not so fast!" shouted a voice, and now a small, lone figure flew out of the shadows and cut off Celeste's advance. "Who would harm a hair on the back of this most noble of werebears must first defeat—¡la Chupakabra! The famous goatsucker of Peru!"

Celeste smiled with contempt. "I have heard of you, goatsucker! You are no match for myself—Chenobia de Celestina! The famous monster slayer of Paragon Mountain!"

"En garde," said Pearl, grabbing her stinger and holding it forth like a rapier.

"En garde." Celeste nodded, and her own blade whooshed out of its sheath. The two weapons clanged as the duel commenced. The stinger and the sword clashed above Pearl's and Celeste's heads, and then they clashed low. Pearl's stinger swooshed through the air, and Celeste jumped high as the Chupakabra's weapon passed beneath her. Then Celeste stabbed forward toward Pearl's heart, but Pearl flew around Celeste's back, making the guardian pirouette like a ballet dancer on one toe. Celeste placed one hand on her hip and crashed her sword against Pearl's stinger with astonishing speed.

"You are . . . a magnificent fighter!" said Celeste.

"I am!" said Pearl. "Indeed, my magnificence is a matter of some renown!"

Gyra stood on the shiny graphite floor of the bumper cars, looking up at Lincoln Pugh and Chandler, who were driving on the ceiling and crashing into each other's cars with enthusiasm.

"Rrrrr," growled a voice, and Gyra turned to see Sparkbolt staggering toward her with his hands outstretched.

"Well, well," said Gyra. "What's big and green and dead all over?"

"*Guardian* belong dead," said Sparkbolt.

"What-ever," said Gyra.

She cracked her whip. But Sparkbolt, with his tremendous strength, just snatched the whip like it was a piece of twine, yanking it from Gyra's grasp. He tossed it out into the street.

"Monster good," said Sparkbolt. "Guardian bad."

Gyra looked at the place out in the middle of Hematoma Boulevard where her weapon had fallen. "You know, there's something I don't quite understand about Frankensteins," said Gyra. "Why do you talk like that, 'monster good, guardian bad'?"

"It accent,' said Sparkbolt, staggering toward her.

"An accent?" said Gyra. "It doesn't sound like an accent. It sounds like you're stupid. Like you don't have any respect for your own language."

"*This* language," said Sparkbolt. "Monster love words. Write poems."

"Yeah? I write poems too," said Gyra.

"Guardian . . . write poem?"

"Yeah. Maybe I'll write one later about whacking you."

"Death first," said Sparkbolt. "Then poetry."

Gyra dove for her bullwhip. She was about to crack Sparkbolt with it when he grabbed her by the foot and whirled her through the air. He let go, and Gyra sailed across Hematoma Boulevard and crashed through the wall of the Hall of Boxing Robot Presidents.

"Guardian—destroy!" said Sparkbolt triumphantly. But no one was listening to him.

Max and Sam were sitting on a picnic table by Zombie Frank's Diner. "Okay," said Sam. "I guess it's our turn. You and me."

"Yeah," said Max. He shrugged. "Listen, I don't want

to tick you off or anything, but you should know . . . I'm not really into *battling.*"

"Seriously?" said Sam. "Oh, man, is that a relief. 'Cause I was totally afraid you were going to expect me to slay you and junk."

"Slay me? No way! Bananas would be good though. If you had any."

Sam thought this over. "I got some jerky," he said.

Max nodded. "Jerky's good," he said.

From the Hall of Boxing Robot Presidents, Gyra cried out in pain. Sparkbolt looked confused for a moment. "Guardian," he said. "Destroy?"

"Help," said Gyra.

"Help?" said Sparkbolt.

The Frankenstein stood in the street uncertainly. He held his hands in front of him, grasping the empty air. There was blood on his fingertips.

Sparkbolt looked at his hands and made a soft, sighing sound, a cry of what almost sounded like pain.

"Ah, ah, ah," Sparkbolt said, and looked at the hole in the wall. The blood dripped from his fingers. "Ah, ah, ah!"

Falcon and Jonny stood by a booth marked POWER. Falcon was flicking switches on a large circuit board. "That's all of them," said Falcon. "Is everything lit up?"

Jonny nodded. "The whole park's on," he said.

"Great," said Falcon, and snuck a peek at the battle on

Vein Street. "How are they doing?"

"I can tell you one thing," said Jonny. "Remember when you told me you'd killed Pearl with your eye? Looks like she's tougher than you thought."

"What do you mean?"

"She's right over there. Dueling Celeste."

"She's alive?" said Falcon, looking around the corner at the two girls, deep in their sword fight. A smile of relief stretched across his face. "She's alive, Jonny! She's alive!"

"Unless Celeste slays her."

Falcon looked unworried. "Nobody can out-fence a Chupakabra."

Jonny looked out at the street where the battles were raging. "You still sure this is the right plan?"

"No," said Falcon.

"It seems like a weird way to stop the fighting," said Jonny, "letting them try to kill each other."

"They won't kill each other," said Falcon.

"Yeah?" said Jonny. "Well, let's hope you're right about that."

"Falcon Quinn," said a voice behind them. "Cluck cluck cluck *cluck*!"

"Squawker," said Falcon, turning to look at the were-chicken, who had discovered the place beside the Five Cent Kandy Korner where he and Jonny had been hiding.

"Monster traitors," said Squawker. "*Rrawk!* Traitors!"

He walked up to Falcon Quinn and then pecked him.

"Ow!" shouted Falcon.

"*Bwwaaaak* Falcon Quinn!" said Squawker. "*Bwaaak* Jonny Frankenstein!" He pecked Falcon again. "Must destroy—traitors!" said Squawker. "Cluck cluck *cluck!*

"We're not traitors," said Falcon. "We're trying to stop the fighting."

"*Bwack!*" said Squawker. "Destroy Falcon Quinn! Destroy!"

Jonny sighed. His eyes rolled back in his head as he got a charge ready.

"Jonny, no," said Falcon. "Don't use the electricity on him. We're trying to stop the violence, not—"

But Squawker was suddenly consumed with flames. There was a bright flash, followed by the smell of roasting chicken. A second later, Squawker fell onto the floor, looking pretty much like a perfectly prepared Thanksgiving turkey. The last thing that happened was that a small plastic pop-up timer in the bird's side popped out. Squawker was done.

"That wasn't me," said Jonny.

"No," said Snick, stepping into the light of the Misery-Go-Round holding a flamethrower. "That was me, angel face."

"Snick," said Falcon. "You didn't have to do that."

"Actually," said Snick.

Snick held up his flamethrower, and the fire that flickered from its tip grew brighter and hotter. He was just about to blast Falcon with it when there was a sudden, forceful breeze. The guardian warrior had to take a step forward to keep from being blown over. His helmet blew off and rolled around on the ground. The flame at the tip of his weapon went out. A small plume of smoke blew off in the wind.

"Hey," said Snick. "What's going on?"

Megan materialized next to Falcon and Jonny. She looked at Snick with contempt. "I'm back," she said.

"Megan!" shouted Falcon.

"Come on," said Megan. "Let's blow them away."

Jonny raised his hands and shot Snick with his lightning bolts. The electricity shook the guardian from head to toe, and then he fell onto the ground, smoke rising from his clothes.

"Jonny," said Falcon. "I said no violence!"

"I know," said Jonny. "But your friend Snick here didn't get the memo. Anyway, I just stunned him. He'll recover."

"Megan," said Falcon. "Are you okay?"

"I'm okay," she said, and the two of them hugged for a moment. It was strange to hug someone who was partly invisible, Falcon thought, and who kept moving and blowing around in all directions. Nice, though.

Then they broke the hug and stood back awkwardly. Jonny Frankenstein looked at them with a knowing, amused glance. "We almost done here?" he said.

"Done?" said Falcon. "The fighting has hardly even started, Jonny."

"Fighting?" said Megan. "Is that what you call that?"

They followed her gaze. In the Antigravity Bumper Cars, Chandler and Lincoln Pugh were crashing into each other's cars. Lincoln Pugh had devolved back to his tiny human shape again. He was laughing. So was Chandler.

"Or that?" said Megan. She nodded toward Celeste and Pearl, who rushed by, weapons clanging, their voices raised in what sounded like pleasure. "Your defensive moves are extraordinary!" shouted Pearl.

"Or them?" said Megan. Now she nodded toward Max and Sam, who were watching Celeste and Pearl battle each other. Sam cast a glance at Max. "More jerky?" he said.

Celeste pushed Pearl back, and the Chupakabra was knocked to the ground. Celeste raised her sword over her head and then whipped it through the air to deal Pearl a mortal blow. But Pearl rolled out of the way, took wing again, and then stung Celeste on the wrist. Celeste cried out and loosened her grip on her blade, which fell from her hand and clanged onto the cobbles of Hematoma Boulevard.

Pearl landed on the hilt of the blade, and Celeste stood before her with a small welt rising on her arm.

"Dude," said Max. "You stung her!"

"I have not used the poison, however," said Pearl. "I have too much respect for her!"

"Wait," said Sam. "She's got poison?"

The Sasquatch nodded. "Oh, she's got poison, all right," he said.

"Poison me swiftly," said Celeste, bowing her head. "I do not fear death. Only dishonor!"

"You shall never know dishonor," said Pearl, bowing to her enemy. "You fight with a courage I find inspiring!" She handed the sword back to Celeste and bowed. "Who knows—perhaps in our next engagement it shall be you who spares my life?"

"I am taken by surprise," said Celeste. "Never did I expect to find an adversary with whom I shared such sympathy! We shall be friends! You and I! To you I pledge my sword, and my honor!"

"And I shall pledge my stinger to you, Chenobia de Celestina! You shall be the friend of ¡la Chupakabra! The famous goatsucker of Peru!"

"They're funny," said Lincoln Pugh and Chandler.

"Rrrr," said a voice, and they turned to see Sparkbolt emerging from the Hall of Boxing Robot Presidents. In his arms he held Gyra.

"The Frankenstein has taken our friend prisoner!" shouted Celeste. "Tell him to unhand her or he shall taste the sword of the monster destroyer of Paragon Mountain!"

"Dude," said Sam. "She's not his prisoner. He's trying to help her."

"Guardian hurt," said Sparkbolt, laying Gyra down in the street.

"I can heal her," said Falcon, and he and Jonny and the still-flickering Megan stepped forward.

"Dude!" shouted Max. "You're not dead! That is so excellent!" Max rushed forward and grabbed Falcon and threw him in the air, then caught him.

"Hey, Max," said Falcon.

"And Megan!" Max now grabbed Megan, but she dissolved like vapor as he wrapped his arms around her. "Whups."

"I'm here," said Megan, re-forming. "It's good to see you, Max. And Pearl!"

"So," said Max a little more cautiously, "is Jonny Frankenstein, like, on our side again?"

"I've always been on your side, Max," said Jonny.

"This comes as news to me, Señor Jonny!" shouted Pearl. "You have betrayed us too many times for me to—"

"Pearl, hush," said Megan. "Heal her, Falcon."

"He can do that?" said Chandler.

"Whoa," said Max and Sam, glancing back and forth from Gyra to Megan. "They're like—twins or something?"

"I for one," said Pearl and Celeste in unison, "fail to see this resemblance!"

"Falcon Quinn—," said Sparkbolt, going over to him.

"Monster betray friend. Should have trusted. Should have faith." He held out his hands, red with blood. "Now monster . . . belong *dead*."

"It's all right," said Falcon. "Sparkbolt friend."

Sparkbolt's face lit up, and he held his hands before him, clasping the air. "Friend? Still? Ah! Ah! Ah!" he said.

"Falcon," said Megan, fading. She nodded toward Gyra. "She's fading."

Falcon drew close to Gyra and shone his blue light on her. Gyra's eyes fluttered closed, then she opened them again.

"Ah! Ah! Ah!" said Sparkbolt.

Gyra raised one hand to her forehead, then looked around at the crowd of monsters and guardians all standing together. "Looks like I missed something," she said.

"Roses red," said Sparkbolt softly. "Violets blue. Guardian—not dead."

Gyra looked at Sparkbolt. "Nice one," she said.

"Okay, listen," said Max. "Sorry to ask, but does this mean we're not trying to kill each other anymore?"

Megan nodded toward Sam. "You're not trying to kill *him*, are you?"

Max smiled. "Are you kidding? I'm going to work in his *diner*!"

The monsters and guardians looked at one another

cautiously. Slowly, nervously, smiles crept across their faces.

Megan picked up Gyra's bullwhip and handed it to her. "Is this yours?"

Gyra took her weapon. "You were right, Falcon," she said. "I'm sorry I didn't listen to you."

"It's okay," said Falcon. "You were just trying to be loyal to your friends."

Celeste looked regretful. "I am glad to have had my eyes opened to the dignity of these creatures. But I am afraid that we may find ourselves in a difficult position when our comrades arrive."

"Yeah," said Max. "I think Count Manson does kinda have his heart set on wiping everybody out."

"Cygnus leans that way too," said Gyra.

"So we have to stop them," said Falcon. He raised his wings. "It's up to us."

There was a moment of silence. "How do we do that?" said Max.

"I have a suggestion," said a voice, and there, leaning against a pillar in front of the House of Wacks, was Mr. Sweeny, smoking his pipe.

"Mr. Sweeny," said Falcon. "We need your help!"

"Oh, you don't need my help," said Mr. Sweeny. "You're doing just fine, my boy. Most impressive."

"Who is this strange creature?" Pearl and Celeste said

in unison. "Is he our friend or our foe?"

"This is Mr. Sweeny," said Falcon, moving toward the grizzled old faun. "He's a friend."

"Rrr," said Sparkbolt. "Him Filcher!"

"Hello, Falcon," said Mr. Sweeny. "And hello, friends of Falcon. 'Tis a fine reunion, surely. But perhaps we'd all better just step inside for a moment?"

"We don't have much time," said Gyra. The DCS began to beep again.

"Sure enough," said Mr. Sweeny. "But you'll be safe for a few moments inside the House of Wacks. Come."

Somewhat uncertainly, they all followed Mr. Sweeny through the doors and into a wax museum that was full of lifelike re-creations of various well-known maniacs. There was Jack the Ripper and Attila the Hun and Jerry Lewis.

"Falcon, my boy!" shouted Mr. Grubb. He and the other Filchers were sitting around a table filled with breads and cheeses, a giant bowl of steaming pasta with homemade meatballs, a roasted duckling, and some moo goo gai pan. There were pitchers of milk, and fresh lemonade, and cold iced tea. Lumpp wagged his tail joyfully as Falcon approached.

"I'm afraid you've rather broken old Lumpp's heart," said Mr. Sweeny. "He found that charm of yours right where you dropped it. Kept it in his tentacles for days and days, thinking you'd come back. When he finally realized you weren't returning, he went out and buried it."

"What," said Falcon. "That amulet?"

"Aye," said Mr. Sweeny. "Didn't you bury it?" The octopus retriever wagged his tail. "He's a good boy."

Mrs. Grubb looked up at Falcon and his friends and sighed. "You didn't tell me 'e was bringin' in a whole army," she said. "I don't have enough to feed that lot! And I think I need glasses."

Fascia was sitting in a corner, fixing a pair of heavy winter boots with a long needle and some thread. Clea sat at one end of the long table, eating cherries.

"Hi, Clea," said Falcon. She turned her head away. "These are my friends—Pearl, and Celeste—"

"We greet you!" they said in unison.

"Max, and Sam—"

Two voices said, "Dude."

"—Chandler, and Lincoln Pugh—"

Lincoln Pugh, who was back to being his little nerd-like self, nodded at Chandler. "His mommy says he's the bravest of all."

"And Gyra." Gyra looked around the House of Wacks to see if there were any hidden adversaries. And as she did so, Megan materialized next to her, flickering in and out.

"Holy cow!" shouted the Squonk. "I think I'm seein' double!"

"There are others here," said Gyra, looking at her DCS. Moving, spherical lights drifted through the air.

"Ah, that would be Willa," said Mr. Grubb.

"Hey, I recognize that guy!" said the Squonk. "He used to be a tweety bird!"

"Hello, Squonk," said Jonny.

"Mr. Sweeny," said Falcon. "We don't have much time. The monsters and the guardians are about to destroy each other. Can't you help us stop them?"

Mr. Sweeny looked at the others. "I'm afraid we're having a bit of a dispute concerning this issue," he said. "Some of us do feel we ought to lend a hand. Others—"

"Let them destroy each other!" said Clea. "Let them rot!"

"Others feel differently," said Mr. Sweeny.

"But this affects you too," said Falcon.

"It doesn't affect me in the slightest!" said Clea.

"They made fun of my warts!" shouted the Squonk. "They said I was ugly! Me! Ugly!"

Max stared at the Squonk's wart-covered body. "Dude," he said.

"Honestly, we'd love to help you, Falcon," said Mr. Grubb. "But we're so busy right now—" He opened a book of poems and began to read. "Road Not Taken Destroy!" he said. "My, my, Mr. Sparkbolt's been busy!"

"That monster book!" shouted Sparkbolt, and grabbed

the "Poetry Book of Rhyming Poems" back from Mr. Grubb. "Filcher steal!"

"Aye," said Mr. Grubb.

"Stealin' poetry's me 'usband's specialty," said Mrs. Grubb.

"But don't you see," said Falcon. "You're part of the world. You can't always live apart. Sometimes you have to return to the world. To bring peace."

Clea made a disgusted sound. "I'm already at peace," she said. "I'm perfectly relaxed!"

"I'm sorry, my boy," said Mr. Grubb. "But it's not our fight."

"Then—," said Falcon. "Couldn't you help us, just as a favor? To me?"

The Filchers all exchanged glances.

"A favor, he says," said Mrs. Grubb.

"Falcon, my boy," said Mr. Grubb. "We'd hate to turn our backs on a friend. But what can we do? We're just a group of—"

"Thieves," said Sparkbolt, clutching his book of poems. "Bad."

"Aye, thieves," said Mr. Grubb. "That's it, plain and simple. And aside from bein' able to disappear all quick-like—"

"And fixing shoes," said Fascia.

"—we 'aven't really got much talent for—for battles

and such." Mr. Grubb looked at Falcon with humility. "You understand, don't you?"

"Hey! I can stop the fighting!" shouted the Squonk. "Me! The lunkhead!"

"You?" said Clea. "You couldn't stop your nose from running!

"I can so stop the fighting," said the Squonk. "All I have to do is—*play my saxophone!*"

Mr. Sweeny's eyes glowed knowingly, and he blew a smoke ring through the air.

"Señor Squonk!" said Pearl, buzzing around the wart-covered creature on her transparent wings. "Surely this is not the hour for a recital of this nature."

"I don't want us gettin' in the middle of this!" said Mrs. Grubb.

"Oh, now," said her husband with a wry grin. "I don't see what the 'arm would be in just letting the Squonk have a blow on his horn."

"The harm," said Fascia, not looking at them, "is that everyone's brains would explode."

"Let him play it!" said Clea. "Let their brains turn to *slime!*"

"That's it!" shouted the Squonk. "I'm going to play the 'Mexican Hat Dance'!"

"This doesn't sound like a plan," said Falcon.

"I'm not so sure, Falcon," said Mr. Sweeny. "The

Squonk's music might make them all stop for a moment. Give them occasion for reflection."

"Dude," said Max. "What about our brains? I don't want my brain to explode, man!"

"Cover your ears then," said Mr. Grubb. "That's what we do."

"Falcon," said Fascia, and he turned to see that the girl was now at his side. She reached out and took his arm. "Here," she said, and pressed something into his hand.

"Wait," said Falcon. "You're giving me—"

"My hammer," she said. "My cobbler's hammer. You'll need this, I think, in the time that is coming."

"But what am I going to do with your hammer?"

"I told you before," said Fascia. "It fixes more than shoes."

Falcon was just about to ask "What does it fix besides shoes?" when Mr. Grubb shouted, "Cover your ears! Everyone cover your—"

But Falcon did not hear the rest of the phrase, because it was at this exact moment that the air filled with the terrible, brain-melting sounds of the Squonk's saxophone, and the cataclysm began.

22

SMARTER NOW

Windows shattered. The Squonk's music shook the ground, peeled the paint off of buildings, opened up cracks in the earth. The Olde Tyme Nickelodeon Theatre shattered into tiny splinters. Robot Abe Lincoln—only recently repaired by Mr. Trunkanelli—began to wander the streets of Hematoma Boulevard, proclaiming that "the South will rise again!" From one end of Monster Island to the other, guardians and monsters alike found themselves sick to their stomachs, clasping at their throbbing temples, losing their sense of balance and falling over, fainting, sneezing, coughing up hairballs, and ripping off their clothes in horror.

Falcon clamped his hands to his ears, trying to blot out the terrible music, but it was no use. He felt his wings spreading, and without knowing where he was going, he took to the air, crashing through one of the windows in the House of Wacks. Falcon beat his wings, circling over the smoldering amusement park. He flew higher and higher, sweeping in a wide arc around the spires of

Dracula's Castle. He reached his hands up toward the sun, then began to fall, an angel hurtling earthward. There was a shattering sound, and a thud, and then blackness. The last thing Falcon heard was the sound of hundreds of running feet, although whether these belonged to guardians, or monsters, or both, he could not say.

When he woke up, Falcon was not immediately sure of his location. There was a large chair upon which he saw a reclining, unmoving figure. Behind it was a painting of a sad clown. Falcon felt a pounding in his head and a pain in his left wing. He sat up. Weird flickering light played off the walls.

A figure walked into the room holding a platter in its hands. "Who wants nachos 'n' baco-bits?" it said.

An audio-animatronic child looked over at its mechanical mother with a frozen, plastic smile.

"How about you, Son?" said the robot mother.

The Unhaunted House, Falcon thought. *I'm in the—*

"Who wants nachos 'n' baco-bits?" The lights in the Unhaunted House flickered on, then off, then on again. A short in the electrical system was playing havoc with the programming of the robots. "Baco-bits?" said the robot mother. Now her head was spinning around and around. "How about you, Son? How about you, Son?"

The mother's head suddenly fell off and rolled across the room to the place where Falcon was lying. It looked at Falcon and said, "How about you, Son?" as sparks flew from its eyes.

"I'm not your son," said Falcon.

"I have no son," said a voice, and Falcon looked up to see Cygnus standing in the doorway, holding a long sword. "My line dies out with me, thanks to you, Falcon Quinn."

"Cygnus?" said Falcon. "What are you talking about?"

"She was mine, Falcon," said Cygnus. "We were pledged to each other. Then she left."

"That's not my fault," said Falcon, getting to his feet.

"True," said Cygnus. "But when we found her, at last, in that miserable Maine town where you lived, that's when we learned what she had done. We were willing to forgive youthful indiscretion, perhaps. But some things are beyond forgiveness."

Falcon felt his dark eye heating up. "Why did you let me live when I was a baby?" he asked. "You could have killed me then."

"Why, indeed," said Cygnus. "Exactly! This is the very question I raised at the time. But she was very persuasive, your mother. She begged for your life. It was some satisfaction to hear her beg, I must say. And so a bargain was struck. We allowed you to live. Gave you over to that terrible woman, the failed banshee, your grandmonster. What was her name?"

"Gamm," said Falcon. He smelled a strange odor in the room as Cygnus drew closer, a sickly fragrance of death and decay.

"Ah yes, Gamma Quinn. We gave you to her and took Vega back to her people. That was the bargain. But I must say, I never thought it was very fair. It all struck me as an injustice."

"Taking my mother away? Trying to kill my father?"

"No, no," said Cygnus. "Letting you live. Because as long as you lived, she could never be mine. You are a constant reminder of her mistake." He grinned and held up the sword. "Fortunately, this is an error that there is still time to fix."

"You think if you kill me you can win her back?" said Falcon.

"No," said Cygnus. "I think if I kill you she will know what it is to suffer as I have suffered all these years."

"Vait," said another voice. "*You* shall not kill Falcon Qvinn."

"I won't?" said Cygnus as Count Manson stepped into the room. "And why is that, Count?"

"Because," said Count Manson, "that wengeance belongs to me."

"He's mine, Count," said Cygnus. "Don't interfere."

Falcon shot a huge fireball toward Cygnus, but the guardian general just stepped out of the way. The fireball sailed across the room and nearly hit Count Manson, but the count, using the force of his will, held up one hand and extinguished the fireball, which then fell in ashes to the floor.

The count grasped the air with his fingers, exerting his willpower on Falcon, who suddenly found himself frozen to the spot. "Perhaps," said the count to Cygnus, "ve might—cooperate, just this vunce? I shall hold him still. As you destroy him vith the *qeres*. That is *qeres* I smell, is it not?"

"Indeed," said Cygnus, drawing out a small vial from his cloak. "The ancient embalming perfume of the pharaohs. Most effective against angels." He poured the perfume on the edge of his knife, and the room filled with the stench of death. "Very well, then, Count, let us join together to remove our mutual enemy. Of course, after the angel is dead I shall have to kill you as well."

"Naturally. And I, Cygnus, vill be obligated to kill you."

"It is good," said Cygnus, "that we understand each other."

"Cygnus," said Falcon, "it's not me you want to kill."

"Vhat is he talking about?" said the count.

"Killing me won't bring her back to you," said Falcon.

Cygnus looked furious for a moment, then his features relaxed. "That may be so," he said. "But you are wrong about one thing, Falcon. It *is* you I want to kill." He laughed. "It is you." And Cygnus rushed forward with the knife.

The blade, shining with poison, slashed through the air and then straight into Falcon's hearts—the two of them, both the guardian and the monster.

For a moment Falcon stood there, looking at the handle of the blade sticking out of his own chest. Then he felt his pulses slow, and then cease altogether, and he fell into darkness.

Monster Island was aflame. Monsters and guardians continued to stagger in confusion, clutching their bleeding ears, some of them falling back to safer positions in Plasma Falls and Abominationland and Yesterdayland.

"Squonk bad," said Sparkbolt, staggering through the drifting smoke. Black soot coated his cheeks. He was not at all sure how he had wound up outside, but here he was, stumbling down Hematoma Boulevard. He paused to cough. There was no sign of the Filchers in the disoriented, screaming crowd.

Gyra, wielding her bullwhip, came out of the smoke, coughing. "Sparkbolt," she said.

"Monster angry!!" He shook his head. "Brain *hurt*."

Max and Pearl now emerged from the smoke. "Max. Pearl," said Gyra. "You guys okay?"

"We're okay," said Sam. "But where's Celeste? And that really big dude?"

"I don't know," said Gyra. "Everything's confused!"

"My mental processes have been roasted by that terrible noise!" said Pearl. "But I have emerged nonetheless! My dignity still intact!"

"Your dignity?" said a voice, and they turned to see Mortlock, standing at the end of the street holding a large flail. "How can a Chupakabra speak of dignity?"

"Is this a challenge?" said Pearl. "I shall sting you on your shiny metal backside! I shall inject you with the poison of humiliation!"

"Mortlock," said Gyra, "the Chupakabra fights with courage and honor! I have seen it myself!"

"That's funny," said Mortlock. "The banshee who killed my mother didn't have much honor at all."

"Please, sir," said Gyra. "If you'll just listen to us—"

"That's enough, Cadet Gyra," said Mortlock.

"I say," said the colonel, now coming up from behind Mortlock. "This is all most irregular. Our party scattered, and everything aflame! Highly improper!"

"Hey," said Sam. "I thought that dude got chased off by that baby elephant."

The colonel continued. "Reminds me of the time back in sixty-two, when I encountered the lamia of Madagascar. Well, there we were—"

"Rrrr," said a voice. A pair of green hands wrapped themselves around the colonel's neck, and the guardian adventurer was thrown through the front window of the Five Cent Kandy Korner, where he became enmeshed in the whirling tongs of the saltwater taffy machine. The colonel was struck by the whirling blades and engulfed with the thick, gummy taffy.

Sparkbolt smiled happily. "Element of surprise," he said.

"Dude," said Sam. "You made candy out of him!"

Mortlock grinned. "You're not making candy out of *me*," he said, then whirled his flail through the air. It wheeled in a whooshing circle over his head, once, then twice, and then came down on Sparkbolt. The Frankenstein jumped out of the way, but Mortlock had anticipated this move and had adjusted his blow accordingly. The flail dealt a glancing blow to the Frankenstein's knee, and with an agonized roar, Sparkbolt fell onto the cobblestones. Now Mortlock whirled the flail around again, and it would have crashed down upon Sparkbolt's shoulders had something not stuck on to the flail's spiked ball, nearly throwing Mortlock off balance. "What the—," he said.

There, clinging to the giant ball, was Chandler. The whirling ball had lifted him off his feet.

"Cadet Chandler, let go," said Mortlock.

"Mortlock," said Gyra, "we're wrong about them."

"Turns out," said Mortlock, "what I was wrong about was you."

Mortlock stepped toward her, Chandler still dangling from the ball of his flail.

"Please, sir," said Chandler. "Can't you show a little mercy? Please?"

"That's what my ma asked the banshees just before they hauled her off," Mortlock said. He shook his head in contempt. "Smarter now."

Dahlia and Maeve Crofton awakened on the edge of Abominationland, where they'd been blown after the blinding music of the Squonk. Dahlia trickled, half in and half out of her water form, as flames shot from the top of Maeve's fingers. They held each other in a hug, making a volcano of hissing steam.

Maeve reduced her flame and then ran her fingers through the waters of her sister's hair. "Where are we?" she asked. "My brain feels like it's been charbroiled."

"You're on Monster Island," said a voice. "With your family."

The Crofton sisters turned, and there they saw their sister Megan, flickering in and out like a candle flame.

"Megan!" the girls shouted, and the Croftons fell upon one another until they thought their hearts would break.

A warm fire, like coals on a winter day, glowed in Dahlia's hair, and Maeve trickled around her sisters in joy. Megan flickered, but stayed visible, made more solid and stable by her family.

"Mom told me you were dead," said Megan. "She said you were drowned."

Maeve nodded. "She thinks you've drowned too," she said. "That's what they do when monsters leave the world. They tell the others they're dead."

"She said it should have been me," said Megan. "That I was the one who should have died instead of you. She said she'd never love me. That no one ever would."

"Oh, Megan," said Maeve, wrapping her fiery arms around her sister. "No one's ever been more loved than you."

Megan looked at the burning spires of Dracula's Castle. Birds circled the towers. "Falcon," she said.

"What about him?"

"We have to help him."

"Why?" said Dahlia.

"Because he saved me," said Megan.

Maeve and Dahlia looked at each other. "Falcon Quinn?" said Maeve. "He saved you? But we thought—"

"You were wrong," said Megan. Her hands drifted like smoke for a moment. "Everyone was. But we can still help him if we put out these fires. The three of us. Maeve, you can control fire—Dahlia, you can put out flames with water—and I can try to steer the wind away from the blaze." She flickered in and out. "That will help."

"Are you well enough?" said Maeve. "You seem kind of wavery."

"We have to help Falcon," said Megan. "Save everyone."

"Guardians too?" said Dahlia.

"Everyone," said Megan. Dahlia and Maeve looked at each other uncertainly.

Then Maeve transformed into flames, and Dahlia dissolved into a rushing stream, and Megan became the wind. And the elements turned upon the burning world.

Jonny Frankenstein, when he came to, found himself in the heart of Dracula's Castle. His head ached as he tried to remember how he had come to be here. *The Filchers,* he thought, looking around. *The Squonk.*

"Why, Jonny Frankenstein," said a voice, and Jonny turned. There before him was Merideath, and Dominique, and Muffy, their eyes dark and moist, their lips slightly open. "I was hoping you'd come."

"What are you doing here?" said Jonny.

"Looking for you," said Merideath.

"Where's Falcon?" said Jonny.

"Falcon Quinn?" said Merideath. "Is he here too? Well, wherever he is, he's about to get wiped out with the others.

I don't think there'll be much left of either side when this is all done, do you?"

"Listen, ladies," said Jonny. "You need to back off."

"Jonny," said Merideath. "Don't be that way. We're offering you a chance to survive this day."

"Boy, are you girls confused," said Jonny. "Don't you know what I am?"

"I know what you've been," said Merideath. "But that can change. After I was expelled, Jonny, I had a lot of time to think about who at that stupid school I'd most like to kill, and whom I'd most like to—" She smiled gently, and her long, shining teeth were visible. "Come on. Join the club."

"I'll fry you with lightning if you take one step closer," said Jonny.

"Oh, Jonny, you don't need lightning anymore. You just need someone to *bite* you. Don't you think it'd be perfectly macabre, if you came over to our side? It's the perfect revenge on all of them for the way they've treated you. Taking bets upon your life! You want to be an outlier, Jonny? It's easy. All you have to do is join *us*."

She stared at him with her moist black eyes and drew very close to him. Jonny could feel her hot breath on his neck. Merideath held him still now with the force of her will.

"Do you remember on the first day of school, Jonny?"

said Merideath, putting her hand on the side of his face. "You showed up with your guitar and your duffel bag, and you climbed up the stairs to the Tower of Aberrations? You sat on the couch playing that little song on your guitar." She leaned forward, her lips full, her eyelids drooping like the petals of a wilting flower. "That day, I knew I wanted you, Jonny. I knew I wanted you *forever*."

She opened her mouth, and Jonny saw her long canine teeth. "Muffy? Dominique?" said Merideath. "Hold him still!"

23

A Beautiful Fish

Falcon drifted in a vaporous whorl. The sun struggled through clouds. He saw his mother lying on a white bed in a white room. The Crow sat at her side, wiping her forehead with a cloth.

"Falcon," Vega whispered. "Where's Falcon?"

The room rose and fell as if the floor had become the surface of a raging ocean. A wave washed through Falcon's vision and he went under. Strange hands reached up from the ocean floor, trying to drag Falcon down. Then he felt himself washed onto unfamiliar shores. Birds sang from trees.

Before him was a long, wooden pier at the end of which was a man with a fishing rod. As he fished, he read a thick leather book.

Falcon approached the stranger. He looked up from his reading and smiled, as if he had been expecting Falcon for a long, long time.

"I'm almost done," said Mr. Lyons. He held up the volume. "*Oliver Twist*. By Charles Dickens."

"Mr. Lyons," said Falcon.

"I am known by that name," he said.

Falcon looked at the librarian and smiled sadly. "This isn't real, is it?"

"Real?" said Mr. Lyons. "I'm not sure I know what you mean by that. Oliver Twist isn't real either, is he? But I have spent many good days following his progress and thinking about his fate. He has brought me much joy, which is more than I can say for a number of these so-called real things of yours. Here." Mr. Lyons handed Falcon the book. "This is for you."

"I thought you weren't finished yet."

"I know how it ends," said Mr. Lyons. He pulled on his fishing rod and reeled in the line. He looked at his lure for a moment, then cast it back out again.

"What are you fishing for?" said Falcon.

"That changes all the time," said Mr. Lyons. "Until a moment ago, I was fishing for you! And look. Here you are. A lunker!"

"Mr. Lyons," said Falcon. "Are we dead?"

"Dead?" said the librarian. "For heaven's sake, Falcon, why would you think you were dead? On such a day as this?"

"They stabbed me, Mr. Lyons. And I think—you must be dead too. We both are."

"Falcon Quinn," said Mr. Lyons. "No man can kill me."

Falcon looked around at the roaring ocean, the strange cloud-filled sky. "Why not? There's some law that you can't kill a librarian?"

"There should be," said Mr. Lyons. "That is a law I would surely endorse. But no. The reason I cannot be killed is not because I am a librarian. It's because I am the Watcher."

Falcon looked at him with wonder. *"You're* the Watcher?"

"I am. The Shepherd of Dreams."

"So this is a dream? We're on—the Island of Nightmares?"

"You can call it that if you like, Falcon," said Mr. Lyons.

"Are my parents here? My father said he was bringing my mom to you. That you could heal her."

"They were here for a time," said Mr. Lyons. "They are both out of danger for now."

"So—you healed them?"

"They healed each other." He smiled. "I must say, I had my doubts, especially about your mother. But she has recovered, mostly, from the poison that she carried." He shook his head sadly. "So much venom in the world."

He held up a broken watch upon a silver chain. The crystal was shattered.

"That's the stopwatch my father used to wear," said

Falcon. "It measured—"

"That curse is lifted," said Mr. Lyons. "They have both suffered enough. All three of you have."

"Where are they now? Did they go back to the castle? Or Shadow Island? Or—"

"I had another task for them," said the Watcher. "They are back in the Reality Stream, in Maine, in fact. There is trouble brewing up north, I am afraid. This is a matter only they can solve."

"What trouble?" said Falcon. "When do I get to see them again?"

The fishing rod twitched and bent. Mr. Lyons began to pull in his line.

"I don't know," he said.

"I thought you knew everything!"

"Oh no, Falcon." He smiled. "I only know what I read."

A large fish crashed through the surface of the water now, and Mr. Lyons reeled in his line. At the end was a large salmon, its silver scales shimmering, its bloodred gills wriggling and writhing. "Hello, my friend," said Mr. Lyons. "Now, now, let's get you unhooked here." He glanced at Falcon. "It's a beautiful fish, isn't it?"

Falcon nodded. "It is."

"All right then," said Mr. Lyons, and threw the fish back into the ocean. They watched as the salmon flashed its tail and then dove.

"What's going to happen to me?" said Falcon Quinn to Mr. Lyons. "Am I going to be all right?"

"All right?" Mr. Lyons looked thoughtful. "I am not sure what you mean by that, Falcon. You will have occasions for great joy, I think, and others of sadness and pain. You will find many things you are searching for and lose others. You will be surrounded by the voices of those who love you, and on other occasions find yourself stranded and alone. You will know great hunger and thirst; and then days will come when the table before you is piled high with warm bread and sweet butter. Above all, dear boy, you will have many choices to make. Perhaps with love, and humor, and the counsel of your friends you will make more right choices than wrong ones." He nodded. "So. If this is what you mean, then I suppose you will be all right, Falcon. Yes. You will be just fine."

Falcon looked out at the waters where the salmon had been released. "What's going to happen now?" he asked.

Mr. Lyons patted Falcon on the shoulder. "I think," he said, "it is time to throw you back. You know what else I think, Falcon Quinn?"

"What?"

Mr. Lyons placed his hand on Falcon's chest, right above his twin hearts. "I think," he said, "that you too are a beautiful fish."

All at once Falcon found himself churning in the waters of the sea. The ocean roared in his ears as he rose toward the surface. As he rushed upward, he felt Mr. Lyons's hand on his chest. His hearts began to pulse, gently at first and then with more force.

He crashed through the surface, and as he did, the world spun around him. The world roared and then grew silent except for two men's voices speaking and a soft, rhythmic thumping.

"And so," said Count Manson. "Ve now turn to each other."

"We do," said Cygnus. "At last."

I'm back, thought Falcon. He glanced down at his chest. There was a hand-shaped pool of blood over his hearts, but as he watched, the stain slowly faded.

Cygnus raised his knife. He was just about to stab Count Manson with it when the knife suddenly vanished.

Cygnus looked curiously at his own hand. He looked around to see if the dagger had fallen on the ground. But such a sharp, thin knife would have made a clattering sound if it had dropped. The dagger appeared to have vanished into thin air.

A set of twinkling lights swirled across the room.

Cygnus and the count looked at the drifting spheres with expressions of wonder.

It's Willa, Falcon thought. *The Filchers.*

Falcon slowly started to crawl out of the room. Willa the Wisp twinkled once more.

"Vait," said the count suddenly. "The boy is alive! He is escaping!"

"Alive?" said Cygnus. "Impossible!" But even as the guardian general turned, Falcon got to his feet and ran.

He ran out the door and into the bingo parlor, where the robot was saying, "The next number is G twenty-three. G twenty-three." Count Manson rushed in right after him. "I have had enough of this, Falcon Qvinn!" he shouted.

"As have I," said Cygnus, coming into the room from another door on that same side of the room. "It is time now to die. And this time, you will *stay dead*."

"Wait," said Falcon. "There's still time to—" But Cygnus wrapped his hands around Falcon's throat, and again the count used his vampiric will to hold the angel motionless. Falcon, feeling his breath being squeezed out of him, looked around the bingo parlor, hoping that the Filchers would intervene once more, but this time there was no sign of them.

The audio-animatronic bingo lady said, "B four. The letter is B four."

All at once, something smashed through the wall of the Unhaunted House. Thundering, lumbering footsteps galloped toward them. "Hey!" shouted Snort. "Everybody spread out! I'm stampedin'!"

Count Manson, then Cygnus, were propelled up in the air by the bulldozing horn of the stampeding were-rhino. They soared across the room and crashed against the robot bingo lady.

"Snort!" said Falcon.

"I didn't *wanna* have to trample them," he said. "Wasn't my idea!" Steam billowed from his nose. "But now they know what happens when ya mess with my friends. Ya get stampeded!"

"Let's get out of here," said Falcon.

"Suit yourself," said Snort. "Climb aboard!"

Falcon was just about to swing his leg onto Snort's back when he heard a loud bark. Falcon looked to his left to see Lumpp, the octopus retriever, standing there in point position. Quimby's amulet, covered with a mixture of dog drool and sand, dangled from his mouth.

"Lumpp," said Falcon. "Where'd you come from?" The octopus retriever wagged his tail.

"Step on it, Falcon," said Snort, looking fearfully at Count Manson and Cygnus, who were getting back on their feet. "They're comin' again!"

"Just a second," said Falcon, bending down to take the amulet. "Where did this come from?" he asked. "I thought you buried it."

"Falcon," said Snort urgently. "They're coming!"

Falcon took the amulet on its chain and held it up to the light. Lumpp whimpered.

Would that stop it? Falcon thought. *Was it even possible?*

He remembered the words that the Watcher had spoken. *Above all, dear boy, you will have many choices to make. Perhaps with love, and humor, and the counsel of your friends you will make more right choices than wrong ones.*

Count Manson and Cygnus were running toward him once again.

"Okay," said Falcon. "Here goes nothing."

And with this, Falcon Quinn placed the amulet around his neck. There was a rushing sound as all the cares and noise and troubles of the world turned into nothing, and Falcon Quinn dissolved into a crimson vapor.

24
THE UNION OF OPPOSITES

The moth man stood in front of the burning House of Boxing Robot Presidents as the cyborg chief executives fled the conflagration, their clothes smoking. A robot Millard Fillmore staggered through the front door with his head spinning around like a top, muttering something about the Know-Nothing Party. From behind him came a synthetic whooping, and an electronic Andrew Jackson barreled past him, his pants on fire. "Look out, Millard!" shouted the robot. "Old Hickory's coming through!"

"The light," said the moth man, looking up at the roaring flames. "So beautiful! So—unattainable!" He raised his hands in yearning.

Out in the street, guardians and monsters ran in panic, many of them still deranged from the Squonk's music. They paused, now and again, to fight with each other, but the confusion was so complete that there were no formal battle lines, and what fighting there was took place between scattered individuals. Mortia and two of her zombie friends, Molda and Crumble, were doing the Zombie Snap.

When you've got a predilection to be real instead of
fiction,
And you want a benediction just to rid yourself of crap.
Then you need a new conviction to destroy this odd
addiction
Then you join my jurisdiction and you do the Zombie
Snap!

"Now, now," said Mr. Drudge. "There's no need for that."

"But you're wrong," shouted Mortia. "Everyone needs—the Zombie Snap!" She and her companions snapped their fingers in unison, and sparks flew through the air. Mr. Drudge had to step very quickly to one side to avoid them.

"Zombies," Mr. Drudge muttered to himself. "Zombies. I can't remember what the proper method is for combating zombies. It's not a silver bullet. It's not a stake in the heart. . . ." He stepped aside again to avoid another spray of sparks from the Zombie Snap. "It's right on the tip of my tongue."

Miss Bloodstone came charging down the street at this moment, still holding her hands to her ears.

"Ah, Miss Bloodstone," said Mr. Drudge. "How nice to see you. I was just wondering—"

"Make it stop!" said Miss Bloodstone, shaking her

head. Her ponytail whipped the air behind her. "Please, just make it stop."

"Ah, watch out for the zombies," said Mr. Drudge as another shower of fiery sparks flew all around them. "I was just wondering—Miss Bloodstone? Are you quite all right?"

"I thought I'd heard everything when I'd heard the scream of a banshee," she said. "But that saxophone—oh my god—it was terrible! *Terrible!*"

"There, there, miss," said Mr. Drudge, patting the guardian teacher on the shoulder. "It's all fine now. Don't you see? Now, I hate to be pushy, but I was wondering if you could remind me of the proper method of dispatching zombies? It's been so long that I've quite—"

"Zombies?" said Miss Bloodstone, blinking. Her eyes focused on Mortia, Molda, and Crumble, moving steadily toward them in a phalanx. "Zombies. Why, everyone knows how to kill a zombie. You cut off the head, destroy the brain." She pulled out a sword. "All right, you three!" she shouted. "Time to go back to being dead now! You've had your fun."

But the zombies just sang:

If you find an aberration in this sudden conflagration
And your mind's a destination that you can't find on a
*   map.*

*Then you'll find your immolation unless you're French
    or half-Croatian
You'll just lose your deformation when you do the
    Zombie Snap!*

"Of course, of course, destroy the brains," said Mr. Drudge. "What was I thinking?"

Miss Bloodstone slashed her sword through the air, aiming for Mortia's neck, but at the moment she did this she found herself knocked over by the sudden appearance of the lower half of Quimby's body.

"Oof," said Miss Bloodstone. A shower of sparks from the Zombie Snap fell upon her. "Ow!"

"Heavens, who brought along Quimby?" said Mr. Drudge.

"That stupid colonel," said Miss Bloodstone, dusting herself off. "Honestly, I'm going to have a word with him when—" She looked at the advancing zombies. "My, this is an aggressive lot, isn't it?" She and Mr. Drudge took a step backward. There was a clattering sound as they backed into something.

"Oh, now look what you've done," said Mrs. Grubb, standing there with a huge silver platter. "Knocked my fresh gingersnaps right off the tray and into the street. It's what I expect, of course! No thanks, ever, for the work I do!"

"Wait," said Miss Bloodstone. "Who are you? Have we met?"

Mrs. Grubb took her huge silver platter and bonked Miss Bloodstone on the head with it. Her eyes rolled back in her head, and then she fell down.

"We 'ave now," she said.

"I see," said Mr. Drudge. The zombies were almost upon him again. "Will you excuse me, ma'am?"

"Excuse you?" said Mrs. Grubb. "What for?" She swung her tray through the air again, but Mr. Drudge ducked.

"Ma'am," he said, and then began to run.

Mrs. Grubb looked at the guardian as he fled from her. A look of satisfaction crept over her face. "It's actually rather pleasant," she said to Clea, who appeared at her side, "bein' involved in things. I'd almost forgotten what it was like, bein' part of the world!"

"What's pleasant about it?" asked Clea.

Over at the Hall of Boxing Robot Presidents, the moth man continued to stand, transfixed, before the roaring flames. "So beautiful!" he murmured. "So, so beautiful!"

Robot John F. Kennedy stepped out of the fire. "We choose to go to the moon!" he said. "Not because it is easy, but because it is hahd!"

Mortlock wheeled his flail through the air as Chandler held on to the spiked ball.

"I'll kill you, I swear!" shouted Mortlock.

"What's wrong with you?" said Gyra.

"Me?" said Mortlock. "There's nothing wrong with me, Cadet Gyra."

"You're doing the same thing the banshees did to your mother," said Gyra. "Don't you get it? *You're* the monster."

"But he's gone over to the *enemy!*" Mortlock shouted.

"He hasn't gone over anywhere," said Gyra. "He's just trying to stop the fighting." She nodded to the group of monsters around her—Sparkbolt and Max and Pearl. "We're all trying to stop it."

"Señorita Gyra has spoken the truth," said Pearl. "We are hoping that our peoples can see that we have much to gain by not murdering one another!"

"There's more in the world," said Gyra, "than just getting revenge."

Mortlock shook his head. "Not to me," he said. He whirled the flail again, and Chandler, at last letting go of the ball, flew through the air over their heads and disappeared beyond the borders of Yesterdayland.

Now Mortlock swung the flail toward Gyra. But just as the ball was about to smash into her head, a purple tentacle wrapped around it and flicked it out of the guardian warrior's hand. "What the—?" he said.

Mr. Hake squiggled toward the scene on his many rubbery arms. One of his tentacles encircled Mortlock and then sent the man sailing through the air in the same direction as Chandler.

With another tentacle he picked up Mortlock's flail and waved it around exuberantly. "I like flails," he said. "They're happy!"

"Poor thing," said Mrs. Redflint, looking at Mortlock soaring toward Yesterdayland. "You know, all guardians miss their mothers."

Now a group of young guardian warriors stepped forward. They seemed awkward in their heavy armor, and some of them squinted at the rising sun, as if they had never seen it before. One of them looked at Mr. Hake and gasped. "It's—a Smaulgtron!" he said.

"We need the Twinkling Shield of Plus Four Stamina," said another.

"Attacking with Enchanted Level Twenty-seven Arrows," said a third. A volley of arrows from the Snoids' bows flew through the air and imbedded themselves in Mr. Hake's rubbery skin.

"Oh," said Mr. Hake. "Now I'm sad." He reached forward with a tentacle, grabbed two of the Snoids with his sucker disks, and dropped them into his hideous Kracken mouth. "But it's all right to feel sad sometimes! Sharing feelings makes me happy!"

"How many lives do we have left?" asked a Snoid.

"Lives?" said Max. "This is *reality*. You only get one life!"

"Ha, ha!" said the Snoid. "You're funny!"

There was the roaring of many voices as dozens more guardian warriors now rushed toward the battle, led by Miss Bloodstone. There were zombie-slaying swordsmen and vampire killers armed with crossbow-mounted stakes. A platoon of bowmen ran forward to act as a buffer between the monsters and the guardians, and for a moment the two gathering armies squared off, eyeing each other with hate.

"Hey," said Sam, pushing forward to join his friends. Celeste was at his side. "Everybody knock it off! We don't have to do this! We can learn to get along."

"Not me," said Snick, right behind him. "I'm not learnin' nothin'!"

"My word," said Miss Bloodstone, looking at Mrs. Redflint, her monster double. "Just look at that disgusting woman!"

Mrs. Redflint looked at Miss Bloodstone. "Well," she said. "Disgusting is as disgusting does."

"Guardians, *attack*!" said Miss Bloodstone.

"Monsters, *forward*!" said Mrs. Redflint.

"It prepares," said the moth man, staggering toward them, his eyes wide and hypnotized by the fire. "It prepares to go into the light!"

Cygnus and Count Manson stood in the Unhaunted House, looking at the place where a moment ago Falcon

Quinn had been and where now there was only drifting smoke.

"Where did he go?" said Cygnus. "What have you done with him?"

"I?" shouted Count Manson. "I have done nothing but act in good faith! But I should have expected treachery— and betrayal!"

"Look out!" shouted Snort. "I'm stampedin' again!" The wererhino charged toward them, horn lowered; but this time Cygnus and Count Manson stepped aside, and Snort crashed through the wall and charged on out onto Hematoma Boulevard.

"So much for the wererhino," said Cygnus.

"Yes." The count grinned. "So much for—" The count paused and looked at his own hands. "Whoa," said the count, but the voice was Falcon Quinn's. "I'm inside— Count Manson."

Cygnus shook his head. "Why are you imitating the boy's voice?"

"I am not imitating the boy's—," said Count Manson, shuddering. "Woice."

A look of bewilderment came over the vampire's features. Falcon, looking at the world through Count Manson's eyes, fleetingly saw the world the way a vampire saw it. He sensed the count's longing for blood, the weariness that came from deathlessness, his hatred and envy of those who were mortal. For that instant Falcon felt compassion for the count. He could almost understand the man, could almost forgive him for all he had done. He thought of the words Quimby had engraved inside the crimson madstone. *To seek to know another's pain, first spend some time inside his brain.*

Count Manson's hand picked up the amulet and for a moment held it before him. Its red jewel glittered darkly in the Unhaunted House.

"Now you see," said Count Manson to Falcon. "Now you understand."

"I do," said Falcon. He looked at Cygnus. "I'm sorry."

"Sorry?" said Cygnus. "For what?"

Count Manson placed the amulet around his neck and vanished into a mist. The crimson madstone fell with a clink onto the floor.

Cygnus found himself alone in the room with only Lumpp, the octopus retriever. "Where did he go?" He looked to his left and right, suspecting a trick.

Lumpp whimpered softly.

Then the cloud of glowing vapor surrounded Cygnus.

Falcon Quinn fell out of the cloud of crimson mist and looked around the room in confusion. "I'm me again," he said. Lumpp wagged his tail.

"Vere—," said Cygnus's body. But it spoke with Count Manson's voice. "Vere am I?"

"You're—in *my* brain," shouted Cygnus, clutching at his temples.

"No," said Count Manson to Falcon. "You cannot leave me trapped in the body of the enemy!"

"Get out of my brain, Count!" shouted Cygnus, waving his blade around. "Or I'll stab you!"

"But you cannot do this vithout stabbing yourself!" said Count Manson from inside Cygnus. "Please, Falcon Qvinn. Release us from this haunting! Ve shall accept your terms! Von't ve, Cygnus?"

The guardian nodded to himself. "I will," he said. "Please. Get him out of me!"

Falcon stood up. "I'll give you terms," he said. In his pocket he still had Fascia's hammer, and now he drew it out. It was not a large hammer, being designed originally for the fixing of shoes, but it was large enough. Falcon picked up the amulet, held it against a bingo table, and then whacked its red jewel with Fascia's hammer. The amulet's center shattered like glass, and its hundreds of glittering pieces fell onto the ground.

"The terms," said Falcon, "are to get along."

"No!" screamed Count Manson, through Cygnus's mouth. "Anything but that!"

"The count is right," said Cygnus, seizing control of his body once more. "We shall slay each other before accepting this fate." He pointed the sword at his own heart.

"Have it your way," said Falcon. "Slay each other then."

The creature—Count Manson? Cygnus?—paused for a moment, trying to decide whether its love of its own soul was greater than the loathing it harbored for its enemy. The knife hovered just above its heart as it weighed its love against its hate.

Out in the plaza before Dracula's Castle, there was a terrible roar from a wide variety of throats, both dead and undead. Mrs. Redflint took a deep breath, filling her lungs with fire. Mr. Hake wriggled his tentacles through the air, and the Snoids strung their Bows of Plus Sixteen Deadliness. Zombies warmed up the Zombie Snap, and banshees prepared to wail. Guardians strung their bows, readied daggers of silver, steeled themselves against tears. But just as the forces began to rush toward each other, just as the final cataclysm began to unfold, there was a shining white light. A winged creature flew into their midst, carrying someone in its arms. Falcon Quinn beat his wings, then lowered Cygnus to the ground.

Cygnus turned to the crowd. He spoke with Count Manson's voice.

"Vait," said the creature.

"Cygnus?" said Miss Bloodstone.

"I am not Cygnus," said the man.

"You are not Count Manson," said Mrs. Redflint.

"Although you sound like him."

"I am neither of these," he said. Then his voice changed, and he sounded once more like the guardian leader. "Or perhaps I should say—I am *both*. I am—Count Cygnus!"

"What did you do to him?" said Mortlock, returning once more, his face covered with blood.

"Vhat has been done to me," said Count Cygnus, "I have done to myself." He looked at the gathered warriors, at the guardian lieutenants and the monster instructors, the fledglings and the young monsters. "I did not see before." He shook his head. "But now I see. Ve must learn to live as vun."

His body shook, and the voice changed back to Cygnus's. "Disgusting as that may sound!" he added.

Then his Count Manson side took over again. "Indeed, the prospect seems—rewolting. But the truth so often is."

The Crofton sisters swept past the gathered crowd. The elementals—of wind, and water, and fire—combined to quell the flames that had roared from the rooftops of the buildings. The guardians and the monsters watched as Megan and Dahlia and Maeve brought the flames under control. The fires died down and smoldered and then went out with a hiss.

There was a clanking, clattering sound from the Hall of Boxing Robot Presidents, and a burnt, smoldering robot Abraham Lincoln walked gravely out of the main doors.

Everyone fell silent as the smoking Lincoln eyed them somberly. *"Werp,"* he said, and then cleared his throat.

"With malice toward none," said the smoking robot president, "with charity for all, let us—*werp*—strive on to finish the work we are in, to bind up the nation's wounds."

"Whoa," said Max. "That is *so true.*"

The guardians looked at Mortlock and Miss Bloodstone, who in turn looked back at Count Cygnus. "Is this truly your wish?" said Mortlock.

"It is," said Cygnus's voice, and then in the count's, "it is *our* vish."

"Fine," said Mortlock, but it was clear he wasn't happy about it. "Have it your way. Let's get all the hurt people together and see if we can't help them out. I guess we'll meet up with our new"—he shuddered—*"comrades—* again, on a future date, I am sure. Maybe then we can talk a little bit about"—his fingers traced the scar upon his neck—"redressing our *grievances.*"

The guardians began to withdraw. Gyra and Sam and Celeste gathered around Falcon. "Nice job, man," said Sam, clapping him on the shoulder. "Sticking your count inside Cygnus's brain. I mean, whoa. Didn't see that comin'."

"Indeed," said Celeste. "You have turned things inside out."

Gyra took Falcon by the arm. "Listen," she said. "I'm

sorry I didn't come with you and Jonny when you asked. I wasn't ready."

"It's all right," said Falcon. "You had to do what you had to do."

"Why did you trust me?" said Gyra. "Before you knew me?"

The wind blew through Falcon's hair. "I don't know," he said. "You reminded me of someone I used to know, I guess."

"I say," said a voice, and they turned to see a strange, gooey-looking creature approaching them. "Bully! Seem to have found myself in a sticky situation, as it were."

"Colonel?"

"Rather," said the creature. "The whirling blades of that infernal machine have—I do say!—stretched me rather thin. Reminds me of the time back in eighty-four when I faced the ice platypus of Greenland. No—wait. It was eighty-three. Same year I had the frostbite. Well, there I was—"

Chandler, back from the place he'd been thrown by Mortlock's flail, appeared at the colonel's side. "My mommy was right," he said. "I am brave!"

"Quite," said the colonel.

"Come along, fledglings," said Miss Bloodstone. "Let's head back to the ship. We have repairs to make."

The guardians retreated toward the harbor, leaving Hematoma Boulevard in the hands of the monsters.

"Dude," said Max to Falcon. "You did it."

"You used the amulet," said Pearl. "To cause the enemy captains to meld with each other! How exceptionally ingenious! And yet it is no surprise that such an action should come from your hands, Falcon Quinn! The hands of an angel! And my sworn companion!"

"Boy," said Max. "What a mess. This place is totaled!"

"Monster Island will be rebuilt," said Mr. Trunkanelli, surveying the damage. "Bigger and better than ever." He trumpeted. "I've been meaning to make some improvements, actually. Bring in some clowns."

"Please!" shouted Pearl. "No clowns! This is the one thing that, indeed, most freezes my heart with fear!"

"Okay, no clowns," said Mr. Trunkanelli.

"Well, well, Falcon Quinn," said Merideath. "Looks like you saved the day again." She was walking toward them now with Muffy and Dominique and Jonny Frankenstein. Her skin seemed slightly green, as if she was not well.

"Of course he did," said Muffy with contempt. "He's a little angel!"

"Hey, man," said Max. "Maybe you guys should have a nice big glass of *shut up.*"

"Fine," said Dominique. "We never speak to our inferiors if we can avoid it, anyway!"

"Ugh," said Merideath, holding her stomach. "I need to lie down."

"Jonny," said Falcon, rushing up to his friend, who looked strangely pale.

Merideath walked away unsteadily, her hands clutching her stomach. Muffy and Dominique followed in her wake.

"What's wrong with Merideath?" said Destynee. "Is she okay?"

"Oh, she'll be all right," said Jonny. "She just bit something that *disagreed* with her."

From high in the air, they heard a voice, singing.

"Would you like to ride in my beautiful balloon? Way up in the air in my beautiful balloon? Thank you, Monster Island, thank you!"

They looked up, and there they saw Quimby's head, floating along on the breeze. "Boy," said Quimby. "Do I have this—*deflated* feeling."

Quimby began to hiss, and he shrank smaller and smaller as he let his air escape. He was just about the size of a bowling ball when a pair of hands reached out and grabbed him. "Hey," said Quimby. "Put me down."

But the hands that held him were his own. Quimby's headless body, which had been stumbling around Hematoma Boulevard for most of the battle, at last took hold of its head and placed it back upon its neck.

"My body," said Quimby. "I've got my body back!" He looked at himself critically. "Heavens, I've put on weight. Be honest, Falcon. Do you think this body makes me look fat?"

"You look fine, Quimby," said Falcon.

Falcon felt a breeze blow through his hair. He turned to his right, and there, flickering in and out, was Megan. She reached toward him with one translucent, wavering hand.

"Falcon," she said gently. "It was you who rescued me from that windmill, wasn't it? Not Jonny."

"I don't know," said Falcon. "We did it together, I guess."

"Listen. Remember when we were up in the tower, last spring?" said Megan. "That night Quimby got loose?"

Megan blew toward him gently, a soft, circling force. With one gusting hand she reached out toward him.

"Yeah," said Falcon. "I remember."

"I just wanted to tell you that night," she said. "I was trying to tell you that I . . ."

Their faces drew slowly, slowly together.

"That you what?"

Falcon could feel the breeze against his cheeks, and in his hair.

"That I—"

Then there was a soft *whoosh*, and she was gone again.

Falcon looked around. "Megan?" he said. "Hello?"

25

BITE ME IN ST. LOUIS

A day later, the *Destynee II* sailed back toward Shadow Island, bearing its crew of Chupakabras, Sasquatches, zombies, and ghouls. At the bow, looking at the horizon and considering the days ahead, were Jonny Frankenstein and Falcon Quinn.

"So it's back to the Academy?" said Jonny. "You sure this is the right move?"

"For now," said Falcon. "Anyway, Count Cygnus said there were going to be exchanges in the future. So maybe Gyra and Sam and Celeste will spend a semester at the Academy."

"Hope that works out," said Jonny, who still looked more than a little pale. "I got a feeling not everybody's on board with the whole peace and love thing."

"What about you?" said Falcon. "You on board?"

"For now," said Jonny.

Sparkbolt, who sat amidships with his back against the mast, writing in his "Poetry Book of Rhyming Poems," growled to himself. "Rrrr. Poem belong *dead*."

"What's wrong?" said Weems. "Still trying to find a rhyme for 'orange'?"

"Found rhyme," said Sparkbolt. "'Porridge'! 'Door hinge'! 'Forage'! Many rhyme 'orange'. But many rhyme— bad. Destroy."

"I don't see why you keep writing poems," said Destynee. "If you hate it so much."

"Monster write," said Sparkbolt. "Express feeling." He moaned.

"Upon what cursed text have you been working?" said Ankh-hoptet.

"It song from musical. 'Scrcam, Scream, Scream Went the Human.'"

"You're writing a musical?" said Weems. "How macabre. What is the name of this musical of yours?"

"Bite Me in St. Louis." Sparkbolt blushed. "It need work," he said.

Quagmire boiled on the deck. A series of bubbles rose from his glop, floating in the air. As each one burst, it released an unpleasant odor.

"Whoa," said Ankh-hoptet, waving her bandaged hands in front of her face.

"Who died?" Lincoln Pugh roared.

"Die?" said Weems excitedly. "Did someone die?"

In the middle of the deck, Quimby's body stood, trying to grasp its own head, which had detached itself again and was now floating just out of reach of its hands.

"One's head should always exceed one's body's grasp," said Quimby. "Or what's a heaven for?"

"Rrrr," said Sparkbolt.

Falcon and Jonny Frankenstein walked over to the place where the others were standing.

"Ladies and gentlemen," said Quimby. "Falcon Quinn."

"Hello, Quimby," said Falcon. "How about a new fortune? Now that the war's finally over? I don't think I'm going to be torn in half anymore."

"A new fortune?" said Quimby, looking momentarily perplexed. "Oh, all right. Let me see. How's this? *Falcon Quinn, his wings so grand, finds enemies new in a northern land.*"

There was a moment's silence.

"What??" said Falcon.

"Oh no," said Destynee.

"Another satisfied customer!" said Quimby.

"Hey," said Max. "Am I interrupting something?"

"Señor," said Pearl, who buzzed over the Sasquatch's shoulder. "Perhaps we should withdraw! Our companions seem to be in a most agitated condition!"

"It's fine," said Falcon. "Quimby's just telling fortunes again."

"Always the life of the party," said Quimby. His hands

reached up and placed his head upon his shoulders once more. "Jonny," said Mortia. One of her eyeballs was hanging in its socket by a single muscle. "You don't look good!"

"I'll be all right," said Jonny. "Merideath bit me. I'm down a couple pints."

"But surely this does not mean you have joined the vampire peoples!" said Pearl. "With their fussy sleeping arrangements and their dislike of garlic! Because I for one would find this most peculiar!"

"I said I'm fine," snapped Jonny. But what Pearl said was true. He did not seem quite himself.

"My friends," said Pearl, "it appears that each of us returns to the Academy in a state of injury or of loss! It is my hope that we shall all return to our same selves with the passing of days!"

The sails of the ship luffed for a moment, and then a wind blew among them, and Falcon felt Megan's presence. Then the sails of the *Destynee II* filled once more, and the ship hurtled headlong once more through the Sea of Dragons.

"I kind of miss Megan having a body and stuff," said Max. "Is that bad of me to say? I mean, I know she likes being the wind. It's just hard to have a conversation with somebody who's all—not there."

"I miss her too," said Falcon.

"Perhaps she shall learn," said Pearl. "Upon our return

to the Academy! A more dependable way of occupying both her corporeal and elemental selves!"

"I could play a tune to cheer us up," said Mortia. She played a chord on her guitar. "You all want to hear a song?"

"Who needs cheering up?" said Max, and roared. "I feel *great*!"

Falcon looked at the faces of his friends. There were Destynee and Weems, Lincoln Pugh and Ankh-hoptet, Sparkbolt and Pearl and Max and Jonny Frankenstein and Mortia. And Megan Crofton, free once more, was filling the sails and blowing all around.

Mortia started to sing "I Wish They All Could Be Zombie Mutants," and Falcon's friends sang along.

Well, the Sasquatch girls are hip,
I love their fur all splotched with crud;
And the vampire girls, with the way they bite,
They knock me out when they suck my blood.

Max threw back his head and roared. "Our lives," he said, "are unbelievably, amazingly great!"

Falcon smiled. "You know what, Max?" he said. "You're right."

The *Destynee II*, bearing its crew of Sasquatches and Chupakabras, friends and lovers, zombies and an angel, sailed on across the Sea of Dragons, toward Shadow Island, and home.